Harlem Moon
broadway books
new york

Sanctified Blues
a novel

Mable John
and
David Ritz

Published by Harlem Moon, an imprint of Broadway Books, a division
of Random House, Inc.

PRINTED IN THE UNITED STATES OF AMERICA

Visit our Web site at www.harlemmoon.com

Book design by Elizabeth Rendfleisch

Library of Congress Cataloging-in-Publication Data
John, Mable.
Sanctified blues : a novel / Mable John and David Ritz.—1st ed.
p.   cm.
1. Women blues musicians—Fiction. 2. Women evangelists—Fiction. I. Ritz,
David. II. Title.
PS3610.O26S36   2006
813'.6—dc22
                                                          2005055039

ISBN-13: 978-0-7679-2165-7
ISBN-10: 0-7679-2165-8

10 9 8 7 6 5 4 3 2 1

First Edition

In memory of
our dear friend Ray Charles,
who introduced us
thirty years ago and,
in his own way,
made this project possible

acknowledgments

I thank God for allowing me the space and time in this life to do something I never dreamed of doing. I thank Him for the good fortune of being introduced to David Ritz.

I thank my dear mother and father, Mertis and Lillie John, my husband Sam, my children Jesse, Joel, Otis, Limuel, Sherry, Paul, Sharon, and John; my grandson, Jesse, and my granddaughter, Jasmine; and a great lady and friend I watched grow up who said, "Mab, you can do this!"—Ms. Susaye Greene. Last but not least, Dr. Charles Queen, my Greek and Hebrew teacher. To God the glory!   —Mable John

Much love and gratitude to my co-author Mable John, whose sweet spirit opened my eyes and my heart; Janet Hill, wonderful editor and creative partner; my forever friend and loving wife, Roberta; my daughters, Alison and Jessica; my sons-in-love, Henry and Jim; my granddaughter, Charlotte Pearl; my grandson, Alden Bryan; my sisters, Elizabeth and Esther; my dad, Milton; my agents, David Vigliano and Elisa Petrini; my publisher, Stephen Rubin; and my brothers, Alan Eisenstock, Harry Weinger, and Leo Sacks. Special thanks to Skip Smith, whose contribution to my spiritual life is incalculable.
          —David Ritz

Sanctified Blues

Part One

"He made known to us
the mystery of His will. . . ."

—EPHESIANS 1:9

Say a Little Prayer

Start out every morning in prayer, setting my life out in a motion that moves toward the Lord. Then I get quiet and simply listen. Sometimes I don't hear Him, though, because Justine, my next-door neighbor, is already knocking at the door. Knocking hard. Justine is something else.

"Hold on, baby," I say. "Getting there fast as I can."

"You look tired, Albertina," says Justine. "Didn't sleep well?"

"Haven't had my morning coffee."

"I'll make us a pot. It'll be ready by the time Maggie goes on."

Maggie, of course, is Maggie Clay. Every day of the week Justine comes over to watch *Maggie's World*. Couldn't stop her if I wanted to. Truth be told, I like watching the show with Justine. Justine puts on more of a show than Maggie.

"When you watch Maggie," says Justine, who has marched into my kitchen and is busy making coffee, "you learn everything you need to know about how a Black woman can get rich in white America."

"I don't see it that way, sweetheart. I was reading in the book of Joshua the other day—"

"Here we go again with the Bible—"

"I don't know any other book so packed full of wisdom."

"Alright," Justine says with resignation. "Go on. Tell me about Joshua."

"It's a passage—Joshua 1:8—that's basically saying that God is the source of wealth and success. There's no true prosperity without Him."

"Well, it looks to me like Maggie is sure enough prosperous. Whether God is behind it or whether it's her own genius brain, I just don't know. All I know is that Maggie's the richest Black woman in the history of blackness."

"It isn't about Blackness or whiteness, baby. It's from one blood that God created all nations, all men, all women."

"You get that little nugget from the Bible as well?"

"Acts 17:26. Someday you really oughta take a look at that book."

"Why do that, Albertina, when I have you around quoting all the good parts to me?"

"You'll see yourself in so many of the stories."

"Right now I just want to see what color her hair's gonna be today. First of the month comes around and Maggie has a new shade. It's April first and I'm guessing red highlights. *Heavy* red highlights."

"April first will fool you, Justine."

"Maggie don't fool me none. She's going for red, I know she is. She has to. She's tried everything. What's left?"

"Before you start tearing up Maggie, I think we better pray."

"You usually get your praying out of the way before I get here."

"I'm having a slow morning, baby. Just give me your hand."

Justine raises her eyebrow skeptically, as if to say, *Here she goes again*, but gives me her hand. We're standing by the stove where the fragrance of fresh coffee floats in the air.

"Father God," I say, "we thank You for this day. We thank You for the breath we breathe. You *are* the breath we breathe. You are the breath of life. We thank You for our friendship and our families and the food we eat. You say in Isaiah 53:4 and 5 that You bore our grief and by your scourging we are healed, right here, right now. So we thank You. We thank You for Your suffering, we thank You for our salvation, we thank You for life eternal. We magnify You, we glorify You, we praise You. We thank You for the gift of Your life because You are our life. And we say all this in the precious name of Jesus. Amen."

"Amen," Justine repeats. "That was sweet. Does that get me off the hook for what I did last night?"

"I'm not sure I want to know what you did last night, baby."

"Herman."

"Again?"

"Again."

"Lord, have mercy," I say.

"He's back," says Justine.

"For now."

"Now is all I know."

"You know more than you like to let on. Sugar, you know all about Herman," I tell her.

"You say accept folk the way they are. You say, we can't change people, only God can."

"That's what I believe," I say.

"Well, I believe it too. Herman is Herman."

"And self-respect is self-respect."

"What's that supposed to mean?"

"The coffee's ready. Want some toast?"

"I'll make it for you, Albertina."

"You act like I can't make toast."

"You're seventy. I'm fifty. I'll make the toast."

"Think I can butter it myself?" I ask.

We sit at the kitchen table. Outside my window the sun is peeking through the clouds and warming the ferns sitting on the ledge behind the sink. I'm not good with plants—not the way my mother was, bless her heart—but the ferns are growing in spite of me. Looks like another nice day in South Central Los Angeles.

"The thing about Herman," says Justine, "is that he's sweet. Deep-down sweet. And, unlike many men, he's not prejudiced against large women."

"You don't have to explain, Justine."

"I feel like I have to. I feel like you're judging me."

"The Lord said in John 12:47 that He did not come to condemn the world but to save it. I'm no judge, sugar."

"But you're a minister, Albertina."

"A minister without a sanctuary and without judgments."

"Judging is what ministers do for a living."

"Fortunately I don't make my living from ministering."

"You got your song royalties. Thank God for your song royalties. Don't you miss singing?"

"I still sing on Sunday mornings."

"I know, but you're singing with nine or ten people sitting in your living room."

"Home-church singing is some good singing, baby."

"But how 'bout those days when you were singing in front of thirty thousand people in football stadiums?"

"Those folks were listening to James Brown or Elton John, not me. I was just singing background."

"But how 'bout those days when you were singing on your own?"

"Chitlin circuit singing. Singing the blues."

"Didn't you love it?"

"I loved it, sure I loved it. But I found I loved something more."

"You aren't going to make me pray again, are you?"

I laugh. Justine is buttering my toast and spreading on blackberry jelly. "Justine," I say, "you don't have to do that, honey."

"It pleases me to please you. Don't you say we're here to serve each other?"

"In serving each other we're serving Him."

"We're not talking about Herman, are we?" Justine asks.

"No, we are not talking about Herman."

"I want to talk about Herman. I think it's different this time."

"Based on what?"

"He's doing stuff to me he's never done before. Can I tell you about it?"

"That's hardly necessary, baby."

"Well, you can imagine."

"I could, but I don't want to. . . ."

"And that tells me he's changing. He's willing to take the time to please me. Isn't that a good sign?"

"I'm not sure how good I am at reading signs," I say.

"You read everything right. You solve everyone's problems. That's your gift."

"That's not me. That's God."

"Well, God willing, Herman's picking me up again after work tonight and we're going clubbing."

"You mean to say that after dealing with all those Target customers till ten at night you can still go clubbing?"

"Herman recharges my batteries."

"Alright, Miss Energizer Bunny, Maggie's about to come on. Let's move to the living room."

I sit in the big blue easy chair that's older than me. It needs reupholstering, but I can't stand the idea of being without it, even for a day. It belonged to my daddy's daddy, a man I never knew.

Maggie's theme song is playing, her announcer is calling her name, and there she is, making her way down the central aisle through her adoring audience.

"*Told you!*" Justine is screaming. Justine has jumped off my couch and is pointing at the screen with her four-inch-long star-encrusted glitter-gold fingernails. "Her hair ain't red, it's orange! It's hideous! My God, what is that woman thinking?"

Justine loves to diss Maggie's hairdos, but this time she's right. A former woman's basketball star for UCLA in the late seventies and a high-fashion model in the early eighties, Maggie is six foot three and a stunning beauty. Wire thin with high cheekbones, flashing green eyes, and a honey cream complexion, she is famous for her bold style and dramatic flair, but this is off the charts. This is plainly wrong. At fifty, Maggie usually looks thirty-five. Today she looks fifty-five.

"Girlfriend looks like Clarabelle the Clown with Shirley Temple curls," says Justine. "What is that child thinking? She's gone off the deep end. She's done lost her mind."

"Today's show," Maggie starts to say, her eyes darting away from the camera, "will be focused on many things, but right now I can't think of any of them."

There's a deadly silence. The camera turns from Maggie

and pans the audience. The audience looks as confused as Maggie. The camera swings back to Maggie.

"I'm kidding, of course," she says. "Today's show will focus on . . ." Another awkward pause. "Let me ask my producer. Cindy, what are we focusing on today?"

"Hey, Albertina," says Justine as the camera pans to a thirty-year-old woman standing in the wings, "isn't that Cindy, your niece?"

"Sure is, honey."

"I thought they never show the producer on camera."

"Well, they're showing her today," I say as I watch the camera catch a glimpse of Cindy, who looks absolutely adorable in a simple pair of jeans and a *Maggie's World* sweatshirt. She's standing in the wings and mouthing the words "mental health."

"Mental health," repeats Maggie. "Nothing is more important than mental health. And today we have a number of experts and a number of people who have recovered. Or maybe they haven't recovered. Who knows if anyone ever really recovers?"

"What in God's name is wrong with this woman?" asks Justine, now planted a few inches in front of my television set with both hands on her hips.

"Please move, Justine," I say. "Can't see through you."

"Maggie's out of it," says Justine. "Maggie's falling apart."

Just as Justine says the words, the screen goes blank. *Maggie's World* always broadcasts live from Dallas—a point of pride with Maggie who built her reputation on bucking the tradition of pretaped shows—so all this is happening in real time: 9:05 a.m. on the West Coast, 11:05 a.m. in Texas, 12:05 p.m. back East.

"Due to technical difficulties," an announcer says, "*Maggie's World* will not be aired today."

The theme song to *I Love Lucy* starts up.

"Call Dallas," urges Justine. "Call your niece. See what's happening."

"Cindy's in the middle of it right now. I don't want to bother her."

"This is amazing. The great Maggie Clay is sure enough breaking down on national TV."

"Don't go jumping to conclusions, Justine. She might just be dizzy with the flu."

"Pah-leeeze, Albertina. Did you see her eyes? She's lost it. I'm telling you, she's gone. This story's gonna be all over *Access Hollywood, Entertainment Tonight* and *Extra*. Those blood-hungry tabloids will eat her alive."

"Calm down, baby. You sound almost happy about it."

"Well, she's supposed to be the happiest human in the world. Besides, she's had every happiness guru from Bombay to Brooklyn preaching on her show. She has written best sellers telling *us* how to be happy. The woman's gotten rich on happy. So how can she *not* be happy? Ain't it funny how things turn around?"

"If she's hurting she needs our prayers."

"You really think Maggie wants *our* prayers? Us little people?"

"I don't know what she wants, Justine, but I can't be happy that she's hurting."

"Sorry, Albertina, but I ain't no perfect saint."

"None of us are, baby."

A Little Dream

The telephone wakes me out of a dream.

I usually don't nap, but after lunch today my heart felt heavy and my head cloudy with worrisome thoughts. I fixed myself a little tuna sandwich, made myself a cup of green tea, took my Bible over to the couch and started to read the Word when my eyes closed and I drifted back to Dallas. In my dream I'm in the Dallas of my childhood. The Dallas of the forties. The Dallas of prejudice and pain. The Dallas of my innocence, when my loving parents are still alive. It's my favorite time of day, almost dinnertime in the little bungalow where we live just off Lemon Avenue. Mama is cooking. I'm peeling potatoes. Daddy's smoking his pipe. My brothers, Calvin and Fred, are playing in the yard. Suddenly it's dark and raining with thunder and lightning and just as suddenly it's clear but here comes the roar of wind and I look outside and see a funnel cloud rushing toward us. Our house is shaking and Mama is screaming and through our window I see the tornado is only a block away. I run out to grab my brothers but the terrible wind has sucked up their bodies and is about to smash our house and me, Mama, and Daddy when a ringing telephone startles me awake.

"Tina, it's Calvin."

My brother is calling. I'm amazed at the coincidence.

"I was just dreaming of us all," I say, "you and Fred and Mama and Daddy."

"I needed to call you," Calvin replies, ignoring what I just said, "because I figure that you're the only one who can make sense out of this."

"Out of what?" I ask him.

"What happened today."

"What *did* happen, baby?"

"Did you watch *Maggie's World*?"

"I saw that the show was cut off."

"Maggie's cut herself off from everyone. Even Cindy. Now Cindy doesn't know what to do. No one does."

"I don't understand."

"It's like Maggie's fallen into some kind of trance. Cindy says they're calling it clinical depression. But Maggie won't do nothing about it. No doctor, no hospital. She just gets worse. Cindy's afraid of losing her job. And, well, to tell you the truth, Albertina, Cindy's been supporting me. Without Cindy, I'd lose everything. The business. The house. Everything."

My heart starts beating fast. From the second I heard my brother's voice, I knew he needed something for himself. Poor Calvin doesn't operate any other way. I feel a lifetime of pain welling up inside me. I can't help but remember how he wormed money out of our brother, out of me, even out of our mother and father when they were at the assisted-living home.

I remember a dozen scenarios from the past when Calvin lied and cheated his way from one hustle to another. I thought the stroke he suffered a few years back might bring him to the Lord. But once he regained his strength he was back on the streets with another get-rich-quick scheme. I want to ask him, *What happened to your latest brainstorm to franchise fast-food chicken-and-waffle shacks?* but don't have the heart to do so.

"Not sure what I can do about any of this, honey," I tell my brother.

"Cindy feels like you can talk to Maggie Clay. Cindy says you're the kind of woman Maggie Clay would respect."

"Maggie Clay has no idea who I am."

"Cindy's told her. Cindy brags on you, Sis. You know that you're her hero."

"I'm not so sure about that. Anyway, it's been a while since I've heard from Cindy."

"She's been crazy busy," says Calvin. "Doing this show. Making her career. She's a brilliant young woman, Albertina. She takes after you."

Calvin's flattery rubs me the wrong way. The more he wants, the more he flatters. But I hold my tongue.

"So you'll be here by the end of the week?" he asks.

"Calvin, I can't just pick up like that and jump on a plane."

"Why not?"

"Well, I have a life here."

"You're needed here."

All my life my brothers have tried making decisions for me, starting when I was a girl. Nothing has changed.

"Make your reservation," Calvin insists. "I'll pick you up at the airport."

"It's not that easy, baby."

"You're making it hard, Tina, not me."

I stop and take a couple of deep breaths. The last thing in the world I need to do is argue with my brother. He's my blood. He's under stress. Doesn't matter whether he lacks consideration for me or not, I don't need to hurt him. I think of Ephesians 4:26 where it talks about being angry without sinning and warns us to lose the anger before the sun sets. Holding on to anger, the Good Book says, gives the devil a foothold.

"Look, Calvin," I say calmly and pleasantly, "if Cindy needs me, just tell her to call."

"She needs you in Dallas."

"Then please tell her to call."

"So you're coming."

"I'm praying."

Or at least I should be praying. My mind should be on the Lord. Fact is, my mind should be on Bible class tonight. The women are coming over at seven and two of them are bringing their teenage daughters. Nothing makes me happier than seeing young people seeking God. We're deep into Galatians. I'm studying the passages in Galatians 5 where Paul discusses the fruit of the spirit. But my eye drifts down to Galatians 6 where I read, "Bear one another's burdens, and thereby fulfill the law of Christ." I don't want to think how that applies to me and my family in Dallas. I don't want to think about Dallas at all. Dallas represents a past that I overcame and nightmares that I do not wish to relive. This July it'll be fifteen years since Mama died. Daddy died barely a month later. After both funerals, I told myself I would not be going back to Dallas. I've kept that promise. I will not be going back to Dallas.

"Father God," I say, "how can I bear the burden of a woman I don't even know? Maggie Clay is a stranger to me. I don't know her, I can't help her. I'd be lost in her world of media moguls and multimillionaires. You know that, Lord. You know that I'm not an interfering woman. I don't go where I'm not wanted, and I don't believe I'm wanted in Dallas. Not really. It's not my domain. It's not my business. So keep me from being a busybody. Keep me home, Father God, where I belong. Dallas will just make me crazy like it always does. I don't need to be crazy. I need to be in . . ." Here I hesitate before I say the words, "Your will. I need to be in Your will."

What is His will?

I hear myself telling friends like Justine how we need to recognize our willfulness. Rather than be willful, we should want to be willing. Willing to listen to God's will. Willing to do His will. Then I get asked the $64,000 question. "Well, how do I know His will?"

"Life will reveal His will," I say. "Just open your heart and open your ears."

My ears need to hear His voice reassuring me, telling me that there's nothing for me to do in Dallas. But instead of His voice, I hear the telephone ringing off the hook.

"Aunt Tina, it's Cindy."

"Hi, sugar," I say. "Been thinking of you today."

"Daddy said he called you. I wish he hadn't. I didn't want to bother you."

"You're not bothering me, baby. It's good hearing your voice."

"I know how you feel about Dallas, which is why I asked Daddy not to call. You don't need to come here. I'm not sure it would serve any purpose."

I'm relieved. "I'd have to agree," I say. "I don't even know this woman."

"What woman?"

"Maggie Clay."

"Actually it's not about Maggie."

"It's not?"

"Then I misunderstood your father."

"My father doesn't know what's going on. He thinks it's about Maggie. But it's not."

"Then who *is* it about, baby?"

"Me."

"What about you, sugar?"

"I'm sick, Aunt Tina. I'm very sick."

Author of My Life

Understanding the ways of God is impossible. I gave up long ago. It's enough to know that God is good. It isn't that He offers love; He *is* love. To focus on Him is to focus on love. I try to focus on love and don't always succeed. When I fail I try to accept that failure. Sometimes, though, I don't always succeed in that acceptance. So I feel bad about myself and wind up with a case of the blues. I used to sing the blues. I made good money singing the blues. Made even better money writing a song that became a hit. I called it "Sanctified Blues." God used that song to change my life. I didn't understand it at the time. I was convinced He was giving me something I always *thought* I wanted—big-time success, big-time fame. I was gonna be as famous as Aretha Franklin. More famous than Ray Charles. I was gonna be *it*. But the Lord had other plans for me. It took a while for me to stop fighting Him so that His plans could unfold. It took a while to surrender.

When I did surrender, I saw how He wanted to use me, live inside me and express Himself through me. I saw that He, not me, is the author of my life.

There are times like today, however, when I forget that fact. I slip back into my old thinking that says, *I'm the author. I'm running my own show. I'm writing my own story.* In the story I'm writing I don't have to go back to Dallas ever again. In that story I've already paid my Dallas dues. I've had enough of that city. I've endured it and I've surpassed it. I've moved on. In my story I get to stay in Los Angeles as long as I want. I might go to Chicago to visit my daughter, Laura. Or I might go to New York to visit my son, Andre. If my heart gets heavy, I can drive up to Oakland and sit by the grave of my baby boy, Darryl. I have family in Detroit and Atlanta and Charleston, South Carolina. I'll gladly travel to any of those places, but Dallas is off the map for me. Dallas is too deep, too hurtful, the drama still too fresh. I need to avoid Dallas at all costs. Me and Dallas are through.

Just when I've convinced myself that I'm in charge of my story here comes God with *His* story. Here comes God saying, *"I'm the author of your book. I'm the light that directs your path. I'm the energy that gives you life."* God doesn't say that with human words—I don't have visions and I don't hear voices—but He says it through people. He says it through my beautiful niece Cindy who tells me that there is cancer in her ovaries and that she is frightened and feeling alone. God is saying to me, *"Go where you must go. Do what you must do."* And if I hesitate, if I fill my head with doubts, if I resist, I have only to look to the example of Jesus whose obedience was perfect. "I do nothing on my own," said Jesus, "but speak just what the Father has told me."

The Father has taught me to put away my blues, to stop

feeling sorry for myself, to stop trying to control everyone and everything and respond, like Jesus responded, to perform the simple task in front of me. That task might not be easy. It might—and surely it will—upset my schedule and upset my life. I don't have to like it. I just have to do it.

I'm walking through the American Airlines terminal at Los Angeles International Airport thinking about how I don't want to think about where I'm going. At least I've had a chance to go to my hairdresser, Hazel, who gave me blond highlights. I've always been partial to blond highlights. My hair is looking okay, but my attitude about getting on the plane for Dallas could be better. I try the self-service boarding pass machine but the thing is broken. The line leading up to the counter is longer than a football field. When I finally get the pass, the line for security is even longer. Heading for the gate, I happen to glimpse the magazine store. Maggie Clay's picture is splashed across every single tabloid. The headlines are screaming, "Maggie's Major-League Meltdown!" "Queen of Daytime TV Dethroned!" "The Big Breakdown: Is Maggie Out of Her Mind?" I break my rule of ignoring those publications and buy two of them. My curiosity is greater than my guilt. Seated in the middle section in the back of the plane, I munch on a small bag of peanuts and try reading the articles. It's not easy. The feeling is nasty. The editors have picked the worst pictures of Maggie imaginable—when she was twenty pounds underweight, when her eye shadow was running and the wind messing with her hair. The writers use harsh words to describe her—"spoiled," "insensitive," "demanding." Because she has kept her private life private, there are few details to report except for the excess of her lifestyle. There are pictures of her penthouses and mansions and private jet. There are rumors that she has a boyfriend who's younger than she is, or a girlfriend who's older, or a secret husband who stays hidden at her two hundred-acre ranch near Austin. I think of Proverbs 26 that says, "Without wood a fire goes out; without gossip a quarrel dies down." I think of all the quarrels in this nasty old world that would die down if only the gossip would stop. In disgust, I put down the tabloids. Who knows what is or isn't true? All I know is that the woman has a devoted audience—me included—because Maggie is a brilliant conversationalist and her shows are intriguing. I remind myself that my trip is not about Maggie Clay; it's not about me and my feelings about Dallas; it's about my niece Cindy.

As the plane starts to descend and I look out the window, I find myself, in spite of myself, staring out at my past. I can't help but remember when my hopes for life were so high. Dallas is where I grew to womanhood with so many expectations. Dallas is where I learned to love the music of my people—the blues and jazz and gospel music that excited my heart and thrilled my soul; Dallas is where I sang in public for the first time, where I declared my love for the Lord in the church of my parents. Dallas is where I met Dexter Banks, the man who . . .

Dallas is where I get off the plane and turn off memory lane.

My brother Calvin is dressed with his usual flair—snappy cap, cashmere blazer, mirror shine on his alligator shoes. His limp is more pronounced and his speech slightly slurred by his stroke. For a man of seventy-five, though, he looks pretty good. When we get to his Cadillac he turns to me and says, "Damn, Tina, I sure have missed you."

"Same here," I say.

"You have to admit it's good to be home."

"It's good to be with family" is the closest I can come to agreeing.

"You need to see Maggie Clay right away. Can't happen too soon. Cindy will arrange it."

Since Cindy told me that she has kept her condition a secret, even from her father, I say nothing. Cindy didn't think he could handle the news. I offered to stay with her, but she thought it better that I stay with her dad. I didn't argue. "Whatever makes you comfortable, baby," is all I said.

Cindy's mother died at age thirty-one of uterine cancer. Cindy was only eight. At the time I was on the road singing rhythm and blues. Calvin went through four more wives before he gave up on marriage. I worried that my niece, an only child, would suffer from so many disruptions, but she turned out to be one of those miracle children. She made the best of any situation, even when her father served a year in prison for forgery. I remember Cindy writing me that she was living in the home of a schoolmate whose parents had accepted her as their own. She was in high school by then, a straight A student and editor of the paper. The next year she received a full scholarship to Yale and four years later graduated with honors. I went to her graduation in New Haven, Connecticut—Calvin couldn't make it—and cried with pride. Two years later she got her master's in journalism from Columbia University in New York City. One job led to another, and she wound up working for Maggie Clay who had established her media empire in Dallas. Cindy was back home. Now I'm back home.

Calvin pulls into his driveway. He lives in an apartment in the same Love Field Airport neighborhood where we grew up. Memories are crowding my mind.

"Got some fried chicken I can heat up," he says.

"That's fine, baby."

Before we eat, I say I'd like to pray.

"Go ahead," he says.

"Father God, I thank you for getting me here safely, for allowing me to be here with my brother, for blessing my brother, for watching over us, for feeding us with Your mercy and grace. You know my heart, Father, You know my mind. You know what I'm thinking and You know what I'm feeling. As I settle back into a place that I haven't seen in so long, I want to feel You more and more. I want to let You live through me. In Jesus' name, Amen."

"Amen."

During dinner Calvin tells me about his latest project. It isn't a chicken-and-waffles franchise; it's a magic formula for shampooing rugs. "Guaranteed to make a mint," says Calvin, "and put us all on easy street." I nod and wish him success. I don't want the details but Calvin needs to list them. Calvin needs to convince himself that this scheme can't miss. So he rattles on about his wealthy partners and his surefire profits. I'm saved by a phone call from Cindy.

"Is he talking shampoo formulas?" she asks.

"Yes indeed."

"Is he wearing you out?"

"No, he's just being Calvin."

"Can I see you tomorrow?"

"That's why I'm here, sugar."

"I have a doctor's appointment."

"We'll go together."

"I'd like that, Aunt Tina. I'd like that a lot."

Calvin doesn't ask me any questions about my life or my church or, for that matter, anything. Instead he goes to the store to buy lottery tickets. I'm feeling a little restless.

"How long has it been since you've been home?" he asks when he returns.

"Fifteen years."

"The city has changed. Gotten bigger. Richer. Want to take a little ride?"

"Might be nice, baby."

Golden Angels

Mid-April is a good time in Dallas. The heat hasn't hit and the evening is cool. Calvin takes Lemon Avenue toward downtown where the skyscrapers glitter like giant jewels. I'm starting to relax. Dallas has a sparkle it didn't have when I was growing up. There are new buildings and fancy shops, people living in town houses and lofts, outdoor cafés and cute little bistros. When we reach downtown there are even people on the street, something unusual for Dallas. It's almost eight o'clock, and on Main Street well-heeled tourists are filing in and out of Neiman-Marcus. My heart sinks.

Calvin is driving past the Deep Ellum neighborhood, now populated by music bars and art galleries. He's headed to the warehouse where he wants to show me his rug shampoo inventory. He's explaining how much he's going to sell this year, but my mind is back at Neiman-Marcus. I'm reliving some fifty-five years ago when the store stood as an island of exciting elegance in the middle of an unexciting city. I was a teenage girl excited by the glamour I saw in fashion magazines. I loved silk blouses and velvet skirts and long dresses like the ones worn by Lena Horne in the movies. I wanted to be Lena Horne. I wanted to be around beautiful people and beautiful things. Mama sewed me beautiful things, and I appreciated her talent, but she didn't have silk or velvet to work with. She worked at the Adams hat factory during the days when men were still wearing hats. Her job was sewing brims. Daddy's job was fixing cars. He had a friend we called Mr. S who operated the elevator at Neiman-Marcus. Mr. S wore a uniform. I'll never forget his immaculate white gloves. Mr. S told us we were always welcome at Neiman-Marcus. He said anyone could walk through the front door to see the brilliant diamond necklaces and fabulous floor-length mink coats. "It's the most famous store in the world," he said. "People from France, from England, people from all over the world come to Dallas just to shop at Neiman-Marcus."

I wanted to shop at Neiman-Marcus. I wanted to see the diamonds and furs and latest Parisian styles. One Saturday afternoon, after completing my chores, I put on a clean white blouse, a nice blue skirt, and a hand-me-down raincoat and caught the bus that stopped right in front of the store. I was fifteen years old. Part of me felt like I was about to trespass, but I fought that feeling. I took a couple of deep breaths and walked right in. It was early December. The main floor was set up like a winter wonderland, red carpets, streams of silver tinsel, a dazzlingly decorated Christmas tree. It looked like heaven. To me it was heaven. The scent of perfume in the air sent me reeling. I was dizzy with the wonder of it all. A woman in a green velvet gown was playing carols on a pipe organ. Golden angels, big as life, danced on strings hung from the ceiling. My eyes darted from the jewelry counter to the cosmetic display. The saleswomen looked like actresses. The customers looked like royalty. I looked for Mr. S, but he was nowhere to be seen. Rather than ride the elevator, I took the escalator to the second floor where I wandered through a forest of fur coats. They smelled divine. I was caressing the back of a silver fox stole when, out of the blue, a hand reached out and grabbed me.

"What are you doing in this store?" asked a white man in a dark suit.

"Let go of me," I said. "You're hurting me."

His hand squeezed my arm even harder.

"What'd you put in your raincoat?"

"There's nothing in my raincoat."

"I'm taking you to the office."

"For what?"

"You're coming with me."

"Let go."

He wouldn't. He dragged me and the stole out of the fur department so viciously that customers stopped to stare. He kept squeezing my arm until the pain was unbearable. I screamed for him to stop. People were looking, people were pointing. I was crying. I was horribly humiliated. I had never been in trouble before at school—not once. It seemed forever before he pushed me into an office and slammed the door shut.

"What'd you steal?" he asked.

"Nothing."

"Why else would a nigger girl come in a store like this?"

"Is there a law against coming in a store?"

Rather than answer me, he started putting his hands all over me, all over my breasts and legs and private parts.

"Stop it!" I screamed.

"I'm searching you."

"Stop it!" I screamed even louder so my voice could be heard beyond the closed door.

He slapped me.

I slapped him back.

That's when he slugged me with his fist. I fell to the floor, my jaw aching. Another man walked in wanting to know what had happened.

"I caught her trying to walk out with this stole," said my assailant.

I tried to protest but my mouth wouldn't move. It took two months for my jaw to heal. It took seven months for the case to come to court. My folks spent their meager savings to pay a lawyer who believed me when I said I hadn't even put on the coat, much less tried to walk out with it. The lawyer argued that because I never left the second floor I could hardly be accused of stealing. The judge agreed. But what about my broken jaw? I had been assaulted. I had been seriously injured. Who would pay for the doctors?

"She's lucky she's not going to jail," I heard Mr. S tell Daddy one day. "I've seen many a colored put in jail for less."

Less than I did? All I had done was touch a stole.

My folks believed me. They were infuriated but didn't know what to do. They were adamant in defending me, but I wanted to attack back. I wanted to sue. They knew we could never win. In the fifties, what were the chances of a Black family winning? It would just cost them money they didn't have—that is, if they could even find a lawyer who would accept the case. Sometimes I went from anger to guilt. I berated myself for even walking in the store. My judgment had been poor. But my parents assured me that I'd done nothing wrong.

"It's this city," said Mama.

"It's this country," Daddy added.

In the many months it took to heal, I hurt in many ways. The swelling and bruising were extreme. The wire contraption holding my jaw together was ugly. My schoolmates made fun of me. I felt their animosity. Some presumed I was guilty. They wanted to find something wrong with me because I was a good student and good students excite jealousy. A few called me names to my face. Others talked behind my back. My mother said all this would only make me depend more on the Lord for my strength. She said someday I'd understand how He is sovereign over all things. But I didn't understand. All I felt was rage. I wanted to hurt the man who had hurt me. I tried to pray, but prayer didn't ease my pain or release my fury. It wasn't right; it wasn't fair. The man had lied about me. I had been falsely accused. Persecuted.

"So was the Lord," said my mother, who spoke of the fellowship of suffering. That was the first time I heard the phrase.

"Aren't you proud to come from the city," Calvin asks, snapping me out of my reverie, "where the original Neiman-Marcus store is located right there on Main Street?"

Obviously Calvin has forgotten the incident or he would never ask such a question. I could remind him, but what good would that do? Besides, he doesn't want to remember. He's happy talking about the riches of Dallas.

"The riches of this world," Mama used to say, "will tarnish and fade, but not the riches of the soul. They last forever.

Those are riches you can't earn. They're gifts that come wrapped up in the package of God's grace." Mama was right. She was also right about the fellowship of suffering. Pain can bring us closer to God. So can persecution. Accepting that truth, though, does not endear me to Dallas. It didn't then. It doesn't now.

Fearfully and Wonderfully Made

I'm looking at my niece Cindy and thanking God for her life. She's bright, pretty, and perky. The Lord gave her one of those sunshine personalities that lets her light the way for others. She has a world of friends from all walks of life so I'm especially flattered that she has asked me to go to the doctor with her. For all her positive energy, though, I can feel her troubled spirit.

It's never fun sitting in a waiting room. You leaf through an out-of-date magazine, you look at other patients, you wait for your name to be called. Cindy has brought along a novel by Toni Morrison. I'm reading the Psalms.

"Which one?" asks Cindy.

"The 139th that says, 'For You formed my inward parts; You wove me in my mother's womb. I will give thanks to You, for I am fearfully and wonderfully made. Wonderful are Your works, and my soul knows it very well.' "

"That's a good one."

Cindy smiles back before letting her eyes rest on the book she's reading. My niece can't weigh more than a hundred fifteen pounds. She's wiry thin and maybe a little taller than her dad, who has to be five feet ten. Her hair is cropped close to her head. Her head is strikingly shaped—high forehead, high cheek bones, strong chin. Big hoop earrings and a bold turquoise bracelet are the only jewelry she's wearing. Her clothes are never showy, always simple but well made. Today it's grey slacks and a blue t-shirt with an image of the pioneer educator Mary McLeod Bethune that says BLACK WOMEN IN HISTORY CONFERENCE: STANFORD UNIVERSITY.

After five minutes or so, Cindy says, "This doctor is always behind schedule."

"I'm fine just sitting here, baby," I say.

Cindy's cell phone starts ringing. "Sorry," she says, "forgot to turn this thing off."

I don't have a cell phone. I should for safety's sake. But I don't. I don't like 'em.

"I can't get over there now," Cindy says. I can hear someone shouting on the end of the line. "I'd love to," Cindy continues, "but it's just impossible. Sorry, but it will have to wait till this afternoon. I know, I know . . ." The shouting gets louder.

I want to tell Cindy, *Tell the caller you're at the doctor's. Tell them to leave you alone,* but I bite my tongue.

When she gets off the phone she says only one word. "Maggie."

"You didn't want to say you're at the doctor's?" I can't help but ask.

"Didn't want to worry her. She has enough problems."

"Cynthia," the receptionist announces. "Dr. Singer will see you now."

A half-hour later I'm called from the waiting area to meet

the doctor myself. Darlene Singer is a middle-aged African-American woman of dark complexion and serious eyes. No nonsense. Her small office is simply decorated with a wall of diplomas above her desk. She speaks with a strong Boston accent.

"While your niece is getting dressed and filling out forms, she asked that I speak to you directly. She further asked that I be blunt. Her endometrial cancer is especially pernicious. We label it papillary serous carcinoma. It is highly aggressive. The cancer has spread from the uterine lining to the lymph nodes of her pelvis and groin. We hope that it has not invaded her vital organs. CAT scans scheduled for tomorrow will give us that information. If it has spread to her vital organs, the cancer will have reached Stage IV, the most serious stage. Either way, a combination of chemotherapy and radiation is required. The physical side effects—nausea, vomiting, hair loss, energy depletion, mouth sores—often lead to emotional devastation. I know you understand."

"I do."

"She tells me that her mother died of a similar cancer."

"She did."

"Of course we will do everything we can. This is a remarkable young woman with a marvelous future in front of her. She has a sterling character and a positive attitude. Maintaining that attitude in these coming weeks will not be easy. Are you a spiritual woman, Miss Merci?"

"I am."

"Then that spirit will be called upon in a powerful way."

"The Spirit never fails," I say.

Natural Spunk

Cindy and I are having lunch at a fashionable outdoor café at NorthPark, an upscale mall. From where I'm sitting I can see a Neiman-Marcus department store. I thank God for allowing me not to focus on the past but on the present, on my niece. *Thank you for letting me be where I am,* I say silently, *not where I was.*

Cindy and I order salads.

"Neiman's," Cindy says, noticing the store. "I'll never forget that horrible story about you and Neiman's."

"Funny how the mind works," I say. "If we think about the future we're filled with fear. Think about the past and we're filled with regret. But the Holy Spirit isn't about the past or the future. God told Moses, 'I am the I am.' "

"Present tense," Cindy confirms.

"And presently the sun is shining and the sky is blue and you and I get to be together. For that I thank God."

"I want to stay present," says Cindy. "I really do. But it's hard."

"Very hard, baby. Seems like all our lives we focus on what went wrong and fear what's coming next."

"You're right, Aunt Tina, but right now how do I *not* think about the future?"

"I think about the unsettled mind. When my mind is unsettled, I bring my thoughts back to Christ. I allow Him to enter my mind and settle my thoughts. It works, sugar. Works every single time. That's why I want to ask you about your love walk, your relationship with the Lord."

"I've known Him since I was a child, Aunt Tina. And I've loved Him ever since I was a child."

"That's good, honey. That's wonderful."

"You might not know this, but you had a lot to do with that. After Mama died, you came and spent two weeks with me and Daddy. Do you remember?"

"Of course I remember, baby."

"The way you talked about the Lord's love made such an impression on me. It wasn't so much what you said but the feeling I sensed when you said it. You were so calm. I felt the Lord's love coming out of you. That's when I felt the Lord's love coming into me."

"And it never stops, sweetheart. It just keeps on coming."

"Now I need it more than ever."

"You have it. You always have that love, Cindy. And you also have all that natural spunk that you've had since you were a little girl. I remember how you would play ball with the boys even when they told you no. I remember you beating them at their own game. You could throw, you could hit, you could do anything you set your mind to. You were as fast as the wind. No one could catch you. You even won that national championship running track at college."

"Regional championship," Cindy corrects me.

"And when did you start that business of jumping out of planes?"

"Five or six years ago."

"That took some nerve."

"It's actually quite safe."

"Takes courage. And courage is your specialty."

"Well, I'm not sure about that."

"I am."

The salads arrive.

"Father God," I pray, "thank you for keeping us safe and keeping us present. In Jesus' name, Amen."

Cindy takes a few small bites of lettuce before breathing deeply and speaking softly. I have to lean in to hear her voice. "I haven't been sleeping well," she says.

"That's understandable."

"I want to tell you some things about my relationship with the Lord," Cindy adds.

"I'm eager to hear whatever you have to say, sugar."

"Maybe these are my confessions."

"Everyone has the need to confess."

"When I was at college at Yale I didn't profess my love of the Lord. I was hanging out with different groups of people, some very political, some very artistic. I guess I just didn't think it'd be hip to talk about my love of the Lord."

"I can understand that," I say. "We're all subject to peer pressure, baby, aren't we?"

"Then there were evangelical groups at Columbia during my time in graduate school. They went around New York City, even down in the subway stations, trying to convert people. I didn't want to have anything to do with them. I didn't like their methods. I thought they lacked sensitivity."

"Some of them probably did."

"But when I began working in the real world and saw the stress and strain of life in the media, I realized I needed the Lord more than ever. When I saw people who had no relationship with God, and how that lack of a relationship kept them in turmoil, I understood what a gift God is."

"Amen."

"That's when I started professing my faith a little more openly."

"That's beautiful."

"And when Maggie started struggling, I even went as far as mentioning you as someone she might want to meet."

"Thank you, sugar."

"I told her how much I admire you."

"Not any more than I admire your courage and strength, Cindy. I love your spirit. Always have. That spirit comes from God."

"And my mother."

"She had great spirit, yes she did."

"I wish I had more memories. I don't remember her last days at all. I remember that you were there with her."

"She was at peace, sugar, I can tell you that."

"Did she and Daddy have a happy marriage?"

"I'd call it a troubled marriage."

"I remember them arguing. Bickering. Was my father faithful?"

"He was young. I'm not sure he knew what he wanted."

"You're being diplomatic."

"Just being honest, honey. I really never knew the details."

Cindy puts her fork down and studies her salad. Sunlight reflects off the glass of water she holds in her hand. She looks up at me and says, "I'm frightened, Aunt Tina. Especially at night. I don't want to be, but I'm terribly frightened."

"You're only human," I say. "You're entitled to feel the way you feel. But if you read Paul's second letter to Timothy you'll see he says that God has not given us the spirit of fear. Fear comes from somewhere else. It's the absence of faith. The more we believe, the less we fear. Remember the Twenty-third Psalm?"

"I love the Twenty-third Psalm."

" 'Though I walk through the valley of the shadow of death, I shall fear no evil.' Give the Lord your fear, Cindy, and grab hold of His faith."

Vision of Light

I've never seen a house this big—and believe me, I've seen big houses. Cindy insisted I accompany her to Maggie Clay's mansion. Part of me wanted to stay away, but another part of me was downright curious, even eager.

"How is she?" I asked Cindy on the way over.

"She's hurting. Hurting in a way none of us understand."

"Has she been hurting for a long time?"

"First of all, Aunt Tina, I have to say that Maggie really is a genius. I don't use the word lightly. I had professors at college who were brilliant scholars. One even won the Nobel Prize. I've been exposed to extremely smart people. But Maggie's type of intelligence exists on another level. She was an athlete and a model, yes, but also a Fulbright Scholar with a graduate degree in media relations from Columbia University. She's the reason I went to Columbia. She not only possesses an understanding of American popular culture—which is unpredictable and complicated enough—but she also has mastered the intricacies of operating and owning her own media conglomerate. The woman's a financial wizard. Her business sense is incredible. In journalism school I learned about reporting but never took business courses. Maggie is all business. Which is why what has happened to her is so baffling. Right now she's ignoring business. She's ignoring everything. She either goes off on nonstop talking binges that hardly make sense or she slips into darkness and doesn't say a word for days. Doesn't even get out of bed."

From the driveway, Maggie's house is a vision of light. It's all glass, all windows, a radical design that looks like a major museum of modern art. The windows have no curtains and are two stories tall. Inside, hanging on the walls I can see gigantic canvases of abstract art in every color of the rainbow. There are gigantic pieces of abstract sculpture sitting in the center of enormous rooms. The gleaming wood floors remind me of basketball courts. Everything inside the house is completely visible from the outside.

"I thought this is a woman who protects her privacy," I say to my niece.

"Just wait till you get inside."

A security man, who acknowledges Cindy respectfully, lets us in. We walk through a long suite of rooms. From inside, the house looks even sleeker than from the outside. The furniture is hard-edged, chrome, frozen. There are no cushions or easy chairs, nothing is soft. The walls are painted gunmetal grey.

"This way," says Cindy as we walk through the gleaming stainless-steel kitchen into the backyard. Behind the house is another house, not as large, but certainly not small. This house, made of granite and marble, has few windows and looks like an elegant fortress. By the front door is an electronic pad. Cindy punches in a code but the door doesn't open. Cindy tries again, but it still doesn't work. She presses the doorbell, and, after a long wait, a voice from the small loudspeaker asks, "What do you want?"

"It's Cindy."

"You're too late," says the voice that I now recognize as Maggie Clay. "Where were you when I needed you? Well, I don't need you now. I don't need anyone. Get out. You're fired."

Cindy breathes deeply. I look at her quizzically. I don't know what to think. Neither does she.

"Let's go, Aunt Tina," she says. "This is a waste of time."

Telling the truth should be simple. Jesus said, "You will know the truth, and the truth will make you free." But sometimes you have to sit on the truth.

For example, Calvin and I are sitting in his living room watching the nightly news. Cindy dropped me off an hour ago. Naturally Calvin wants to know what happened. I'm not about to tell him that his daughter has been fired.

"What did you think of Maggie Clay?" he asks.

"Can't hardly tell."

"Are you getting the woman to come to her senses?"

"Too soon to say, baby."

"How long did you talk to her?"

"Not long at all."

"Are you going back tomorrow?"

"I'm letting Cindy decide. She knows her. I don't."

"She's totally dependent on Cindy," says Calvin. "Can't run her show without her. Fact is, can't run her life without her."

"I see."

"For all her brilliance, Maggie is a mental case. Maybe some people are too smart."

"Maybe. And maybe something we don't understand has claimed her attention."

"Meanwhile, Sis, I'm under some pressure here. Got a payment due at the end of the week. Need to pay the guy who's making the shampoo. We have orders for nearly $50,000 of the stuff, so paying you back is no problem. I'll have the money May first."

"How much do you need, Calvin?"

"Five hundred dollars."

I should know better, but I don't. I write out a check.

Later that night sleep does not come quickly. I toss and turn. I can't find a comfortable position. I can feel the springs under the thin mattress of Calvin's sofa bed. When sleep finally comes, I fall into another crazy dream.

Cindy is a fashion model. I'm in some European city—Paris or Milan—and Cindy is walking the runway in a fabulous gown of red silk. Camera flashes are popping and people are cheering. I'm seated in the first row. I'm beaming with pride. Other models strut back and forth but they look emaciated, sick, hollow. Cindy is the picture of health. Just as Cindy turns on her heels and walks back to the dressing area, Maggie Clay jumps onstage in front of her, blocking her path. Dressed in vampire black, Maggie starts screaming obscenities and grabbing at Cindy's dress. I leap to my feet. I run to protect Cindy from Maggie's assault, but Cindy's gown has caught fire and the whole place is going up in flames. I wake up in a sweat.

My first husband, Dexter Banks, used to call it the hour of the wolf. Blues singer Howlin' Wolf used to sing a song called "The Wolf Is at Your Door." The Wolf is trouble and trouble comes in the midnight hour. It's midnight when I wake up from my dream and can't go back to sleep. It's midnight when I get attacked by bad thoughts, fearful images, a head filled with worry. In my dream my niece is healthy. In real life she isn't healthy at all. In my dream Maggie is attacking my niece physically. In real life Maggie is attacking her emotionally. What can I do? I pray. "God, you said Your yoke is easy and Your burden is light. Well, my burden feels heavy. Here in the midnight hour my mind is heavy with thoughts of death and anger and burning fires. I give you these thoughts, Father. Allow me to feel the light of Your love. And your peace. I offer You every negative thought running through my head. I offer them up to You because I know You can handle them. I can't. They weigh me down with worry. They upset my stomach. They make me crazy. Father, I won't be crazy with worry. I won't rage against a woman I don't even know. I won't fuel resentment against my blood brother. But these are feelings running through me, Father, and I know You accept them. I know You accept me. I know You can handle everything I can't. I know Your son died so I can live. And I know You want my life to be free of grief and filled with joy. So I'm claiming the victory, Father, the victory that You gave me. I'm chasing the Wolf away from the door. I'm claiming victory in the midnight hour, knowing that joy comes in the morning. In the precious name of Jesus, I say Amen."

In the morning Calvin is telling me Justine's on the phone.

"Just checking up on you, Albertina," she says. "You okay?"

"Fine, baby, just fine."

"You meet Maggie?"

"Not exactly."

"Well, what are you waiting for?"

"It's gonna have to be God's timing," I say, "not mine."

"Well, tell God to hurry up. I wanna hear what that crazy woman's really like."

"I never found that telling God to hurry up does much good."

"He listens to you, but I'm not sure He listens to me."

"What have you been telling Him?"

"That I want Herman to propose. And I think it's gonna happen, Albertina, I truly do. We're going to Vegas this weekend. He got us a suite at Caesar's Palace. We're seeing Gladys Knight at the Flamingo."

"Great."

"Can you get us VIP tickets?"

"I'm not sure, honey. . . ."

"You know her, don't you, Albertina?"

"From years ago. Back when she was on Motown."

"Well, I'm sure she remembers you."

"Maybe, but that doesn't mean I'm comfortable calling her for a favor."

"It's a favor for me, Albertina."

"Justine, I love you, baby, and I hope you have a wonderful time in Vegas with Herman. But I got a lot on my mind now and—"

"You don't have to call Gladys. Herman has contacts. He knows everyone. He'll get us good seats."

"I'm sure he will."

"So keep me in your thoughts, Albertina."

"I always do, Justine. Are you watering my plants?"

"Every day."

Mockingbird Station

It's my fifth day in Dallas and Cindy has asked me to move in with her. We've just learned from Dr. Singer that the cancer has reached Stage IV, the most serious stage. Cindy is shaken and doesn't want to be alone, and I'm here to see that she isn't. We still haven't said anything to Calvin. He thinks Cindy and I are busy discussing Maggie. He doesn't know that Cindy has been fired, or that she's sick. Someone said you're just as sick as your secrets, but these secrets are for Cindy to reveal, not me. I can't tell her how to manage her relationship with Calvin. I can barely manage my own relationship with him.

Cindy drives me to the loft she bought last year in a section of the city called Mockingbird Station, just off Central Expressway. I can feel her apprehension. I can see how tightly she's clutching the steering wheel of her little Porsche sports car. Everything in me wants to say, "Don't be afraid, baby," but saying that won't help. Words won't help, not now. The news is too fresh. So I say a silent prayer, asking God simply to allow me to sit still and be a loving presence. Sometimes silence is the biggest comfort of all. Most of the time we talk too much, especially when we're nervous.

Mockingbird Station is a complex with multiplex movie theaters, a Virgin megastore, sleek restaurants, edgy clothing stores, coffee shops, and a new building of lofts made to look like industrial New York City. Cindy's loft is on the top floor and it's big and comfortable. She has thick Persian carpets everywhere, and the furniture is made of corduroy and lived-in leather. The kitchen is old-fashioned white tile and the master bedroom is light blue. I like the Tiffany lamps and little candles she lights and places on the wicker tables. On the living room wall, in the most conspicuous spot of all, is an elaborately framed poster of my last long-playing album, *Sanctified Blues*. In the picture I have an Afro and a bit of an attitude. I'm looking a little bit too sure of myself, though I admit that the green and gold dashiki I'm wearing is something of a knockout.

"Boy, does that ever bring back memories!" I admit. "Where did you find that thing, sweetheart?"

"You. You gave it to me."

"I guess I did, but are you sure you want it right here in the middle of the room?"

"I love looking at it right there. I'm proud of my aunt."

"Thank you, honey," I say as I look over the dozens of books in the teakwood case that lines her dining room. I see the complete works of James Baldwin, Richard Wright, Zora Neale Hurston, and a few books by Charles Dickens. On her CD rack are Miles Davis, De La Soul, Aretha Franklin, Jill Scott, D'Angelo, John Coltrane, Alicia Keys. Everything about her place makes me comfortable.

"I'm going to have to rest," she says. "You don't mind, do you?"

"Not at all."

"If a guy named Bob Blakey calls, please tell him I'll call him tonight."

"I'll tell him."

Bob Blakey doesn't call. He shows up at the loft while Cindy is still napping. He has midnight black skin, a handsome bald head, a big husky build, and sweet brown eyes peeping through oversized gold-framed glasses. His vested pinstriped suit is nicely cut. He can't be older than thirty-five.

"You must be Aunt Albertina."

"I am. I just hope the buzzer didn't wake her."

"Sorry, if I knew she was napping . . ."

"She's been napping for a while. I'm sure she'll be up soon. What can I get you?"

"I'm fine. I just stopped by to check in on her."

"Sure you don't want a cup of tea? I'm making a pot."

"Cup of tea would be great," says Bob.

I make the tea and serve us on the dining table. I put down a tray of English butter cookies from the pantry. They're delicious.

"I just want to say, Albertina . . . May I call you Albertina?"

"Of course, honey."

"Okay, Albertina, I just want to say I'm honored to meet you. My uncle was in the music business. So I've known about you since I was a young kid looking through his LPs."

"Are you also in the music business?"

"Only tangentially. I'm a lawyer."

"Here in Dallas?"

"Yes, ma'am. I work for a large firm here. That's how I met your niece. I do work for Maggie Clay. Or at least I think I do."

His pained smile tells me he's been having his own problems with Maggie.

"Have you met our esteemed Miss Clay?" he asks.

"Not yet."

"She's crazy about Cindy."

"So I hear." I don't say anything about Cindy being fired. It's not my place.

"How is Cindy doing today?" Bob asks.

I don't know what Bob knows, so, again, I say little. "She's tired."

"She's been through a lot," he says in a voice filled with concern.

"Well, the Lord never gives us more than we can handle."

"I forgot that you're a minister."

"Guess I can't help sounding like a minister."

"You sound like a devoted aunt."

"More tea?"

"Please," Bob says.

A prolonged silence sits between the two of us. I feel a sweetness coming from Bob. I can't explain why, but I also feel like he wants to pray. I feel like he needs to pray. But I don't know the man. So the best thing I can do is sit there and not presume what he wants or needs.

A few minutes later Cindy walks out of the bedroom. Yawning and rubbing her eyes, she leans over Bob and kisses him on the cheek.

"You met my aunt," she says.

"I have."

She sits next to Bob and gently takes his hand. "Been meaning to call you," she tells him. "Sorry."

"No problem," he says. "You've got other things on your mind."

"Has Albertina told you about our encounter with Maggie?" Cindy asks.

"We just started talking," says Bob.

"She was there when Maggie fired me," Cindy recounts. "She did it over the intercom at her house. Not even face-to-face."

"Who's going to put the show back on the air?" asks Bob.

"Virginia Hogobin could take over. She knows the ropes. But you'll have to ask Maggie," says Cindy.

"She's not taking my calls," Bob announces.

"You're the only one she trusts."

"*Used* to trust," he says.

"How are we going to reach her?" asks Cindy. "How are we going to help her?"

"*You're* going to concentrate on getting well," Bob insists.

"But who's going to concentrate on helping Maggie?" Cindy wants to know.

"The Lord," I say. "The Lord's concentrating on helping us all."

Bishop

"**H**e's alive! *He's alive! He's alive! He's alive!*"

With unrelenting rhythm, the choir is standing and shouting those two words over and over again. Music is raining down from heaven.

"He's alive! He's alive! He's alive! He's alive!"

City of Faith megachurch is more mega than I ever imagined. The sanctuary looks like it seats half the city of Dallas. On either side of the purple-draped pulpit are giant screens like you see at the drive-in. The choir has at least a hundred members, and they are firing on all cylinders. The sound is supercharged, electric. The sound is like rolling thunder, the rhythm section cooking, the saxophonist flying, the choir reaching higher and higher. God is being glorified by glorious voices and for the moment all of us—Cindy, Bob Blakey, and me—are standing and clapping and celebrating the anointing we're feeling from head to toe. The worship is putting a smile on our faces. Whatever was bothering us before isn't bothering us now. God is with us now. God's anointing is all we know. God is in us.

When the music stops and the sermon starts, God gets a little lost. At least I feel like I'm losing Him. The preacher, a tall elegant man in a blue silk suit, is nationally known and one of Bob's clients. The preacher is talking about prosperity, and he looks mighty prosperous indeed. So does the congregation. The preacher says, "God desires prosperity for all His children." I think that's right, but I'm not sure God means monetary prosperity. Spiritual prosperity is our guarantee. Grace is our guarantee. But lots of money? I'm not so sure. But I'm not delivering this sermon. I'm not leading this church. I'm a guest, and as a guest I settle back in my chair and tell myself to quit judging the preacher. It's hard. I think he's slick. I think he's way too impressed with himself. He has a golden tongue, that's for sure, but preachers aren't supposed to be actors. Preachers are supposed to be sincere and let God speak through them. Preachers aren't supposed to exalt themselves; their job is to exalt God. But my job isn't to judge the preacher. My job is to be here with my niece and her friend Bob and rejoice in the opportunity for us to worship together.

After the service there's a reception in the preacher's office, which turns out to be twice the size of my house in Los Angeles. Bob makes the introductions.

Bishop Henry Gold has silver hair, intense dark eyes, medium brown skin, and a glittering diamond watch on his left wrist. He nods, gives me a half smile, and focuses all his attention on Cindy.

"Bob tells me that you're Maggie Clay's producer," he says.

I'm glad that Cindy doesn't correct him. Glad she has the good sense not to tell her business to a stranger.

"And I understand," Bishop Gold continues in a voice ooz-ing with syrupy sincerity, "that Miss Clay is under great pres-sure. Please let her know that I stand ready to help her in any way possible. I understand the importance of privacy for someone in her position, so please reassure her that she need not come here. I'd be delighted to meet her wherever she is most comfortable. In addition to my divinity credentials, I have advanced degrees in psychological counseling. I have counseled prime ministers and presidents, princes and cap-tains of industry. I can assure her of absolute discretion."

Cindy politely nods without committing herself. But the good bishop isn't through. He keeps talking about himself, his many books, and his wondrous ways with celebrities. I'm still trying hard not to judge the man, but I'm doing a lousy job.

"Bishop comes on strong," says Bob as he drives me and Cindy to the Adolphus Hotel where he's treating us to lunch. "But I guess if I had the number one syndicated religious pro-gram in the country, and if I had the number one Christian book on the best-seller list, I might come on even stronger."

Hmmmm . . . is all I think.

Cindy is quiet. For the last two days I've been taking her for chemotherapy. She seems to be tolerating the treatments remarkably well. We're all encouraged. But just after we arrive at the hotel she turns pale and says she has to sit down. I sit beside her on a couch in the lobby. She closes her eyes. I take her hand. "Take all the time you need," I tell her. When she tries to get up, she falls back down, this time in a dead faint.

A week later Cindy's phone is ringing off the wall.

"Put her on," says the caller without identifying herself.

"Who should I put on?" I ask.

"Cindy that's who."

"She can't come to the phone."

"Tell her to get on the phone, *now*! Tell her it's Maggie Clay."

"I'm sorry, Miss Clay, she can't."

"Who are you?"

"Her aunt."

Click! She hangs up on me, just like that.

Breakdown or Breakthrough

"Have you made sure that your niece is saved?" asks my nephew Patrick, who's calling from Los Angeles. Patrick's father is the brother of my second husband Arthur. "Have you told her exactly everything that comes in the salvation package when you accept Christ?"

Patrick is twenty-nine. He majored in philosophy and recently graduated from Trinity Divinity School. He's on fire for the Lord. He's assistant pastor at a small congregation in Watts, and when I'm out of town he's good enough to conduct Sunday services in my home.

"Well, I'm not here to preach, Patrick, just to comfort."

"Isn't that the same thing?"

"Not always."

"But you do want your niece to be saved."

"She told me she loves the Lord. That's all I needed to hear."

"But you need to be more specific with her than that."

"I do?" I ask.

"You can't ignore Romans 10:9, Aunt Albertina. 'Because if you shall confess with your mouth Jesus as Lord, and shall believe in your heart that God raised Him from the dead, you shall be saved.'"

"I'm not ignoring Romans, baby. I love Romans."

"Then don't you need to remind her of Romans?"

I change the subject by mentioning Bishop Gold.

"My God," says Paul, "he's the biggest preacher in the country. The man is huge. He's brilliant. You actually met him?"

"Yes, I did."

"Was his sermon brilliant? It had to be."

"It was fine."

"Just fine, not brilliant?"

"Brilliantly geared to his congregation."

"Will he minister to your niece? That would be a blessing."

"You're a blessing for ministering to my little congregation while I'm away," I say. "I really appreciate you, Patrick."

"And vice versa, Aunt Albertina. If you can, please buy Bishop Gold's latest book for me and have him autograph it. I'll reimburse you."

"What's it called?" I ask Patrick.

"*Breakdown or Breakthrough, How God Gets Us Through the Tough Times.* It's a best seller."

"So I've heard."

Three weeks have passed and Cindy is getting sicker. I'm cooking lunch and dinner for her every day. That makes me happy because I feel useful. Besides, I like cooking. I'm cooking her healthy greens and fresh vegetables and urging her to eat while at the same time I'm trying not to nag her. She spends a lot of time in her bedroom reading. She likes history books and old novels by Charles Dickens because she says his stories take her mind off herself. She doesn't watch much TV and late at night when I hear her crying sometimes I knock on her door and ask if she'd like company. She usually says yes. If the spirit moves me, I'll ask her if she'd like to hear some Psalms. "The Psalms," I tell her, "are the most comforting words I know. The Psalms calm me down." She goes back to the Twenty-third Psalm. I love it. I love rereading the words, "Though I walk through the valley of the shadow of death, I will fear no evil."

" 'There is no fear in love,' " says Cindy. "I remember you once sent me a card with that Scripture from the Bible. " 'A perfect love casts out fear.' "

Bob Blakey calls every day offering to bring food or whatever else we need. Sometimes she talks to him, sometimes she doesn't. Sometimes she lets him come over in the evening and sit with us while we watch a movie or television. Sometimes she and Bob hold hands. When Bob visits, he turns off his cell phone and gives all his attention to Cindy. If she falls asleep he'll talk to me about his mother, who's dean of a college in New York, or his dad, who died last year after a distinguished career as a corporate lawyer. He tells me about attending boarding schools in Switzerland where his brother, Clint, died in a terrible ski accident when he was ten and Bob was twelve. He says his parents were never religious but he asks me if I would show him how to pray.

"Just speak your heart," I tell him as I take his hand. "I speak my heart to God. I just address the Father and say, thank You for this day. This is the day the Lord made. This is the day when we reach out and touch Your hand and feel Your warmth. This is the day we are renewed by Your strength. We are grateful, Father God, for our old friendships and our new friendships. We worship You as the wondrous and limitless source of love. We rejoice in Your spirit and Your energy. And we say Amen. Bob, would you like to add to the prayer?"

"I just want to say thank You," he says.

"That's a beautiful prayer, baby. Just beautiful."

Cindy sleeps more and more. I answer her phone and take messages. She has many friends. When they call, the genuine concern in their voice tells me how deeply she is loved. Several of them describe the help she has given them over the years. She has found two of her college friends jobs in Maggie's media empire; another friend became Maggie's stockbroker. "It isn't enough that Cindy does well," says one of the caring callers. "She has to make sure that she brings her friends along with her." I see her monthly schedule pinned on a cork board: She participates in two volunteer groups to help mentally handicapped children; she attends a great books class where they discuss ancient history; and before she got sick she signed up for a course on Italian country cooking and played softball every Sunday. She seemed like a woman thoroughly healthy in mind, body, and spirit.

My friend Justine calls to ask about Cindy and tell me how Herman took her to Vegas but didn't propose. She's certain he will. He just needs more time. Vegas was exciting. Justine won eighty dollars at the slot machines and Gladys Knight sang "Midnight Train to Georgia" so beautifully the audience gave her a standing ovation. Justine tried to see Gladys after the show but they wouldn't let her backstage. She tried using my name, but it didn't work. Mary J. Blige was in the audience, though, and Justine got her autograph. Herman has promised to take Justine back to Vegas. He's also taking Justine to Hawaii. The girl is over the moon.

That same day I get an urgent message to call Paulette Simmons, a woman who has been praying with me for only a few months. She's a nurse, her husband, Martin, is a high school football coach, and their son, Chuck, is studying law at UCLA. Martin and Chuck don't get along and Paulette feels caught in between. The father-son relationship is volatile and, according to Paulette, there has been a history of violence. When Chuck was a boy and didn't perform well at athletics, Martin sometimes beat him.

"Chuck has AIDS," Paulette tells me over the phone. "He's had it for three years and only told us yesterday."

"I'm so sorry, sweetheart," I say.

"He says it's under control. Thank God, the medicines are working. But Martin went crazy. He told Chuck that this is proof of how God hates Chuck. He said AIDS was God's way of punishing Chuck for being gay. Do you believe that, Pastor?"

"No, I don't."

"Will you talk to Martin? Will you talk to Chuck?"

"I will if they want to talk to me, Paulette. Of course I will."

"What will you tell them?"

"That God loves us. He loves us in our imperfections. And He has not instructed or enabled anyone to predict or render or even interpret His judgments. No one is capable of doing that."

"It helps me so much to hear that, Pastor Merci."

"God loves Chuck. Chuck didn't earn that love through anything he did or did not do. That love is given to Chuck through the miracle of grace."

"Please call my husband and my son. Please talk to them."

I spend the rest of the afternoon making these calls. Chuck is a sensitive and intelligent man. I feel how much he needs and appreciates the ministry of grace. He is deeply appreciative and thanks me for taking the time to call. His father takes a different approach. He says he's been a churchgoer all his life and knows the Word. And then he asks me if I know the Word.

"I've studied the Word," I tell him.

"In its original language?" he asks.

"Yes," I answer.

"So if you know the Word you know that my son is a sinner."

"I'm a sinner, too, Mr. Simmons," I say. "We're all sinners," I add.

But this sin is precisely proscribed," he argues, "and the punishment is obvious. You have to be blind not to see it."

"Mr. Simmons," I say, "I believe with all my heart that the Word does not have to be argued. So I will not argue with you. I will only tell you that my deepest conviction is that God loves you. He loves your wonderful wife, Paulette, and He loves your brilliant son, Chuck. The God I worship, Mr. Simmons, *is* love. He can't help *but* love."

A few hours later Paulette calls back to say that her husband seems much calmer, more concerned with their son's medical condition rather than his moral status. She wants to know how I did what I did.

"I didn't do anything," I say. "I invoked God's love and let God do the rest."

That night, as a crackling thunderstorm passes over the city, Cindy can't stop throwing up. The chemotherapy and radiation are making her sick. I help her back to bed and place a damp towel over her forehead.

"Thank you for all you're doing for me, Aunt Tina."

"Please, sweetheart, you don't have to thank me for anything."

"I miss my friends," she says. "When my friends are around I'm less focused on myself."

"Your friends are calling all the time. They want to see you."

"I think they'll help my mood."

"Then maybe you want to invite them over, baby."

"I think I want to have a party."

"Child," I say, "say no more."

Living My Life Like It's Golden

I'm frying up a mess of fresh fish and making macaroni and cheese. I'm preparing string beans and squash and, in a burst of energy, baking a couple of pies. Cooking is creative, like singing or writing a song. When you cook you feel like you're giving people life and, baby, I'm cooking up a storm.

"I don't want you serving," says Cindy. "You aren't here to serve."

"Jesus' ministry is all about service. In one way or another, we all need to serve," I say.

Bob helps as well. So do all Cindy's friends. They come over with piles of food of their own. There are men with men, men with women, and men and women who arrive alone. There are Blacks and Latinos and whites and Asians. Everyone calls me Aunt Albertina, and everyone is warm and friendly. They understand their job tonight is to be upbeat and loving, and they do their job beautifully. Cindy wears a lovely lavender spring dress. Her body is alarmingly thin but her energy, at least for tonight, is revived. Hope and healing is in the air. We bring out the food on big platters. Before we start to eat, Cindy asks me to pray.

"Father God," I say, "we just want to thank You for this chance to be together as friends. We thank You for being our friend. We thank You for the love You put in our hearts and the love that You let us express to each other. I thank You for my niece Cindy and all the beautiful people she brought into her life. Bless this food, Father, as You bless us all with your amazing grace. In Jesus' name, Amen."

While we're eating, Cindy puts Jill Scott on the stereo, that wonderful song about "living my life like it's golden." It's a golden moment. The sun sets in golden rays behind the white curtains; the smell of fresh food settles in over the room; Cindy's friends toast her, raising high their glasses of sparkling wine and saying beautiful things about her generous spirit. Surely the spirit of God is present.

I can see that Cindy's energy is beginning to flag, but she's trying and succeeding. She bravely sits in the middle of the couch in the middle of the living room and talks to everyone. She asks them questions about their jobs and their lives as though she's perfectly fine. Bob brings her a plate of food but she hardly eats a bite. I can feel her struggling to stay alert. When someone turns the music up, Cindy gets up from the couch and—believe it or not—does a little dance herself.

"How about some 'Sanctified Blues'?" she asks, looking straight at me.

"Oh no, baby," I say, "no one wants to hear that old song."

"Well, I do," Cindy insists.

And just as Bob finds the CD reissue and puts it on the

stereo, just as the opening notes come pouring out of my thirty-five-year-old mouth, the door opens, a tall, thin, light-skinned black woman walks in, all heads turn, all jaws drop, and the party comes to a screeching halt.

Meet Maggie Clay.

On cue, she stretches out her arms and breaks into song, mouthing every single word along with the record, note for note, riff for riff, all the while doing this crazy dance to the lyrics I wrote another lifetime ago in the midnight hour in a crummy hotel room in Jackson, Mississippi:

Moon is howling outside my window
Wind is crying and I'm staring at the phone
Mama said, "There'll be nights like this, child,
When a man loves you, then leaves you all alone."

    Got the sanctified blues . . .
    I miss the church where Mama raised me

    Got those sanctified blues . . .
    Miss the wisdom that Mama gave me

    Sanctified blues . . .
    This man ain't what he said

    Sanctified blues . . .
    Said he was a saint, then led me to his bed

When that church got to shoutin'
And the Holy Ghost ran up and down the pews
I saw this man with pretty brown eyes
Saying, "Girl, let me spread the good news."

Sanctified blues . . .
Oh, he looked so fine, his words were strong and true

Sanctified blues . . .
Lord, have mercy—if only I knew

Maggie's Move

Wearing an Armani double-breasted heather gray knit suit that seems a half-size too large, Maggie has lost considerable weight since her last TV appearance nearly a month ago. The clothes hang on her wafer-thin frame. The red dye in her hair has started to fade. Her hair needs work; it looks a little wild. Her eyes are also a little wild. It doesn't seem like she's drunk, just manic. It's a party, and certainly a party mood prevails, but Maggie is over the top. She's flying.

"Love that song," she screams. "Play that thing again!"

But before Bob Blakey can hit the repeat button, Maggie takes a good look at Cindy, who's sitting on the couch. "My God!" screams the television star, "you look absolutely dreadful! You look like you're wasting away! What in hell is wrong with you?"

There is a terrible silence. Maggie doesn't know. No one has told her. Until now, she has cut herself off from Cindy,

Bob, and everyone else involved with her show. Many of her assistants and crew members are here. They are shocked.

The silence sinks in. Even in her manic state, Maggie sees she has made a mistake.

"I just thought it was a party," she says. "I didn't know. . . ."

Cindy comes to her rescue. She gets up from the couch and takes Maggie's hand, kisses her cheek, and says, "It *is* a party. It's my party, and I'm glad you came. We're having a ball. Now meet Miss Sanctified Blues herself, my aunt, Pastor Albertina Merci, who has come all the way from Hollywood just to watch you do your fabulous dance."

I'm proud of my niece for being so sensitive to someone who has been insensitive to her.

"So you're Aunt Tina," says Maggie in nonstop stream-of-consciousness mode. "Cindy's told me about you. I didn't think I'd ever get to meet the writer of my favorite song—and my mom's favorite song. She loved it because she loved Reverend Albert Jefferson, the biggest jackleg jackass preacher in Memphis, a city known for jackleg preachers. Mother was always convinced the good reverend would leave his wife for her. That man in your song was a preacher, wasn't he?"

"Actually no. I have too much respect for preachers to ridicule them in a song."

"No matter," says Maggie. "Mom took it that way. What year did the song come out?"

"Nineteen-seventy."

"Precisely. The year Mother finally kicked Reverend Jefferson out of her bed. It took your song to do it. So I salute you, Aunt Tina, for blowing the whistle on a jive-ass turkey in Tennessee. Wasn't for your 'Sanctified Blues,' the reverend might still be making booty calls to Mother, even at age eighty."

"Glad I could be of service, Miss Clay," I say.

"You have no idea. When my dad left us, Mother was inconsolable. My father was one of those white fraternity boys in lust with every sexy Black woman he met. Mom was convinced if she gave him love, he'd give her the good life. But when he learned she was pregnant with me, boyfriend was gone with the wind. That convinced her that only a righteous preacher could save her. When the preacher turned out to be just another dog, your song became our national anthem. Set Mother free. Wait till I tell her I met you."

"I take it she's in good health."

"Better than me. She doesn't drink and won't even take Advil. The woman's a saint. That's why I can't be around her. I trust you don't have the deficiency of sainthood, Aunt Tina."

"No, indeed," I say.

"I'm not so sure," adds Cindy.

"I am," I assure her.

"Anyway," Maggie breaks in, "I could use a drink. What are you having, Aunt Tina?"

"When it comes to drinking, Miss Clay," I say, "I'm afraid this old girl's out of shape."

"Well, I'm *in* shape," Maggie announces, "the best damn shape of my life. I see my attorney Bob is here and I know he's gentleman enough to fix me a drink."

Bob accommodates Maggie. As she circulates among the guests with the grace and poise of a seasoned athlete, she relinquishes center stage and the party goes back to normal. Or almost normal. When Maggie Clay is present, nothing remains entirely normal. Without trying, she sucks all the air out of the room. Even in her state of high joviality, she's articulate and fascinating and seemingly in command. Everyone defers to her. Her mind is quick. She's funny and perceptive and has a way of winning over everyone. I feel like she's won me over, and I'm not even sure how or why. Maybe it's because I appreciate how quickly she saw her mistake in saying Cindy looks like she's "wasting away." She immediately understood the gravity of her blunder—the gravity of Cindy's condition—and rather than belabor the issue she turned her attention to me. For the rest of the evening, she showered me with the same attention, asking about my life after "Sanctified Blues" and my reason for becoming a pastor. Her nonstop chatter is much more hyped up than the calm demeanor she displays on TV. But even in this state of high excitement I see that her interviewing skills are superb. She asks me dozens of questions.

As the party continues, Maggie's employees are more comfortable approaching her. They make casual chitchat. Not only does Maggie know them each by name, she knows to ask after their husbands, wives, partners, and children, also by name. She has the people skills of a first-class politician. Her chatter is incessant, but the screaming monster who fired Cindy over the intercom is nowhere to be found.

An hour later Maggie and I find ourselves in the kitchen. I've started to clean up. Amazingly, she's helping.

"You don't have to do that," I say.

"I want to help. I need to help. But I need to know what's wrong. What does Cindy have?"

I put the dish towel down and look Maggie in the eye. "Ovarian cancer."

"What stage?" she asks me without missing a beat.

"Stage four."

"I understand why she didn't tell me," says Maggie, who's talking faster than ever. "I understand Cindy completely. But here's what is going to happen: Tomorrow morning at ten a driver will be downstairs to take you and Cindy to Love Field Airport. My plane will be waiting. You'll be in Houston in less than an hour. Houston has the country's most advanced treatment facility for female cancers. I know because I built it. The Maggie Clay Center. A team of physicians with international reputations—two have won Nobel Prizes—will give her round-the-clock care. The advanced research team is coming up with remarkable cures all the time. There's a two-year waiting list just to be examined. Cindy doesn't have to worry about that. Cindy doesn't have to worry about anything. Your job is to keep her hopes high. You must assure her that she will not die. I won't let her."

Houston

The last private plane I was on nearly crashed. It was an aging contraption with propellers that stopped working while we were flying over the Ozarks. Booker T and the MG's were on the plane along with Joe Tex, the man who sang "Skinny Legs and All." Joe, may he rest in peace, got so scared he lost control of his bladder. I was nervous—our friend Otis Redding had just died in a plane crash—but I figured that if my time was up, it was up. Praise God, though, my time wasn't up.

Today Cindy, a private nurse, a stewardess, and I are seated inside a jet paneled in rich mahogany. There are a dozen seats, bigger than La-Z-Boy recliners, made of the softest beige suede I've ever felt. On a plasma TV screen we watch scenes of Hawaiian waterfalls accompanied by the sounds of chirping birds. As we lift off and sail into the clear spring sky, Cindy closes her eyes and sleeps. I thank God for the day. This is, after all, the day that God made. I look out the window and catch a glance of the Love Field neighborhood where I grew up. I think I see Calvin's house. In a little while the stewardess comes out with a tray of fruit and sweet rolls. Cindy is still asleep.

Last night when I mentioned the idea of flying to Houston on Maggie's plane, Cindy smiled and said, "Why not? What do we have to lose?" I had the same attitude and was glad Cindy agreed. She asked that I call Dr. Singer and tell her what we were doing. "I'll fax them all the records," Dr. Singer told me, "and I'll hope for the best. I hope they see something or know something I don't. All the same, if you wish to be practical, Pastor Merci, I'd keep your hopes high and your expectations low."

Cindy wakes up in time for the landing. She has a smile on her face. I think to myself, *My niece is an amazing woman. Cancer has not defeated her spirit. In her own quiet, determined way, she's moving forward. She never complains or says, "Why me?" She deals with exactly what is in front of her.*

Houston is humid and hot. The waiting limo rushes us to the Maggie Clay Center, far out in the suburbs, a radically designed ultramodern compound of vaulted glass and strange angles that reminds me of Maggie's house. "It's the same architect," Cindy tells me. We're taken to a two-bedroom suite. The furniture is plush and the abstract paintings on the walls are colorful and bright. The floor-to-ceiling windows look out on a green meadow. There's an entertainment center with big-screen TV and DVD player. I keep thinking of what Cindy told me when I asked her why she hadn't mentioned her illness to Maggie: "She has enough problems."

For the next week, Cindy is examined by a battery of doctors. She's wheeled in and out of rooms equipped with elaborate devices. Bob Blakey flies down midweek to sit with us for the evening. Cindy's happy to see him. Sometimes she has the energy to read *Tale of Two Cities*—she reads it every year, she says—but she mostly sleeps. I feel her fading away. At the end of the week, the doctors confirm Dr. Singer's diagnosis. Chemotherapy and radiation must continue. At this stage, there are no miracle cures.

Maggie calls. "Cindy can't die," she says. "I won't let her." Maggie shows up on the weekend, still talking nonstop, her eyes still very wild. "I hate what the doctors are telling me," she announces as she and I stand in the hallway outside Cindy's suite. "I'm bringing in a doctor from France. She's working on something new for arresting late-stage ovarian cancer. It's experimental but it's going to work. She'll be here Monday morning to take over the case."

Maggie leaves without seeing Cindy.

"Just tell her I was here," she says.

Maggie's state of mind is hard for me to understand. She still sounds hyper and in a hurry, as if to say, "I don't have time for this." She still sounds shaky and agitated, not at all the cool-and-collected Maggie you see on TV. At the same time, here she is, doing all she can to save Cindy's life.

When Cindy sleeps I sometimes go to the cafeteria. One time I notice the local paper carrying a story about spotting Maggie at a posh hotel in Houston. The reporter suggests that, given the sudden suspension of *Maggie's World*, her media empire may be collapsing. A quote from Maggie's attorney Bob Blakey states that "her empire is in excellent financial shape."

One night before retiring I call my daughter, Laura, in Chicago and my son, Andre, in New York. They are concerned about their cousin Cindy. Laura is having problems with her new teaching assignment at a rough high school on the South Side. Andre has decided to drop out of business school at NYU to write screenplays. I listen to them both as closely as I can, but truth be told, my mind is on Cindy. I tell Laura to be patient; I say the same thing to Andre. "God has a plan for you," I tell them both, "and you're living out that plan as best you can. I'm proud of you."

In my heart, my words ring hollow. I want to say more; I wish I could say more right now but I can't.

The next morning my nephew Patrick tracks me down.

"Your neighbor Justine showed up at your house for church on Sunday."

"That's unusual."

"She was crying hysterically. I tried to comfort her but it didn't do much good."

"What was wrong?"

"She wouldn't say. All she said was, 'Only Albertina would understand.' But I wouldn't give her your number in Houston. I told her you couldn't be disturbed."

While a nurse bathes Cindy that afternoon, I call Justine.

"Herman's married," is the first thing she says.

"Oh, no . . ."

"He's been married for twenty years. *Twenty years!*"

"He finally admitted it."

"I finally found out. His wife called. She found my number in his wallet."

"That must have been so awful for you," I say.

"Humiliating. I've never been so humiliated in my life. I feel like my life is over."

"Maybe your life's just begun, baby."

"Twenty years!"

"Justine, please don't blame yourself."

"What could I have been thinking?"

"Romance has a strange way of distorting our thinking."

"He played me, Albertina."

"Whatever happened, happened. It's over. Now it's time for healing."

"I hate myself for loving him. I hate myself for being a fool."

"If God forgives us, we can forgive ourselves."

"I'm in no mood to forgive anybody. Next thing I know you'll be telling me to forgive Herman."

"Forgiveness isn't easy, or quick. Takes as long as it takes. Can't be rushed."

"Well, I wanna rush over to his house and cut out his lying tongue."

"You'll get over him, baby."

"I won't. I can't. He's like a drug inside me."

"People give up drugs. God frees us of our addictions, if we let Him."

"I don't want to hear about God now, Albertina. I want to hear about revenge. I want to hurt the man. I want to hurt him bad."

"What good will that do?"

"It'll make *me* feel good, that's what it'll do."

"I'm praying for you, Justine, but I need to go now. Cindy's awake."

"How is she doing?"

"I believe she is healed in Jesus' name."

Man and Wife

Two weeks later I'm honored to officiate at the marriage of Cindy and Bob. The ceremony takes place in Cindy's suite in the Maggie Clay Center in Houston. The only witness is Bob's mother, Mrs. Gertrude Blakey, a college dean who seems especially uncomfortable. She's a lovely light-skinned woman in her sixties whose formal tweed suit is too heavy for the Texas heat. I admire her for honoring her son's request. I sense she disapproves. Cindy herself was against the idea. "It's sympathy, don't you think?" my niece asks me.

"I think it's love," I said. "He wants to be your husband. He's made that very plain to me. I've never seen anyone so sincere about anything."

"And you don't think it's crazy, Aunt Albertina?"

"No, baby, I think it's beautiful."

Beautiful flowers are everywhere, their powerful fragrance fills the air. Cindy is too weak to get out of bed, too weak to put on a dress. Bob is wearing a blue suit and striped yellow bow tie. He holds her hand as they exchange vows and slips a gold ring on her finger. Cindy finds the strength to reciprocate. My service is short, my prayer little more than an acknowledgment of the grace and grandeur of the moment. By the time it is over, all of us are crying, even Bob's mom.

I call my brother Calvin to tell him how beautiful the day has been. His decision not to attend didn't surprise me. Calvin has not really dealt with his daughter's sickness. Calvin has never been able to deal with reality. In a strange way, his reaction is like Maggie's. "She'll be fine," he keeps saying. Also like Maggie, he doesn't want to see her. I don't argue with him. I understand.

Bob also understands that Cindy needs time alone. The ceremony exhausted her and she sleeps for nearly ten straight hours afterward. By then Bob has gone back to Dallas, at her urging. "You'll come when you can," she tells him. "You don't have to devote your life to this hospital."

Maggie is infuriated when she hears about the wedding.

"Why wasn't I invited?" she asks me on the phone. She sounds hysterical.

"It happened so quickly," I tell her, "there was no time to invite anyone."

"I'm insulted, and I'm furious."

I'm not sure she would have come even had she been invited, but I don't say that. I assure her that Cindy is grateful for her magnanimous help.

The French doctor, Simone Grosz, speaks perfect English and after a long series of exams concludes that it is too late for radical treatment.

"Should I tell the patient," she asks me, "or is this information too devastating?"

"My niece has told me that she wants the truth."

After Dr. Grosz tells Cindy the truth, I walk into the room to see if Cindy wants company. She does.

"When strong people learn they have cancer," she says, "they say, 'I'm fighting it, I'm whipping it, I'm not losing this war.' I never said that, Aunt Albertina. Maybe my spirit was too weak to fight it."

"You have a wise spirit, darling."

"Didn't my spirit need to fight it?"

"There's a thin line between arrogance and acceptance. You're a woman of great intelligence and intuition, Cindy. Your intuition tells you that any situation can be handled, no matter how severe, with calmness and grace. I haven't seen you panic. I haven't seen you rage. Your attitude has inspired everyone. I'm sure your composure is what makes you so invaluable to Maggie."

"Has she been calling and raging?"

"She's been concerned about you, baby."

"But she's too frightened to look me in the face."

"Everyone deals with these things differently."

"Do you have any idea what I must weigh?"

"It doesn't matter."

"Ninety pounds? Eighty pounds? I don't even want to look at myself."

"Sweetheart, to me you look beautiful."

Five days later I was deep in sleep when I knew Cindy had passed. In my dream I felt a warm light surrounding my heart. Someone had departed this earth. Someone had arrived in heaven to great rejoicing. When I awoke, Bob was by Cindy's side. He had slipped in during the night.

When he looked at me, I saw it in his eyes. Cindy had gone home.

"She's with the Lord," I tell my brother Calvin.

A few minutes later, I tell Maggie the same thing. A great silence follows.

Into the Arms of the Lord

I'm back in Dallas, in Cindy's loft, arranging for her things—her books, records, furniture, clothing—to be given to the charities designated in her will. She has given the loft to her father who has already called an agent to arrange its immediate sale. Calvin is dealing with the loss of his daughter by focusing on practicalities.

Bob tells me that Maggie is focusing on the funeral. He says she is doing so frenetically. She's micromanaging everybody and everything, but that's fine; I'm still grateful for her help. She's paying all the hospital bills and flying Cindy's body back on a private plane.

"She insists that City of Faith is the right place," Bob tells me, "and that Bishop Gold is the right minister. I tried to use my lawyerly powers of persuasion to convince her otherwise, but to no avail. I told her that Cindy wasn't even a member of the church, but she didn't care. She had already called Bishop and Bishop has already agreed to officiate. I argued that you're the only minister Cindy would want to officiate. The only time Cindy met Bishop was last month when we went to church together. Bishop didn't know her. You knew her as well as anyone in the world. Because she's my wife, I feel like I should have something to say about this, but Maggie won't relinquish an inch of control."

"Don't worry about it, baby," I say. "You're in a difficult position."

"Maggie's planned everything. She's bringing in Stevie Wonder and Jill Scott to sing."

"Cindy loved their music."

"That's why I couldn't argue with her. I feel terrible about this whole thing. But I did insist that you speak at the service."

"That's not important, Bob."

"It's *very* important. It's what Cindy would want."

"Her wants have all been lifted," I say. "Her wants were left behind in this old world. We still have to deal with wants, Bob, but she doesn't. She's free."

On my way out the door to Cindy's funeral, the phone rings. It's Paulette Simmons. I tell her I have only a few minutes to talk.

"Martin and Chuck are actually talking," she says. "They had lunch. It wasn't perfect, but no one stormed out of the restaurant."

"Praise God," I say.

"Martin said he would take the issue to God. He said he would ask God for guidance. A day or so later, he said—and this is the miracle, Pastor Merci, this is the part I still can't believe—he said, 'Maybe I should listen to Chuck for a while and hear what he has to say. Maybe I shouldn't say anything at all right now.' Can you believe that?"

"I believe God's timing is exquisite, Paulette. I'm on my way to the funeral of a young and beautiful niece who was—who is—near to my heart. Before leaving here today, I cannot think of a gift I'd rather receive than the news you have blessed me with. Thank you for calling me, Paulette. Thank you for thinking of me. God is changing hearts."

"Bless your heart, Pastor."

I sit in the first pew of the church next to Maggie, Bob, and my brother on one side and my children, Andre and Laura, on the other. Bob's mother, Mrs. Gertrude Blakey, is noticeably absent. My son and daughter are infuriated that I'm not leading the service. My brother is too lost in his grief to consider my position. What *is* my position? The megachurch is overflowing with people. Cindy had a large circle of friends, but nothing like this. When word went out that Stevie Wonder and Jill Scott were to sing and that Maggie Clay would be present, the service became an event.

"Isn't this amazing?" Maggie whispers to me, excited in a crazy way. "This is just what Cindy would have wanted. Cindy would be thrilled." Maggie doesn't wait for a reply from me. She moves to the front of the church and sits in a grand chair behind the pulpit. Wearing a large-brimmed black hat and dramatic black silk dress, Maggie projects an especially slender silhouette. She looks like a page out of *Vogue*. I have not been asked to sit in one of the grand chairs. Bob, Laura, and Andre are offended by what they consider an insult to me.

"This is not the time for egos," I whisper to my children.

"Well, how about Maggie Clay's ego?" they ask me.

"I don't even want to go there," I say. "That's between her and God."

But despite what I say, I feel my ego rising up inside. I remember what it was like to sing before twenty thousand people. There are easily that many people in this airplane hangar of a church. I have never preached before twenty thousand people. The prospect is seductive. I love to preach. I love preaching in a church when the congregation shouts back encouragement. I love the feeling of God talking through me. I love praising Him. I love hearing others praising Him. I also know that I am good at times like this. When singer Johnnie Taylor and producer Clarence Paul died, I was asked to lead the service. I've led probably a hundred funeral services. I like comforting the mourners. I like the feeling of being useful. I love being in God's service. Right now part of me wants to tell this huge assembly that I am the relative that Cindy loved best; part of me wants to be recognized, even glorified. These feelings do not make me comfortable. But I sit with them, knowing that they'll pass. Silently I offer them up to God. "We are here for Your Glory," I pray. "Not mine."

I sit through the service with a storm of emotions battering my heart. Stevie Wonder and Jill Scott sing magnificently. Maggie praises Cindy for her integrity, her industry, and her intelligence. Maggie sounds wired, high on an energy that does not feel real. Cindy's friends give beautiful testimonies. Calvin doesn't want to address the church, but Bob does. He speaks with genuine love for his wife. In introducing me, he mentions my dedication to Cindy.

"My niece's favorite passage of Scripture was the Twenty-third Psalm," I say. "I'd like to read it and praise God for His grace, for Cindy's life and the courage she so lovingly taught me." I read the psalm and sit down.

Bishop Henry Gold then gives the eulogy. He speaks for nearly an hour. It's hard for me to follow his sermon. My mind is on my niece. Halfway through, the congregation is up on their feet and waving their arms, hanging on his every word, excited by the heavy cadence of his overwrought message. His message is to have hope. My hope is that I will not rail against a minister who had nothing to do with Cindy. I see how badly Bishop wants to impress Maggie. I see how I want to impress him with my superior character. But my character, I realize, is no different than his. I am a sinner, he is a sinner, we are all sinners. But we are saved by grace. So when I think competitively, when I want to best a fellow preacher, I'm operating out of the flesh, not the spirit. But when Bishop pulls out his big words and speaks in his grandiloquent booming baritone, I have to confess: The man makes my flesh crawl.

I do my best at the big reception afterward. I smile and shake hands and say as little as I can. I feel the blues coming over me. I know the mourning process is long and painful. I've lost loved ones before. I think of my son Darryl. I look over at my brother Calvin, who sits alone in a corner. I go over to join him. My daughter, Laura, is speaking with Jill Scott. Stevie Wonder has already left. Maggie Clay approaches me and says excitedly, "I'll send you a videotape of everything." Does she think this is a TV show? I know she must be grieving on the inside; but on the outside she's racing around like it's a party. Her energy is disconcerting and crazed.

I ask my brother how he's doing. "Okay," he says, but his eyes are filled with pain. When I take his hand, he feels listless. At the end of the week, the night before I'm scheduled to return to Los Angeles, he suffers a massive heart attack. He goes quickly. There is another funeral service. This time I officiate in a half-empty room at a run-down funeral parlor near Love Field. A dozen or so mourners, including Bob Blakey, are in attendance. "I loved my brother," I say, "and I know he loved me."

Maggie's Call

"**D**id they accept Christ before they died?" my nephew Patrick asks me. His tortoise-shell glasses and ultra-serious demeanor bring to mind a college professor.

I'm home in Los Angeles and exhausted. This is not the question I want to entertain.

"How have the services been?" I ask him, hoping to change the subject to my home church.

"Good," he says. "But were you able to get your niece and brother to accept the Lord? Did they confess it with their mouths?"

"Don't know what they actually confessed with their mouths. But I know they loved the Lord. Is formal confession all that important to you?"

"It's vital to *them*. They either have eternal salvation, Aunt Albertina, or they don't."

"Did I ever tell you about my Uncle Melvin?"

"No."

"Uncle Melvin grew up in Alabama. Worked as a black-smith. Loved the Lord with all his heart. I mean, he was *committed* to God. He was passionate about showing others that salvation was possible only through Christ. Melvin wasn't an educated man, but he was God-fearing. Knew the Good Book like the back of his hand. But Uncle Melvin, bless his heart, had him a temper. A bad temper. Well, one Saturday night he met his match. Met a man whose temper was just as bad, a man who flat out refused to accept Jesus as his Lord and Savior. Melvin argued long and strong. The man argued back. The words got hot. Tempers flared. Melvin got so incensed he up and cut the man. The man nearly bled to death."

"Your Uncle Melvin must have been crazy."

"That's what I'm saying, son."

"I don't get the connection."

"You will. We're all connected to God. But it's in how we express that connection that we can help others."

"You're either saved or you're not."

"Well, Patrick, one thing's for certain. You are sure enough saved. And I love you for it."

I'm hoping that puts the matter to rest, but when Patrick learns Bishop Henry Gold led the funeral service for Cindy he gets excited all over again. He has to hear every detail. I try my best to satisfy his curiosity, but finally I tell him I need to rest. It's going to take me weeks to catch up on my sleep.

Sleep comes quickly. I can't remember my dream except to say it's disturbing. It has something to do with my late son Darryl. It has something to do with gunshots and heroin needles and shock treatments and death. When I wake up, the phone is ringing off the wall.

"Just sitting here listening to your 'Sanctified Blues,' " says Maggie Clay.

It took me a minute to figure out if I was still dreaming.

"Tell me more about that song," says Maggie, who still sounds strangely hyper.

"Not much to tell," I say.

"Is it a true story?"

"Afraid so."

"Give me the details."

"I've forgotten most of them."

"That's hard to believe."

I laugh. Of course she's right. The details behind that song won't ever be forgotten.

"Well, Maggie," I say, "this isn't the best time for me to start reminiscing. I know you understand."

"I understand more than you think I understand. Maybe a better time is tomorrow. I'll send a car for you."

"To drive me to Dallas?"

"To drive you to Malibu. I'm just up the road from you in Malibu."

I hang up the phone, astonished and more than a little bewildered.

"What kind of crazy limo is this?" asks Justine. She's looking out my kitchen window as a Rolls-Royce pulls up the driveway.

"A friend has sent for me."

"Who?"

If I tell Justine, she'll go crazy. If I lie, she'll know I'm lying.

"I'll tell you when I get back."

"I can't wait that long."

"You'll have to."

"I'll die."

"You'll survive, baby. I've got to go."

"*Maggie Clay!*" says Justine. "Oh my God, you've become friends with Maggie Clay, haven't you?"

"You're my friend, Justine. She's an acquaintance."

Maggie in Malibu

Luxury is seductive. At least it seduces me. When I was a young girl, as much as I despised Neiman-Marcus for not firing the man who injured me, I loved Neiman-Marcus for introducing me to the world of luxury. Cashmere, I learned, was deeply comforting. Coarse cotton was not. Perfume, with its delicate notes of lavender and jasmine, rarefied the air and lifted the spirits. Tailored gowns turned my head and excited my imagination. When I started out as a blues singer on the chitlin circuit in the fifties, the Holiday Inns refused us service. Those were the dark days of segregation. We were forced to stay in dilapidated boardinghouses and the back bedrooms of private homes without indoor plumbing. Later, when I learned about the Ritz Carlton and Four Season hotels, I thought I had died and gone to heaven. Who doesn't like luxurious sheets, chocolates on the pillow, and cavernous bathrooms of gleaming marble? When you ride in a Rolls-

Royce, you can't help but be seduced by the smell of fine leather. With seats so comfortable, you want to sit there forever. I've brought my Bible for the long ride today, and I fully intend to continue my study of Acts. I love reading about the early church, but who can read when you're sitting in the back of a Rolls watching the world roll by? I can't. I can only imagine I'm a queen or a princess or—forgive me—a superstar like Maggie Clay being silently transported from one glamorous setting to another. I know this is fantasy. Maybe all luxury is fantasy, fooling us into believing the world is all smooth and comfy when the truth is otherwise. I've never taken drugs, but maybe luxuries are like drugs. They make the bad feelings go away, at least for a while. You get a taste of one luxury and immediately crave another. You spend a lifetime pursuing luxuries. No house is ever big enough. Or if you are blessed enough to get the house of your dreams, you start looking for another, in the mountains or by the sea.

On this Tuesday afternoon in June, the sea is sparkling blue. The highway up to Malibu hugs the curves of the coast. I relax. I stop fighting the luxury and let myself enjoy it. I allow myself a breath of gratitude. I don't have to feel guilty about being ushered into the home of a billionaire. The world of extreme luxury does not exclude God. God lives everywhere, in houses great and small; He lives among the privileged and He lives among the poor. My job is to let God lead me where He will.

The house is many miles north of the Malibu pier. It sits on a cliff overlooking the ocean. The property is massive, a beautiful complex of palm trees and exotic flowers, a sculpture garden, a pool, a tennis court, a circular driveway that stops in front of a startlingly modern structure of steel and glass that displays the same traits as Maggie's home in Dallas and her medical center in Houston. It must be the same architect.

"It is," Maggie tells me when I mention this to her over coffee and cake. We're sitting outside on what I'd call a patio, but I'm sure Maggie has some fancy name for it. She's wearing a pale pink cashmere sweater and black slacks. She looks almost alarmingly thin.

The world is spread out before us, the sea calm, the sky hazy blue. Seagulls glide with such grace I want to applaud. Down on the beach, sandpipers scuttle across the sand.

"The architect's name is Massimo Basso," Maggie says, still speaking at her superfast breakneck speed. "Have you heard of him?"

"I haven't."

"Brilliant man. He won the Pritzker last year, *the* most prestigious prize for architecture. He's outrageously arrogant, but they all are. Architects are like film directors or, even worse, preachers. They think they're God."

I smile.

"Don't take that personally, Albertina."

"I don't."

I think of the concept "passive-aggressive." When people use that term, I'm never sure what they mean. Now I know.

"What do you think of Bishop Gold?" asks Maggie. "Surely he thinks he's God."

"I thought you liked him. Isn't he your pastor?"

"Please, Albertina, I see right through him. Besides, the last thing in the world I need now is a pastor."

"I thought you asked him to conduct the service for Cindy because—"

"Because Cindy merited a service of that magnitude. I did that for Cindy and for you, not for me. I wanted Cindy to have the recognition that comes with an illustrious minister. And I knew that in your world, Albertina—the world of evangelical preaching—Gold is more than a bishop, he's a king. Was I wrong?"

I don't have the heart—or inclination—to tell Maggie just how wrong she is. So I leave it alone.

"He's impressive," is all I say.

"I detect a note of jealousy," she adds.

Maybe she's right. I don't know what to say. My mind turns to Cindy, and I'm feeling sad. The great expanse of endless sea suddenly makes me sad.

"I know you loved my niece," I say, "and I know you miss her. I miss her terribly."

Maggie takes a sip of coffee and follows my eyes to the sea. We both stare at the horizon. I feel like she wants to cry but can't let go. I can't hold back the tears. Maggie suddenly changes the subject.

"Let me ask you a question, Albertina. What's your opinion of life coaches?"

"I don't know enough about them to have an opinion."

"Do you know what they are?"

"I saw the show you did on them. As I remember, they get involved in the daily lives of people looking to break free of drugs or drink—"

"Or depression," Maggie quickly adds.

"I didn't realize depression was an addiction," I say.

"No one knows what depression is. Do you know what it is?"

"It's extremely painful, I'm sure. All separation from God is painful."

"Oh please, Albertina. Don't tell me you think all we have to do is connect with God and depression vanishes."

"My belief is that God *is* a miracle worker. Sometimes making the connection isn't easy. Sometimes it comes and goes. But the effort to connect is a beautiful thing. To me that's prayer."

"Did you see my show on spiritual enablers?" she asks me.

"I saw that one too. My friend Justine and I watch your show every day."

"So you know that spiritual enablers are like personal pastors. You hire them to help keep you close to God."

"That's what the man on your show said. I forgot his name."

"Pastor Steven McCalley. Leading spiritual enabler in the country. Six bestselling books to his credit. Enabler to the stars. Do you have any idea what happened to him?"

"I don't," I say.

"He had an affair with one of his star clients. And her husband found out."

"I'm sorry to hear that."

"So much for the legitimacy of spiritual enablers," says Maggie.

"I'm not sure he represents all pastors who give personal counseling."

"Are you applying for the job?" Maggie asks.

"I'm hardly qualified."

"I've had at least two great basketball coaches, but do you know how many life coaches I've had?"

"I wouldn't venture to guess."

Maggie turns her eyes from me and says, "Half a dozen at least. I'm convinced they're all charlatans."

"I'm sorry," I say.

"Sorry for what?"

"Sorry they couldn't help you with your depression."

"You're the one who wrote 'Sanctified Blues,' Albertina. Isn't depression just a fancy word for the blues?"

"I'm not a linguist, Maggie. And I'm not a psychologist either."

"And how about manic depression? Or bipolarity. Are they terms you understand?"

"Extreme highs and extreme lows. I know that's exhausting. And frightening."

"Stop being so sanctimonious, Albertina. Stop trying to be so understanding."

"I don't claim to understand what I haven't experienced. I can only imagine."

"Do you consider yourself a woman with a good imagination?"

"Average," I admit.

"Have you ever read *A Tale of Two Cities*?"

"No, but Cindy loved it. She loved Charles Dickens."

"I know. She got me on a Dickens kick. She was also the one who researched this business of life coaches and spiritual enablers. In that regard, she mentioned you. Before she got sick, when she saw me getting . . . well, when she saw how the pressures of the business were eating at my insides, she was convinced I needed help. Dickens would give me a break from the harsh realities of the twenty-first century. And you, she felt, would be my ideal spiritual enabler."

"I'm not at all sure about that."

"Neither am I."

"Well, then," I say, "we agree."

I hear a rising irritation in Maggie's voice that verges on out-and-out nastiness.

"The idea of a personal pastor is repugnant to me," she says. "I see it as a superindulgence on the part of the super-rich. What could be more un-Christian?"

"If we serve each other—and serve God—the names we

give our jobs don't really matter, do they? I can't believe God is concerned about what we call our positions."

"Don't talk to me about God!" Maggie jumps up out of her chair. Her voice is filled with rage. "Where was God when you called Him to save Cindy? Tell me that, will you? Where the hell was your God of mercy when that poor child was crying for mercy? Where were his miracles, his pity, his magnanimous saving powers? How can you sit there, a woman of the cloth, and talk to me about a God who rewards the wicked and lets good-hearted brilliant young women like Cindy die before their time? Tell me, Pastor Merci, is this the God you would have me fall on my knees and worship, the God who allows millions of souls to starve to death in Africa and die of AIDS, the God who stood idly by as cancer devoured my protégée for no reason at all?"

"You're angry at God. I understand that."

"Please, lady, save me from your piety. Don't pretend to empathize. Your empathy doesn't impress me one bit. I find it self-righteous and downright sickening. You preachers are all the same. You can't look tragedy in the face. You can't call it what it is. You sugarcoat life with a prescription of placebos called Scriptures. They're supposed to make the pain go away. They're supposed to help us make sense of something that makes no sense. And that something is nothing more than this miserable crapshoot called human existence. We're either lucky or we're not. We get cancer or we don't get cancer. The plane lands safely or the plane blows up. We're on it or we're not. No rhyme, no reason, no master plan, no benevolence, no kindly old man in the sky blessing the good and punishing the bad. No nothing. Just blind luck. Cindy's luck was lousy. Can't you recognize that? Can't you admit that your precious God failed you when you needed Him most? Can't you be honest or do you have to go through life believing in this make-believe fairy tale you call religion?"

I don't know how to respond. My heart hammers inside my chest, a million replies race through my mind, but I'm afraid to express them. I'm afraid of what I might say.

"If I were you I wouldn't say anything," says Maggie, "because there is nothing to say. Go back to your little home church and tell your little congregation that all is right with the world, that God is good, that Cindy is happy in heaven, and, praise the Lord, everything is hunky-dory. Go back and spread those deceits and see if you can get your brain-dead congregation to believe them. If they do, I pity them. I pity you, I really do. I feel sorry for someone like you who lives a lie and spends every Sunday feeding poor gullible souls a meal of unmitigated crap."

Finally I say, "I'm not sure why you asked me up here."

"To be honest, I'm not either," says Maggie, who gets up and walks out.

Prayer For Love

Dear Lord, I pray when I get back home and kneel beside my bed, *I want to hurt this woman. You know that. You know my thoughts. You know my heart. You know how I want to call Maggie a vicious witch. I want to tell her how she uses her power cruelly and irresponsibly. I want to call her vain and selfish. I want her to know that I know that she is lonely and frightened. I want to accuse her of using me as a punching bag. I don't need that. I'm better than that. I can punch back. I can hurt her as much as she hurt me. I want to hurt her. I want to argue her down and make her feel stupid. What does she know about Scripture? About God? Who is she to pontificate? Being a multimillionaire doesn't give her the right to spew her venom. I don't have to sit and listen to her rant and rave. I don't have to subject myself to her harangues. I don't ever have to talk to her again. And I won't.*

Take these thoughts, Father, and forgive me for hating. Show me how to deal with her without this hate. Lift this burden of rage. Let me feel for this woman, even though right now I can't. Let me empathize, even though I don't want to. Let me realize You have placed her in my life for a reason. I don't have to understand that reason or even like that reason. I just have to accept that, just as You accepted those who scorned you. Just as You loved those who tortured You. Just as those who crucified You added to Your glory by setting up Your glorious return, Your resurrection, Your rise from death. You said that "all men will know you are My disciples if you have love for one another." Thank you, Father, for showing me how to love this woman because right now I don't. Right now I have nothing but contempt, but I'm looking for love. I'm asking for love. Only You can help me love her. In the precious name of Jesus, Amen."

"Give me every last detail," says Justine. She's at my door with a baked chicken and a homemade apple pie. Who has the heart to turn her away?

"I don't know where to start."

"What was she wearing?"

"A sweater, slacks."

"Does she look emaciated?

"Can't say, Justine."

"What do you mean you can't say? Didn't you see her?"

"I was sitting right next to her, baby."

"So has she lost more weight or hasn't she?"

"I suppose she has," I say.

"She looks awful, doesn't she?"

"I've seen her look better."

"Oh come on, Albertina. Why in God's name do you have to protect this woman? I'm not writing for no newspaper. Give me the 411."

"Her house is pretty."

"Pretty or magnificent?"

"Magnificent."

"Acres and acres of magnificence."

"Many acres."

"So do the scandal sheets have it right? Is she high on drugs?"

"I didn't see any drugs."

"What in the world did she want from you?"

"I'm not sure, sugar."

"Then why did she have you over?"

"I think to talk about Cindy."

"That's sweet."

I'm about to say something, but I don't. I'm not comfortable confiding in Justine about Maggie. Justine wants to hear the worst. Telling her the worst will just get me riled up, and Lord knows complaining is never a good thing. Just look what happened to the children of Israel.

"What else?" Justine asks.

"That's it."

"Will you see her again?"

"I would be surprised. I don't think she likes me."

"If she didn't like you, why did she invite you to her home?"

"I don't know."

"She's impossible, isn't she?" Justine asks.

"I barely know the woman," I say, though silently I agree.

The Tabloids

My son, Andre, sends me a screenplay he has just completed. I'm disheartened because it's filled with violence and sex. The plot is clever and I could see where it could be a successful movie but I wish the theme were a little more uplifting.

"An agent is interested in it," he tells me on the phone. "If I can land an agent I might be able to land a sale."

"That's wonderful, son."

"Dad loved it. What did you think?"

Of course Dad loved it. His dad is Benjamin J. Hunter, my third husband, a man obsessed with violence and sex. Don't want to think about Ben Hunter and his struttin' beauty-shop-owner wife.

"I think it's great you've found the discipline to write," I say.

"You don't like the screenplay."

"I'm not a critic, sweetheart."

"Too much violence?"

"Sometimes less is more."

"*The Passion of the Christ* was one of the most violent movies ever made."

"Jesus suffered violence. That's what it was showing. He suffered violence to bring us new life and deeper love," I tell my son.

"You don't have to preach, Mom. You know I'm a believer."

"And I'm a believer in you, Andre. You'll find your way."

I'm standing in line at Ralph's grocery store trying to avert my eyes from the tabloids. It isn't easy. The tabloids are screaming headlines about Maggie—big splashy headlines, big splashy pictures. Looking frighteningly thin and lost, Maggie is shown walking on the beach by her house. Maggie is said to be entering a clinic specializing in manic depression. "Maggie," says one paper, "is emotionally out of control."

Maggie is on my mind until there is no room for anyone else. Even God. That's not right. Getting obsessed with another earthly relationship isn't anything I want. I want to avoid idol worship. I want my relationship with Jesus to come first. I want Him to live and breathe through me. When that happens, I'm not a victim of the earthly emotions of resentment or envy. I remember Paul's first letter to the Corinthians where he talked about having "the mind of Christ." When we believe in Him, He occupies our minds. His consciousness is our consciousness. We think His thoughts. Sinful thoughts flee. Our old self is crucified with Him and our new self is born with Him. The Holy Spirit came to inform us and direct our path. Right now my path is leading away from the rack of tabloids back to my car. Right now I just want to concentrate on putting my bag of groceries in the trunk of my cute little red PT Cruiser, turning on the ignition, and avoiding an accident as I leave the parking lot. Right now I am willing to let God lift my rancor toward this woman and return me to my right mind. *Father,* I silently say, *I repent for how I feel. I know your Word says that vengeance is yours, not mine. I want to forgive her in Jesus' name. I feel bad that I feel good about how the scandal sheets attack her. I feel bad that I feel vindicated. I want to forgive her and be more generous. I want to forget her.*

When I turn on the TV that same afternoon, though, the challenge is back: an entertainment news program is airing a special on Maggie's crisis. I force myself not to watch. Every fiber in me wants to. I switch to a Christian channel instead, hoping for a little spiritual nourishment, but instead a preacher is selling holy water guaranteed to heal every ailment. The holy water will even help you lose weight. "Jesus is better than Jenny Craig," says the man. "Jesus is better than Dr. Atkins." How did Jesus get to be a huckster? Didn't Jesus chase the hucksters out of the temple? But who am I to condemn this huckster preacher? Didn't Jesus say that he didn't come to condemn the world but to save it?

I need to stop judging myself. I need to confess my faults and accept my forgiveness. I need to stop judging myself for judging others. I know God has changed my nature. Yes, I have a new nature. But obeying Him is a process. It takes as long as it takes. Jesus' work is a finished work. I am a work in process. That work takes as long as it takes. At seventy, I want to be perfect. I'm not. But I am being perfected. The process is taking longer than I'd like. That's life.

Amazing Invitation

Come Sunday and I'm better. Got my little groove back. I'm prayed up and prepared for church. I'm happy to see that, instead of the usual fourteen or fifteen worshippers, my living room is overflowing with nearly forty people, including the three families who regularly attend. My sermon is about acceptance. "I know God accepts my imperfections," I say. "But do I? God can't do anything else but love me. That's God's nature. God *is* love. But I sure do find ways to mess up that love."

I confess my imperfections. I talk about my judging mode. My angry mode. My get-even mode. I want to tell my son what kind of screenplays to write and how to run his life. I want to help God and solve everyone's problems. Meanwhile, I need to obey and let the Lord solve mine. Need to trust Him. Need to relax in the bosom of His grace. Need to praise Him, exalt Him, magnify His name. Need to shout "Hallelujah!"

"You gave a good Word," Wanda Woodson tells me when the service is over. Wanda's a single mother of eight who has been praying with me for the past twenty years. I kiss Wanda and her beautiful eighteen-month-old granddaughter Tanisha who looks at me with smiling eyes and, in adorable baby talk, says something that sounds like "I love you."

"God is good," I tell Wanda.

"All the time," says Wanda's son Kevin, who's studying to be a bookkeeper.

I spend the evening reading about David, one of my favorite characters in the Bible. David's life is more dramatic than any soap opera. David's life proves to me how God uses all our imperfections to teach and expand our awareness of Him. David's love of the Lord touches my heart; the Lord's love for David, I realize, is the same love the Lord showers on me.

I'm up bright and early Monday morning. Feeling fine. Feeling optimistic. Feeling blessed with energy. Grateful for the day. The July smog is heavy, but I can deal with it. Justine comes over for an hour of bellyaching—her hours at Target are too long, her aunt in Pasadena is too demanding, Herman still wants her to be his secret girlfriend—but I can deal with Justine. Today I feel like I can deal with anything—even the prospect of looking for a warehouse for my church, a task I've been putting off for months.

Sometime last year I knew I had to do it. Just like I knew years ago that I had to preach. Preaching wasn't anything I asked for. Wasn't even anything I especially wanted. But my mother taught me when I was very young, "When the Lord calls, you answer." Simple as that. One night in Lexington,

Kentucky, I heard the Lord's voice saying, "Albertina, go home." First I thought I was imagining things. I had to be hearing things. So I ignored the voice—until it came back. "Go home," God kept saying as clear as day. But what did that mean? It took me a while to understand that it meant go home to God. So I did. I went back to school to get a regular divinity degree. I loved the courses even though a lot of the male teachers didn't look kindly on female pastors. That didn't bother me because I wasn't there for their approval. I already had God's approval. I was there to learn. And learn I did. I learned the Bible in Hebrew and Greek so I had the righteous reference for helping people properly. When I graduated I didn't have a church or a congregation, but, thanks to my "Sanctified Blues" royalties, I did have a house. My house became my church.

But now the church is getting bigger than my house and I see the need for more space. More outreach to the poor. More ministers serving young people. I need a small building or a warehouse. The church monies aren't much, but maybe if I use some of my personal savings, I can pull it off. If God wills it, God will see it done.

Riding around Los Angeles, though, I wonder if God knows about real estate prices in this crazy city. Everything's out of my budget, even run-down warehouses in run-down neighborhoods. Everyone's looking for top dollar. Seems like everyone's looking to gouge everyone else. By two o'clock I've seen seven different properties, each one seventy or eighty thousand dollars out of my price range. And that doesn't even take into account the price of renovation, furnishings, insurance, taxes, and a million other things. But I'm not discouraged by what I see. I am encouraged by my faith in the living God.

"There are dozens of other properties," says Sheila, the real estate agent who has been driving me around.

"Less expensive than these?" I ask.

"Not really," she answers, "but I'm sure God will show you a way to work it out."

I think of 1 Corinthians 10:26—"For the earth is the Lord's and all it contains"—and realize that all these buildings, all this land, everything I see belongs to God. When God sees fit to give me a church building, I'll get it. But my impatience keeps popping up. I want to find the property *right now, today, this very instant!* I realize I need patience to do God's perfect work. But impatience has been a lifelong challenge for me. I want what I want when I want it.

I drive up to my house, still thinking how things are never as easy as you expect, when I notice a FedEx envelope leaning against my door. Naturally I'm curious. I don't get many FedEx envelopes. When I open it, I see it's an urgent overnight letter from *Upward Magazine.*

Dear Pastor Merci,

At the behest of Ms. Maggie Clay, it is my pleasure to invite you to deliver the opening invocation at our nationally televised Upward Awards Show on September 1. Ms. Clay, who will be honored with our Lifetime Achievement Award on that very evening, expressed her strong preference that you lead us in prayer. "There is no one," she wrote me, "who will set a more inspiring tone for your gala event. I consider Pastor Merci one of the leading lights in our spiritual community."

Ms. Clay has generously volunteered to pay all your expenses, including first-class travel to New York City and a suite at the Four Seasons Hotel.

My public relations director will be in touch with you shortly to make arrangements.

Very truly yours,
Esther Belwethyer, Editor in Chief

I'm stunned. *Upward* is the most prestigious African-American magazine in the country. I've subscribed for years. And the Upward Awards is also the classiest of the TV specials. Everyone who is anyone attends. I never have 'cause I've never been invited. When "Sanctified Blues" won a Grammy for best rhythm-and-blues song of the year, I was certain I'd be invited to sing it on the Upward Awards show. I wasn't. Later I learned the show's producer considered my song sacrilegious. In all the years I was in show business *Upward* never ran an article about me; they never even ran my picture. I figured that's their right, but I also felt a little hurt. Singers less successful than me got all kinds of coverage in *Upward*. When you're in *Upward*, the whole community sees you. It's a big honor that was denied me. Now, out of the blue, I'm offered an even bigger honor: the opening shot on the biggest African-American TV special of the year.

I want to do it, but I worry that this is a Maggie manipulation. After she scolds me like a child, she suddenly graces me with this favor. Maybe she's guilty. Maybe this is her way of making up. Or maybe—and probably—this is her way of snaring me back into her web of confusion. I ask myself: Shouldn't I avoid all that by turning down the invitation?

The invitation also includes information on the program.

In addition to recognizing Maggie, the magazine is also honoring Sidney Poitier, Harry Belafonte, and jazz singer Nancy Wilson. These are three of my favorite artists in all the world. I imagine that there will be all sorts of private parties, before and after the show. There will also be a red-carpet entrance with the media snapping photos to send around the world. I see that the show will be taped at Radio City Music Hall. The last time I performed there was a million years ago with Elton John. I was in the background. *Upward* is putting me up front. They're asking me to open the show by acknowledging God and God's grace. If I look at it that way, I'd have to admit it is an awesome honor. And a privilege. But of course that's how Maggie wants me to see it.

I need to think about it. And right now I'm too excited to think clearly. All I can think about is do I have the right gown to wear. I turn to the Word. I turn to David. He wrote the Sixty-third Psalm from somewhere in the wilderness of Judah. He wrote, "Because Your lovingkindness is better than life, My lips will praise You. So I will bless You as long as I live. I will lift up my hands in Your name." Isn't that just what God wants me to do at the Upward show? Praise Him with my lips. Bless him with my heart. Lift up my hands in His holy name. Isn't that my mandate?

Showtime

I'm on my way.

It's been so many years since I've flown first-class I've forgotten how much I love it. What's not to love? My hairdresser Hazel worked hard on my blond highlights and my color is exactly the shade I like. I'm feeling fine. My window seat is wide enough for two of me. The footrest extends all the way out. They bring me hot towels and lobster salad and filet mignon. I have my own private DVD screen with a choice of ten new movies. Even when I arrived at the airport there were special lines for first-class check-in and first-class security clearance. No waiting, no hassles. I'm already spoiled. First class will spoil anybody.

"First class!" Justine screamed when I told her about the invitation to the Upward show in New York City. "You've got to go! I'll never speak to you again if you don't!"

By discussing it with Justine I knew just what I was doing. I knew her passion would quiet my doubts.

"I'm not totally convinced it's a good idea," I told her.

"What are you talking about? It's a sign from God."

"It doesn't come from God. It comes from Maggie Clay."

"Well, maybe that's the same thing. You said He uses people."

"Yes, He does."

"You sound like you're mad at Maggie. I thought you liked her."

"Justine, I love everybody. It's her attitude toward me that's troubling."

"I thought she liked you."

"It's not clear who she likes."

"When you went out there, didn't the two of you get along?"

"She threw something of a fit."

"You didn't tell me."

"I didn't want to perpetuate the negative," I say.

"She was probably just out of it. All the papers say girlfriend is out of it."

"She was nasty."

"But you're tolerant, aren't you, Albertina?"

"I try to be, baby."

"And you're God-fearing, ain't that right?"

"I'm God-loving."

"Then love this lady like she needs to be loved."

"I'm not sure it's that simple, Justine."

"Well, you can make it complicated if you want to, or you can see it the way it is. Maggie Clay needs you. Period."

Well, look at Justine! I think to myself. *Maybe she actually has been listening to me all these years.*

"I worry about Maggie's manipulations," I say. "One minute she hates me, the next she's doing me favors. Maybe she just likes to string people along like they're her puppets."

"Albertina Merci, you are not about to mess up the chance of a lifetime. You are getting on that plane, you are going to New York City, and when you get back you are telling me every last delicious detail of everything that happens to you from the time you get to your hotel until the time you get home. Is that understood?"

I laughed. Justine told me just what I wanted to hear.

Now, as the 747 flies over Kansas, I want to hear some gospel music. I slip in a Yolanda Adams song called "Open My Heart." That's what I need to do. Yolanda is young but she sings old. She sings with the wisdom of the ages. She sings with God in her heart. When I was singing, I was pretty good, but I was no Yolanda Adams. The girl is anointed. She sings the truth. She's asking God to guide her. She's saying she's confused. Sometimes we all get confused. We want to do His will. But what is His will? I'm going to New York because the lure is too great to fight. Is that God's will or my ego? My ego is excited at the thought of the glamour and the attention. My ego is also my humanity. Jesus was perfectly human and perfectly divine. I am imperfectly human and my Spirit Man is perfectly divine. All I can do is open up my heart and say, *Dear Lord, I am who I am. Let me follow Your light and trust that I'm doing right.* As Yolanda keeps singing, "You're the lover of my soul," my eyes are shut. Tears roll down my cheeks.

There is a man at baggage claim holding up my name. There is a limo waiting at the curb. In my suite at the Four Seasons there is a button that automatically opens and closes the curtains. There is a vase of fresh flowers, a tray of cheese and fruit, a note from the manager welcoming me. I sleep soundly. When I awake, I feel wonderful. I thank God for the day.

Today is rehearsal. Tomorrow is the show. Today the Radio

City Music Hall is empty except for the TV crew and presenters. I see Bill Cosby talking to Sean Combs and Cicely Tyson talking to Halle Berry. The producer, a light-skinned brother named Reggie Brown, recognizes me and escorts me to my dressing room where I find a huge bouquet of lilacs and a note that says, "Thank you for taking time from your ministerial duties to minister to our community. We are honored and grateful. Your friend, Maggie Clay." What am I to say? What am I to think? How can I not feel gratitude for this woman's consideration? This is a whole different side to her character. Why not embrace it? Why not appreciate it?

When the rehearsal begins, Mary J. Blige tells me how much her mother loves my records. She asks for my autograph. So does Janet Jackson. Old friends like Mavis Staples and Al Green embrace me. It feels like old home week. Since I open the program with a prayer, I'm the first to step in front of the ornate podium. Reggie Brown's voice booms over the big speakers and reverberates throughout the massive auditorium.

"Pastor Merci," he says, "can you get your invocation in under two minutes?"

"Yes."

"That's great. So we'll move on to our first presenter."

"I'd like to pray now," I say.

"Not necessary," Brown replies. "I know you're a professional, Pastor, and you don't need to rehearse your prayer. I'm sure it'll be wonderful."

"It isn't for the sake of rehearsal," I say. "It's for the sake of the Lord."

After several seconds of silence, Brown finally says, "Fine. Go right ahead."

"Father God," I begin, "we thank You for gathering us together in this wonderful forum. We thank You for inspiring us to recognize excellence, just as we recognize Your divine excellence. And Father, we thank You for Your Son, we thank You for Jesus. We thank You for sending Him to redeem us. When we accept Jesus, we accept life eternal, we reject a life of sin and embrace a life of love. When we accept Jesus, we open our hearts to His living presence. He comes to live within us, we come to live within Him, and our life, like His love, is never ending. In the precious name of Jesus, Amen."

Another long silence.

"It'll be longer tomorrow," I say.

"Alright, everyone," says Brown, "let's move on."

Two hours later, when rehearsal is over, an assistant says Reggie Brown would like to see me. I'm escorted to the control room where Brown is seated behind a battery of television monitors. It's just the two of us.

Brown is in his forties, a good-looking man energized by an intense ambition. Seated close to him, I notice how his left eye is brown but his right eye is green. I've never seen this before.

"Pastor Merci, we're all excited to have you on the show," he says.

"I'm excited to be here, Mr. Brown."

"And of course Miss Clay is especially excited. As you know, it was at her request that we extended this invitation to you. As a matter of fact I just spoke with her and mentioned that you were at rehearsal and gave us a preview of tomorrow's prayer. She agreed with me—and I'm sure you will agree as well—that the prayer is critical because it comes at the very start of the show. And because we're interested in reaching a larger audience, I'm sure you'll also agree that the more general the prayer, the less chance we'll have of losing that audience."

"More general?"

"Yes, more general means lowering the risk of alienating our audience."

"And the prayer I delivered earlier was too specific?"

"Far too specific."

"Because it mentioned Jesus?"

"Jesus and sin and all that sort of business. Not everyone in the general audience will be comfortable with that language. So if you could stick with God—everyone loves God, there is nothing offensive about God—that should do it."

"And there is something offensive about Jesus?"

"Not to me, of course. My grandmother raised me on Jesus. But to some people, yes."

"And those are the people we don't want to offend."

"I'm glad you understand."

"I appreciate your position, Mr. Brown, but, to be perfectly frank, I'm not used to having my prayers edited."

"This is a different forum, Pastor Merci. This is network television."

"Well, I will pray on the matter tonight."

"Please do, Pastor, because we would hate to have to edit you out of the show."

His last remark stings. For all Brown's deference, he makes it clear that it's either his way or the highway. I leave the meeting in a state of uncertainty.

Dinner with Andre

That evening I have dinner in Brooklyn at the home of my son, Andre. He has a new girlfriend named Nina. She is a stunningly beautiful actress who is not shy about displaying her physical attributes. Andre has always liked flashy women, and I try not to judge. I'm always trying not to judge. Nina is excited that I've gotten them backstage passes for tomorrow night's show and wants to know about every star I met today. I'm hesitant to run down the list. At the same time, I don't want to criticize her for stargazing. Everyone does it, including me. But when I get through describing my afternoon, Nina wants more. She wants to know whether I will introduce her to Spike Lee and F. Gary Gray, the film directors.

"I don't know them, honey," I say, "or I would."

But Nina won't take no for an answer. She spends much of the evening questioning me about the people I do know. Andre is embarrassed by her behavior and tries to get her to back off, but the girl is unrelenting. When she learns that it's Maggie Clay who has brought me to New York, she makes me promise I'll introduce her. Nina has a DVD of a recent movie in which she portrays, as she puts it, "the other woman." Would I like to see it?

"I would," I say, "but not right now. Right now I'd like to catch up with my son and see how he's doing."

"Oh, of course," says Nina, "I didn't mean to go on and on about myself."

"Not a problem," I say, "I'm glad to know that you're doing well."

I wish I could say the same for Andre. He seems down, mainly because his screenplay hasn't sold. He's been offered a job as a marketing analyst in a small advertising agency run by a friend from business school. "I'm going to have to take it," he says, "in order to pay the rent."

"That doesn't mean you have to stop writing," I tell him. "Your talent won't go away." Andre appreciates the encouragement.

After a delicious dinner of fresh pasta and salad, prepared by Andre himself, the phone rings. It's Benjamin J. Hunter, his dad. Nina and I clear the table and start washing the dishes. I try not to listen in, but the apartment is small and I can't help but hear Andre telling his father everything he told me about his screenplay and job offer, only in more detail. I can feel how close he is to Ben, and I can feel how I'm uneasy with that. It's good that Ben has kept up his relationship with Andre. It's what a man should do. He's right to be a concerned dad. And he's done right by Andre. But, far as I'm concerned, that's the only right thing the man's ever done in his life. I don't want to hear about Benjamin J. Hunter, not now, not ever. I pray for him.

"Dad says to tell you hello. He's glad to know you're doing well."

"Thank you, son."

I should ask, "How's your dad?" but I don't. I don't believe one parent should bad-mouth another. So the best I can do is keep my mouth shut.

Back at the hotel, I look at the eleven o'clock news. A late-summer heat wave is due to hit the city tomorrow. Subway fares are rising. A young boy has drowned at Coney Island. I pray for his parents, pray for all those who lose children in accidents too terrible to understand. I try to understand my own mood. I'm not happy that Nina has accepted Andre's invitation to live with him. He told me so just before I left. They've known each other only six months. I think he's making a mistake, but it's not for me to say. Maybe my bad feeling is due to the fact that I was looking forward to spending the evening alone with my son. I didn't know he had a serious girlfriend until I arrived. I'm sure his father knew. The truth is that Andre is closer to his father than he is to me. That has always been the case. And I'm a little jealous. I'm also thinking about Reggie Brown. I've been stewing all evening about his directive to excise Jesus from my prayer. I had wanted to discuss the matter with Andre. He's a sensitive soul and he'd understand. But I was hardly comfortable talking about something so personal in front of Nina. So I kept quiet. Seems like a lot of my life is about keeping quiet. That's something else I resent.

As I kneel beside my bed before going to sleep, I silently say, *Lord, purge me of my resentments. Let me just serve You, Lord, and do Your will.*

My Opening Prayer

The next morning is devoted to hair and makeup. Maggie has assigned her people to come to my room. They do a great job. Nothing fancy, nothing garish. They understand I want to keep a simple look. The taping starts at six, but at noon Maggie is hosting a private luncheon downstairs in the Four Seasons dining room. I wear a blue suit with gold stitching. Maggie is decked out in an elegant black and silver pants suit. She's wearing striking silver jewelry, dangling earrings and an exquisite diamond necklace. She greets me like a long lost friend. She is still speed talking but seems a little more in control of herself. All the stars are in attendance. I'm seated at Maggie's table next to Bill Cosby. Cosby does all the talking. That's fine with me. Maggie asks everyone if they remember "Sanctified Blues." They do. She goes on to explain the good work I've done with my ministries—feeding the homeless, helping abused children, finding jobs for rehabilitated prisoners. She has made a point to learn the details of my work. When lunch is over, she turns to me and whispers, "Thank you for understanding the format of the show. Thank you for compromising."

I dress early. My gown is a good fifteen years old but, thank God, it still fits and, at least as far as I'm concerned, it still looks good. The city is sweltering and even in the short walk from the front door of the hotel to the car I feel my makeup melting. In my dressing room at Radio City Music Hall, my makeup is reapplied, my hair restyled and my mind focused on the Lord. When the taping begins, I'm escorted to center stage. The audience, looking especially affluent in fancy formal wear, applauds me heartily. I am introduced as Pastor Albertina Merci.

I close my eyes and pray that my words will be the right ones. "Father God," I say, "we pray that tonight our focus be on You. You are our glory, You are our light, You are the source of creativity that we celebrate here tonight." I pause for a breath, I open my eyes and I continue. "Through Jesus Christ we are strengthened and we are saved. Through His completed work on the cross, we ourselves are completed. Through His redemptive Word, we are redeemed. His cross is our cross, His Ascension our ascension. His precious blood sets us free of sin, and His infinite love feeds our spirit and lights the path of our lives, now and forever."

"Show's Starting! Everyone Quiet!"

Three weeks later, Justine is jumping out of her skin. She has invited forty people over to her house. She has set up two TV sets, one in the living room, one in the dining room. She has baked three chickens and a mess of dumplings. You'd think she was the one who was going to appear on the show tonight, not me.

When I arrive at her house the party is already under way. The minute I walk in, I'm applauded. "Come on, y'all," I say, "let's not get carried away." Everyone wants to hear about the taping in New York. I spare them the story about how I defied the producer and prayed the way I wanted to pray. I don't tell them how at the after-party Maggie came over to me and said, "You were wonderful, Pastor." I appreciated her support. She put my mind to rest and allowed me to enjoy the rest of the evening. The producer, Reggie Brown, even gave me a forced smile and a weak handshake. I flew home the next day knowing that I had done the right thing.

So now I'm in great spirits, here among friends and church members, enjoying Justine's down-home cooking. No one can bake a mile-high chocolate cake like Justine. We're eating and jabbering and having a grand ol' time when, at eight o'clock, Justine yells out, "Show's starting! Everyone quiet!"

I'm sitting on the couch in the living room. The music comes up. The excitement builds. The announcer mentions all the stars who will make appearances. I'm to appear first.

But I don't.

Bishop Henry Gold, the silver-haired smoothie from the City of Faith in Dallas, appears. He prays in his puffed-up manner. Jesus is not mentioned. God is barely mentioned. And it's over before it starts.

"When do *you* come on?" asks Justine.

Others are asking the same thing.

"I don't," I say.

"Well, what on earth happened?" Justine wants to know.

"I wound up on the editing room floor."

"Why in the world would they do that?"

"It's a long story, baby," I say. "Let's just enjoy the show."

Arthur

I have a special place in my heart for my daughter, Laura. She's my middle child and an absolute doll. I also have a special place in my heart for her father, Arthur. Everyone calls him A. A. was my second husband and the best man I've ever known. He had great compassion for people. Laura inherited that compassion, which is why she's such a great schoolteacher. The knuckleheads in her classroom would drive most people crazy, but Laura hangs in there with them, and, despite getting discouraged now and then, she always winds up inspiring five or six of her students to go on to college.

Arthur was like that, always encouraging. His problem was liquor. I suspected that when I married him, but I was still in show business where everyone drinks and does drugs and it's easy to overlook the obvious. When A. drank, though, he never became loud or rowdy. Just the opposite. He just got sweeter. He was the road manager for a tour I was doing with Bobby

Blue Bland, the great blues singer. Arthur was so good at his job—so considerate and concerned with everyone else's welfare and comfort—that you couldn't help but love him. By the time the tour ended he and I had fallen in love. Six months later we were married. He found work as a record promoter, which suited him fine. He was a good salesman, honest and sincere. Atlantic Records promoted him several times. But I could see that the drinking was taking its toll. He'd never admit it, he'd always say he had it under control, he said it was only beer and wine. But beer and wine can kill you quicker than the hard stuff because it doesn't look as bad. It lets you think you don't have a problem. And besides, on weekends A. traded off beer and wine for gin and vodka. All this was breaking my heart because I could see his body deteriorating. He was reed thin to begin with. And the more he drank the less he ate, until he looked like a skeleton.

I'm not a nag by nature, but I confess to nagging A. to get help. Finally he went to AA but he didn't like it because he said the program was based on God. Like I said, Arthur was a loving man but stubborn when it came to religion. He got religion mixed up with God. I'd tell him, "Arthur, it ain't about religion, it's about a relationship with God. God doesn't care about religion. Fact is, Jesus didn't start a religion. He just started a love revolution." Arthur listened but he didn't listen. The drinking got worse until the day the doctor said his liver was beyond repair. He died quickly—I'm glad he didn't suffer long—and one of my strongest memories is sitting in the hospital room with him and hearing him say, "Tina, you know that I didn't care much for those AA meetings. But one thing I do remember is how they kept saying, 'Be careful of expectations. If you expect life to go the way you want it to go, you're in trouble. Take life on life's terms. Beware of expectations.'"

My expectation was that A. and I would be together until old age. He died at forty-five. And sitting here today, thinking of love lost and loving days gone by, I know my problem was that I expected to be on that awards show. I fully expected that my prayer would open the show. I expected that all my friends would see me, applaud me, admire me, tell me how wonderful I looked and how wonderfully I spoke. Of course those expectations were natural, since I had every reason to believe I'd be included in the broadcast. Maggie implied as much when she congratulated me at the after-party. At the same time, I knew I'd gone against the producer's wishes and direct instructions. I could have seen what was coming. I could have at least guessed I might be cut. But my expectations got in the way. And the truth is that I was crushed, at least for a minute.

But I'm over it. I tell myself, *Baby, you will not let this get you down. You got a free trip to New York, you hung out with the stars and that's enough.*

My nephew Patrick, on the other hand, is convinced I should sue. When I tell him the circumstances, he's ready to call a friend of his from divinity school, an editor of the religion section of the *Los Angeles Times*, to break the story.

"No," I say, "let's let the story die. 'Vengeance is mine, saith the Lord.' God will work it out."

"But you need to let the world know," he insists, "that Jesus can't be pushed aside for the sake of public relations and big ratings."

"Baby, Jesus has big enough ratings of His own," I say.

"Our job is to increase those ratings," Patrick argues. "That's what it means to spread the Gospel. That's our sacred assignment."

"We have to pick our fights wisely," I say. "And this is the wrong fight for me. It's *their* program. I was *their* guest. It was *their* choice whether to include me in *their* broadcast."

"You're too understanding, Aunt Albertina. This is a time to fight for the Lord."

"This is a time for me to finally find a building for my church."

Which is what I'm doing right now.

My real estate agent Sheila has called to say she has found something perfect for me. Sheila is a lady with a bubbly personality—I guess all real estate agents have bubbly personalities—and she's always optimistic. She's convinced that today is the day I'll discover the property of my dreams. She's a little lady who drives a big Lincoln Town Car—she can barely see over the steering wheel—and loves the Lord so much that gospel music is blasting from the stereo so loud I can't hear myself think. When Sheila pulls up to the corner of Crenshaw and Adams boulevards, a hip-hopper in a Jeep is booming rap music. Sheila gives him a dirty look and cranks up her gospel. It's LaShun Pace versus Fifty Cent. LaShun seems to be winning because the hip-hopper acknowledges the power of God by lowering Fifty Cent a few decibels. Sheila smiles victoriously.

We turn east on Adams and after a few blocks stop in front of a beautiful old bank building. It's a small one-story structure and looks like it dates back to the twenties. The front has big windows and the façade is decorated with bas-reliefs of birds and flowers. Over the front door the name of the bank is carved in stone. Time, however, has eroded the lettering. Only one word remains intact: "Trust." The lot next to the bank is vacant. The neighborhood is in transition.

"The building is beautiful," I tell Sheila as we get out of her Lincoln. "And it looks perfect, but it's got to be out of my price range. It's got to be at least two or three hundred thousand."

"It's a lot less than that," says Sheila.

"You're kidding."

"Wait till you see the inside, Pastor."

The main room, which would be the sanctuary, is paneled in deep mahogany. The floor is marble. There are also four smaller rooms and a little kitchen in the back. The place is dusty and needs painting but the old-world workmanship is magnificent. It's a neglected old jewel.

"I can't believe it's under two hundred thousand," I say.

"Much, much less."

"Why? Are there foundation problems? Plumbing problems?"

"No, Pastor, the inspection report says it's amazingly strong. When they built these old buildings, they built them right."

"Then why is it cheap?"

"It isn't cheap, it's actually all paid for. In cash. For you."

"I don't understand."

"Your friend Maggie Clay. She told me to find the perfect place for your church and send her the bill. So this is it."

"I can't accept this."

"Then you're going to have to give it to someone else. 'Cause it's paid for and registered in your name. Signed, sealed, delivered, baby, it's yours."

House of Trust

Sometimes I wonder why we get the blues. And sometimes I wonder why, when the blues wash over us, it's hard to shake them. The blues are deep. I say that because I'm a blues singer. That doesn't mean I don't love the Lord. And it doesn't mean I don't love praising His holy name. Doesn't mean I haven't devoted my life to putting God first. It just means that I know about the blues. I was born with the blues inside me, and I consider that a gift. Today I'm singing the blues and I'm listening to the blues on my stereo. I'm listening to Bobby Blue Bland and thinking about my beloved Arthur and my beloved Cindy. I wish they hadn't left when they left. I wish I had had more time with them. Wish they were here with me today. Wish a lot of things. I'm listening to "Stormy Monday Blues" because today is Monday and Bobby says Tuesday is just as bad. Wednesday is worse, and Thursday is oh so sad.

"How can you be sad?" asks Justine, who's bringing me a

couple of those big glazed cinnamon buns from Starbucks 'cause she knows they're my favorite. "This woman has answered your prayers. Not only will your church have a building, Albertina, but you won't have any mortgage. Is God good or what?"

"I'm not sad, baby," I tell Justine. "Just wanna make sure I'm doing the Lord's will."

"The Lord doesn't want you to have a building for your church?"

"But look who's paying for it? That's what concerns me."

"Albertina, you're inventing a problem where there isn't one. I'd agree with you if she'd put stipulations on that building. But she hasn't. She gave it to you. You could turn it into a skating rink if you wanted to. It's yours, honey, free and clear."

"I'm not comfortable being indebted to the woman."

"That's just the point. There ain't no debt."

"An emotional debt," I say.

"An emotional debt that's in your head, Albertina, not on paper."

"She's feeling guilty that she cut me out of the show, sugar, so this is how she overcompensates."

"I'd say that's pretty good overcompensation. Anyway, I don't think it was her who cut you out. You said it was that producer."

"Maybe I'm wrong, but I suspect she had the power to include or exclude whomever she wanted. It was her show. Everyone knows that."

"Look, Albertina, if you don't want the building, just give it to me. I'll take it in a heartbeat. I'll turn the thing into a nightclub and make a mint. I'll take the whole thing off your hands. That way you won't have to worry about being played by Maggie Clay."

I have to laugh. Justine has to add, "You see, you ain't

about to do that because you know that's not what God wants. God wants you to have that church and you're not about to argue with God, are you?"

Justine's right. If the lady wants to buy me a church, let her. If she wants to come pray in the church, she's welcome. Everyone's welcome. If she doesn't want to come and pray, that's fine too. She can pray from her palace in Dallas. Not that I'm angry. Why should I be angry at someone who's giving me a building? I'm just tired of trying to understand the woman. Who knows what makes her tick? Time to forget about her motives. Time to move on. I've got work to do for the Lord. Contractors to meet. Plans to approve. Schedules to supervise. I want to whip this sanctuary into shape in a hurry. I've had a vision for years, and now, praise God, it's time to turn that vision into reality. Time to get going.

" 'Trust' is the one word that has remained over the door," I tell the congregants at a church meeting in early September, "so 'Trust' it is. Why not call it the House of Trust?"

"Amen."

"Let's praise God," I say, "and thank Him for the blessing of this new building. May it be a sanctuary where His glorious grace is celebrated for centuries to come."

Soon the building is busy with workers. We're scrubbing and painting and mopping like mad. We're on track to worship here by Thanksgiving. Ain't no stopping us now.

Message From Maggie

I **don't believe** in coincidences. I think there's a plan. I believe God creates the plan, and, in our limited way, we try and understand it, but that's usually not possible. Or just when we think we understand the plan, it changes up on us. So we live our lives in faith. The faith is simple—that God is good. That His plan is good. That the people He places in our lives are there for a reason. That the wisdom we get from our consciousness of Christ lets us discern who to embrace and who to avoid. Sometimes the avoidance is as great a spiritual act as the embrace. By avoiding the negative we embrace the positive. By avoiding darkness we embrace the light. But we can't always avoid ambivalence or uncertainty—our human nature won't let us—yet it is certain that God is not ambivalent about His love for us. That love leads to light, clarity, and focus on Him.

On Halloween I was focused on handing out candy to the

kids. I like seeing their bright faces and big smiles when I open the door. I like looking at their cute costumes. I like seeing the ballerinas and clowns and ghosts and Spider-Men. I like hearing them scream "Trick or treat!" in their high-pitched voices. I like seeing their moms and dads hovering over them. I just like the energy and excitement of an evening devoted to making children happy. In the middle of evening—around eight o'clock—one woman, whose little girl is dressed up as Tweety Bird looked at me twice and said, "Excuse me, but are you Pastor Merci?"

"I am."

"Well, this is a really nice coincidence. I didn't know this was your house. I'm Dorothy Wright. This is my granddaughter Louise."

"Hi, sugar," I say to Louise.

"I saw you at Miss Clay's not long ago. At the house in Malibu. I've kept house for Miss Clay for two years now."

"It's good meeting you, Dorothy. You have a gorgeous granddaughter. And how is Miss Clay?"

"To be honest, Pastor, I'm worried sick about the woman. Weeks go by when she doesn't seem to want to get out of bed. Just mopes around. Won't even read or turn on the television. Sleeps for days. When I've worked at night, I've seen how sometimes she'll be talking nonstop on the telephone for hours on end. I have no idea who she's talking to. But she'll just talk herself to sleep. I was hoping she was talking to you because I know you're a woman of God. I was hoping she was reaching out to you because, God bless her soul, she needs someone who cares, someone who doesn't want to use her but just wants to help the poor lady. I do believe she's lost."

———

Bright and early the next morning my phone rings.

"Aunt Albertina, it's Bob Blakey."

"Bob! Been meaning to call you, baby. How are you?"

"Been fine. In fact, I'm in Los Angeles for a couple of days and would love to take you to dinner."

"I'd love it too," I say.

Bob wants to send a car but I tell him that's ridiculous. At six that evening I cruise over in my trusty PT Cruiser. He's waiting for me in the lobby of the Regent Beverly Wilshire. After we embrace, he tells me I'm looking younger. I tell him he's a liar but I love him anyway. We walk down the street to a quiet Chinese restaurant on Rodeo Drive.

When we sit down, the first thing Bob says is, "I miss her so much."

"I know you do, baby. I miss her too," I say.

"I ask myself the question—how long does the mourning last?"

"Lasts as long as it lasts. We can't cut it off. We can't pretend we're through mourning when we got more mourning to do. I'm still mourning folks who died a long long time ago."

"May I ask you to pray, Aunt Albertina?"

I take his hand and say, "Father God, we come before You with heavy hearts. We miss our Cindy so much, Lord. We don't have to tell You. You know our hearts. You feel everything we feel. And that makes us feel better because we feel understood. You understand grief and pain. Lord Jesus, You suffered the worst pain of anyone who has ever lived. You died the worst death. But the worst death was the best death because it led to our redemption. We know that our precious Cindy was born again in You, that she lives in You, just as she lives in our hearts, just as You live in our hearts, with all Your compassion, love, and amazing grace. Thank

You for the food we're about to eat, Lord, thank You for our many blessings, for our beautiful relationship and the clarity of our minds and the strength of our spirit. In Jesus' name, Amen."

Dinner is delicious. Some of the best spareribs I've ever devoured. Bob speaks about how he's setting up a journalism scholarship in Cindy's name. I think that's wonderful. I think Bob's a wonderful guy, but I'm feeling he has another agenda. He is, after all, Maggie's lawyer.

"I was talking to someone yesterday who knows Maggie," I say. "She tells me Maggie is still struggling."

"She is," Bob confirms. "That's one of the reasons I wanted to see you, Albertina. I've come to deliver a message from Maggie."

"Let me guess. She's paying Billy Dee Williams to marry me? When I get home, he'll be waiting at my door!"

Bob smiles. "I didn't know you're still in the marrying market."

"Unmarried women are always in the marrying market, baby, whether they admit it or not. It's just that at seventy my market value isn't what it used to be."

"I disagree."

"You're prejudiced, sugar. Now what can I do to help Maggie?"

"She wants to hire you."

"My cooking also isn't what it used to be."

"Seriously, she wants to hire you as a combination life coach and spiritual enabler."

"Oh, come on, Bob—"

"The job would be on a per month basis at thirty thousand dollars per month plus all expenses. The first month paid in advance."

"Someone could see this as spiritual prostitution on my part."

"You could see it many different ways. It could be that someone in desperate emotional straits is reaching out the only way she knows how. She can't whip this depression. Her mood volatility has intensified. She's either over the moon or down in the dumps so low I worry whether she'll ever come back up."

"I want to help her, Bob. I want to help anyone who's hurting, but I'm not sure I can. I'm not sure how she really feels about me. I'm not sure about her motive for hiring me."

"I genuinely believe she has but one motive here, and that's to get her life back. Right now it's in tatters."

"What makes her think I can help?"

"I've told her so. And so did Cindy. Those are two opinions she respects."

"Thank you for your votes of confidence."

"She already cast that vote when she arranged the purchase of the building on Pico. She genuinely likes you."

I let out a deep sigh. I don't know what to think.

"She buys me a church," I say, "and then a few months later offers me a fortune to leave the church."

"Only temporarily."

"I'm not sure, Bob."

"This is a seriously sick woman, Aunt Albertina. The irony is that were she poor you'd probably do all you could to help her."

Bob's remark stops me cold in my tracks. I have to think about what he has just said.

"Those doctors have failed her," he adds. "She needs a different kind of doctor."

"We all need the same doctor, honey, Dr. Jesus, and He's available to everyone, free of charge, twenty-four/seven."

"But sometimes He needs to be introduced by people who know the right way to introduce Him."

"Your lawyer skills are no match for me, Bob."

"I'd never want to coerce you into doing something you don't feel is right."

"Baby, you never could."

Rhonda and Lisa

It's Sunday evening and I'm just settling down to watch *60 Minutes* when my nephew Patrick shows up at my door. He looks terrible. He's just been fired from his post as assistant pastor at his church in Watts. He's all torn up inside.

"I can't believe it, Aunt Tina," he says. "No review. No severance pay. After service, the head deacon called me aside and showed me the door. I mean, he was cold-blooded."

"There had to be an issue, baby."

"There was. But I wasn't even given a chance to voice my position. You see, I didn't know this couple was gay."

"Two men?"

"Two women. Rhonda Bolden and Lisa Adams. You've met them."

"Over at your house, yes. Lovely ladies. Aren't they schoolteachers?"

"Rhonda's the principal at Wiltern Place Elementary. And

Lisa teaches history at L.A. High. I thought they'd be perfect to head up my committee on religious education. They've been revamping the Sunday school, making sure our teachers are better prepared, reevaluating the books we use, reenergizing the program at all levels. Rhonda and Lisa are perfect people for the task. Devout Christians. Highly educated. But then the deacon saw a picture of them in the newspaper at a gay rights parade. They were holding hands. He confronted them and they refused to discuss it, saying it was their business, not the church's. The deacon was incensed. He said I had put lesbians in a position of poisoning our church youth. He said I had knowingly gone against Scripture and God's natural laws. The truth is that I knew they roomed together but I didn't know they slept together. Fact is, I still don't know."

"And shouldn't care."

"But the deacon cares."

"You can't control the deacon's mind, sweetheart."

"But he controls my job—or what used to be my job."

"You'll find another."

"Rhonda and Lisa have been asked to leave the church."

"If you give me their phone numbers, baby, I'll call and invite them to my church."

"You don't mind the controversy?"

"I don't see it as controversial, Patrick. I don't have a sexual survey form for members to fill out before they're allowed inside. My understanding is that our Lord reached out to everyone and we are to do the same. It's no more complicated than that."

"Given everything that's happened, finding another job might be complicated for me."

"Maybe yes, sugar, maybe no. The House of Trust can always use a brilliant preacher."

That night my dream is complicated. I'm set to perform at the Neiman-Marcus store in downtown Dallas. The store has been turned into a beautiful concert venue with plush red velvet seats and gold curtains. It looks like an opera house. I'm in my dressing room getting ready when someone knocks on the door. It's Cindy. "You can't preach," she says. "Maggie wants you to sing. She wants you to sing 'Sanctified Blues.' "

"Tell Maggie I'm preaching," I say. "And tell her to mind her own business."

"If I tell her that," says Cindy, "she'll fire me. She'll fire all of us."

My second husband Arthur, who is seated on the couch across from my dressing table, gets up and whispers in my ear. I'm so happy he's alive that I want to listen to him, I want to agree with him when he says, "This is not the place to preach."

Cindy leads me to the stage. I see my brother Calvin in the first row. The band strikes up a chord. I open my mouth, not sure whether to sing or preach, when Maggie Clay steps in front of me and recites the Lord's Prayer. I begin to cry. Maggie's voice gets louder and louder. The audience is on its feet applauding her. I fade into the background. I wake up.

Rhonda Bolden and Lisa Adams look to be in their early thirties. They are attractive women who dress with simplicity and elegance. I am glad to see them seated in the first pew of the House of Trust on the Sunday before Thanksgiving. I'm happy that the congregation has grown to nearly sixty members. My friend Charles Green, who once accompanied the rhythm-and-blues singer David Ruffin, is playing the second-hand upright piano I purchased last week. He's playing magnificently.

We've held Bible class in the old bank building before, but this is our first Sunday service. The sanctuary isn't fancy, but, to my eyes, it's stunning. The walls are painted off-white and the cross above the pulpit is royal blue. Mary Green, Charles's wife, is an artist who designed two beautiful banners that hang from the ceiling. One depicts a white dove, the other a glowing sun. One says, "Know Him," the other says, "Make Him Known."

"I've known for a long time that God is faithful," I tell the congregation. "My mother lived that faith. She was the one who said, 'Honey, don't *force* your way through life, *faith* your way through.' Well, that's how this church has come about. We *faithed* our way through. We can do that because we serve a faithful God. We serve a worthy God. He has certified our worth through His grace. He has blessed us with His grace and expects nothing in return except that we worship Him. To do so is a joyful thing, a comforting thing, an exciting thing. When I grew up, we didn't have much but that didn't matter because Mother taught us we had everything. We had Jesus. I saw how one praying mother can save a whole household. That's the strength of prayer. That's the strength of believing in Jesus.

"Now I've always believed I would have a church building. I didn't know how it would happen. It happened in a way I could never have imagined. But I believe it's because of trust that we sit here in the House of Trust. It is because of God's goodness that we have a beautiful sanctuary in which to express that goodness. God's miracles continue. Every day He reveals Himself in new ways. Sometimes—maybe even often—we don't see what He's doing. We don't want to see because He's not doing it in a way that's comfortable for us. He does it in a way that challenges our plans and challenges our attitudes. That's when we have to surrender.

"My plans, for example, were to spend this holiday season with you in our new church. My plans were to have my children come here for Christmas so they could see this sanctuary and spend the holidays with me. My plans were set. But then God came in and said, 'Albertina, not so fast. Can't you see I'm moving you in a different direction?' At first I didn't see that. Didn't want to see that. But, like they say, when the handwriting is on the wall you better read it. So I'm leaving next week on a trip I never planned. But I'm grateful. It's Thanksgiving, a season to focus on gratitude. I'm grateful that my nephew Patrick will be leading this congregation in my absence. That's a blessing and, I'm certain, also part of God's plan.

"I'm even grateful for the idea of gratitude because without it I'd be lost. We all would be. We'd be complaining instead of complying, pleading instead of praising, nay-saying instead of praying. My prayer is that I please God. I don't need to please people. I don't need to please myself. I need to please God. God can't die, lie, or change. He simply is. He is the great 'I Am.' Through His Son, He became what we are so we can become who He is. For His Son, the lover of my soul and light of my life, I am forever grateful.

"I ask for your prayers on my journey. Know that you, my brothers and sisters, are always in my heart. Know that I love each and every one of you."

Part Two

A man's discretion makes him
slow to anger, and it is to his glory
to overlook a transgression.

—PROVERBS 19:11

Paradise Lost

Maggie Clay is depressed. Deeply depressed. Since I arrived on the Caribbean island of Maraqua a week ago, she has remained depressed. Her house sits on a cliff overlooking the vast blue sea. She sits in a chair in the living room, just staring. I sit in the den, my Bible open to passages on patience. I need more patience than I presently possess. I need the patience of Job.

Getting here required a special act of patience. When I told Bob Blakey that I had decided to accept the offer, Maggie rescinded it. She said she had given me a week to reply and I took eight days. I didn't know there was a time limit—neither did Bob—but I didn't argue. I was relieved. I'd get to be home for Christmas after all. But then Maggie called that night and told me to be in Dallas on Thanksgiving day. Dallas, of course, was the last place I wanted to be. But by then I was resigned to do what I had to do. Waiting on line at the airport

I heard myself being paged. When I got to the phone, I heard Maggie telling me, "I've decided to spend the holidays on Maraqua. Bob will change your ticket. You'll meet me there tomorrow. You'll love it. It's paradise."

I didn't relish spending Thanksgiving on a plane. I didn't relish being tossed around like an old football. I didn't relish any of this. I had never heard of Maraqua. Had no idea where it was. When I got to LAX Thursday morning, the flight to Miami was delayed for two hours. I missed my connection and wound up spending the night at the airport hotel. By the time I got to Maraqua the day after Thanksgiving I was beat and Maggie was in a rage. She was angry that she had spent Thanksgiving alone. But, in fact, she wasn't alone; she had a housekeeper and cook. I wanted to ask her whether she had thanked God—or thanked anyone—for her countless blessings, but I didn't.

Those first days I just left her alone. I quickly understood that I was there as an overpaid babysitter and that, as time went on, God would reveal exactly what He wanted me to do. My prayer was that I'd be sharp enough to perceive His revelation. I didn't feel sharp. I felt confused. Maggie stayed in her bedroom. She ate alone. During the day she slept for hours on end. She barely talked to me. Her depression was profound. She medicated herself with wine. She watched old movies in the elaborate screening room but did not invite me to join her. She barely acknowledged my presence.

I realized this was part of her hostility. I was there to suffer her hostility, just as I had suffered it before. Going in, I knew that was part of my job. But knowing that didn't make it any easier. I felt like a fool, sitting in the gorgeous guest bedroom that overlooked the gorgeous sea; sitting out on the gorgeous veranda that faced the gorgeous mountains; enjoying the gorgeous weather; eating gorgeous meals prepared by Maggie's superb Maraquan cook. Delicious fish, fresh fruits and vegetables, homemade breads and cakes.

I told myself this was a well-earned vacation, but was it? Depression is a contagious disease, and, in spite of all my efforts to resist, I felt my own spirit deflating. It was a ridiculous situation. How could I complain about being paid a king's ransom to hang out in paradise where I had nothing to do but look out at the blue sea? Did I want to swim? Maggie's house led down to a private beach. She also had a pool out back. Did I want to exercise? Maggie had built an enormous exercise room next to the garage. Did I want to read? Maggie's library, next to the dining room, was fully stocked. I found a beautiful book on the life of our Lord that I read slowly and with great delight. Through the author's poetic language, Christ's miraculous mission was brought to life. I never tire of the story of stories. The book returned me to a state of gratitude—gratitude for having been brought to this island of such natural beauty. I was deep into Jesus' final arrival in Jerusalem when I was told I had a phone call.

Justine was on the line.

"But how did you get the number here?" I asked her.

"That man Bob Blakey. I told him it was a matter of life and death."

"Is it?"

"Maybe."

"I thought you were on your vacation, Justine. Weren't you going to North Carolina this week?"

"That's where I'm calling from, Albertina. I'm at the fatty farm. I've already lost three pounds."

"Great."

"Not so great."

"Why?"

"The instructor says he's fallen in love with me."

"That sure was quick, sugar," I say.

"It happened the first night."

"What happened?" I asked.

"You don't want to know."

"Okay."

"He's my soul mate, Albertina. The most wonderful man I've ever met. His name is Walker Jones and he was a football player for the Detroit Lions. He went to school to become a nutritionist and then a weight-loss expert. He used to weigh three hundred pounds. Now he weighs one-eighty and, believe me, it's all muscle."

"I believe you, baby."

"The man is also psychic. He sensed everything about me. He knew I'd been hurt. He said things to me only a person who'd known me my whole life could know."

"That's good."

"Well, not so good."

"Why?"

"He's married."

"Oh, sweetheart . . . not again—"

"But he didn't lie about it, Albertina. He didn't try to hide it. He said it right away. 'I have a wife,' he said, 'but we're not really living as husband and wife. It's just a business arrangement.' She runs the office here."

"You've met her?"

"I see her every day. She's a scrawny little thing. She looks like a mouse."

"And does she know?"

"I don't think she cares."

"But what you think and what you know are two different things. Be careful, Justine. This is a messy business."

"That's why I'm calling you. I want to avoid a mess. That's why I skipped out of the fatty farm today. I'm calling you from a pizza parlor in town."

"You're eating pizza?"

"Just one slice. I just talked to Walker. He wants me back. He says if I don't come back he's coming to get me. See how romantic he is?"

"I see."

"How's the life-coaching business? Have you coached her back to sanity?"

"She's mainly sleeping."

"Well, that makes it easy. How's the house? Something out of a magazine?"

"Very beautiful."

"You're very blessed, Albertina. You know that, don't you?"

"I do, honey. But what are you going to do?"

"Resist the second slice of pizza. Resist getting further involved with a married man. Isn't that what you would tell me?"

"Well, baby, if he's hitting on his clients the first night they arrive that is not a good sign."

"He didn't hit on me. He fell for me."

"Can you get a refund?"

"I'll have to ask his wife."

"That could be awkward," I say.

"*Oh my God!* He's pulling up to the pizza parlor right now! He's found me! He's getting out of his car! I gotta go, Albertina—" And with that, she clicked off.

I still haven't heard back from Justine.

And I still haven't found an opportunity to sit down and ask Maggie what she expects from a life coach/spiritual enabler. Meanwhile, I'm feeling the splendor of the living God in the great expanse of sky and sea. I'm sleeping like a baby.

Gumbo

I don't know if the sound is coming from inside my dream or is in the real world. Whatever it is, it wakes me up. It's a steady sound, a bouncing sound that's coming from outside. I draw back the blinds enough to see Maggie on the driveway shooting baskets into a hoop set up on the garage. The glow of a full moon sheds all the light she needs. In loose-fitting sweats, Maggie stands and makes one free throw after another. She never misses. When she's bored with free throws, she tries her hand at hooks. She misses a few of those. Then it's her jump shot, then her layup. She's a fine, steady player with a sure hand. I smile and think to myself, *This is good, this is the kind of therapy she needs, exercise will help her feel better.*

Next morning Maggie calls me into the den where she's watching tapes of some of her old shows on the enormous plasma screen. Outside the sun is shining. In Maraqua the sun is always shining. Inside the shutters are closed tight and the den is dark. Maggie is sullen and silent. In spite of last night's workout, she still hasn't been able to shake the blues. She wears a white t-shirt and slacks that reveal her long thin frame. She asks me to sit beside her. I do. I'm interested in which shows she has chosen to watch. They all concern mental health. Each has her interviewing experts—psychotherapists, hypnotherapists, New Age gurus, Buddhist monks, reformed rabbis—who give their views on dealing with depression and other emotional maladies. I watch Maggie on the screen and am amazed by her curiosity, sharpness, and probing questions. She's generous with her guests, careful to avoid arguing, and great at clarifying their points for her viewers. She's the ideal interviewer, and, as I observe her charming and cheerful manner, it's hard to believe that the woman on the screen is the same person as this painfully depressed woman sitting across from me.

"What do you think, Albertina?" she asks me when the last show is over.

"I think you're excellent at your job."

"I hardly think you're qualified to give me a job evaluation. That wasn't the point of my question."

"Sorry. Guess I missed the point."

"You certainly did."

"Then what was the point, sugar?"

"I was asking you about this house, my lifestyle here in Maraqua."

"It's idyllic," I respond.

"Oh come on, you're bored to death sitting around doing nothing."

"I'm fine," I say. "It's a privilege to see this part of the world. It's absolutely beautiful."

"You're playing games with me, Albertina."

"I'm really not. I don't play games—not with people's emotions."

"I'm touched. But I still don't think you know what you're doing here."

"Honey, I'm the *first* to admit that."

"You're keeping me company, that's what you're doing."

"And for that I'm grossly overpaid."

"You're right about that."

"And how long will you require my company?" I ask.

"That's my decision, not yours."

"I'd like to feel useful. I'd like to help you in some way. I'd like to know how *you* see me helping you," I tell Maggie.

"Can you make gumbo?"

"A good one."

"Then do it."

Maggie doesn't like the gumbo. She eats two bites, says it's too salty, and gets up from the table and leaves. This is after I've been preparing the dish for a couple of hours. What am I supposed to say?

That night, despite wonderful sea breezes sweeping in from the open window, I sleep poorly. My dreams are jumbled and disturbing. My children are infants who are swept up by waves; Cindy is calling me from the other side of a chasm but I can't hear what she's saying; my nephew Patrick is an astronaut on a rocket ship lost in space. When I wake up in the morning and go to the kitchen to make coffee, Maggie is already sitting there, watching the *Today* show.

"I hope you don't mind taking over the kitchen," she says. "I've fired the cook. The woman didn't know what she was doing."

"I liked her meals," I say.

"I didn't. And I was the one paying her. I like my eggs over easy."

I think about this for a couple of seconds. I breathe in a deep sigh and put on an apron.

Actually the cooking makes me feel useful. I enjoy it. I've always enjoyed cooking because cooking brings Mama to mind. I learned to cook by watching Mama in the kitchen. Those were some of our best times together. Cooking put Mama in a good mood. That's when she would reminisce about *her* mother who had been a sharecropper and the daughter of slaves. Maybe it's the warmth of the stove, maybe the fact that food is what sustains our bodies, but there's something about cooking that puts me in a positive frame of mind. Cooking says to me, *Life goes on; life is good.*

I feel the same way about shopping for food, especially in Maraqua where the open market down the road from Maggie's house is a carnival of brilliant colors and fabulous aromas. The women wear their native garb and the spices, flowers, and fruits are displayed with artistic flair. With the sun beating down and the sound of steel drums pulsating from a band of musicians playing at water's edge, it's hard not to be happy. I buy a bunch of stuff—the fish looks incredible—and decide to make a fish fry.

When I get back to the house, I see a guest has arrived. As I carry in the groceries, Maggie does not introduce me. She and her guest are sitting at the kitchen table. I recognize him from television. He is Dr. Oliver Porter, the best-selling self-help author and therapist—at least I think he's a therapist—who first started appearing on Maggie's show before landing a show of his own. He solves everyone's problems with his positive can-do, don't-be-a-victim, take-charge philosophy. He's a short man with a pleasant smile, a big pot belly, a small head covered with thick curly gray hair, and a super-thick Boston accent. His latest book, *Mind Over Matter: Making Every Day Count,* has been sitting on the living room coffee table since I arrived. After offering to make them a pot of coffee, I'm still not introduced. Moving around the kitchen, making the coffee and putting away groceries, I can't help but overhear their conversation.

Dr. Porter has a hard time talking about anything but himself. He tells Maggie how he's been on a whirlwind book tour and how his books are selling like hotcakes. He tells her of the thousands of e-mails he receives every day from people whose lives have been changed by reading his book. The president of the United States, the prime minister of Canada, even the pope, he tells Maggie, are all reading his book.

"But enough about me," he finally says, "how are you doing?"

"Enjoying the island, Oliver. Just relaxing."

"You look wonderfully relaxed," he says, "but then again, you always look wonderful."

Maggie seems less depressed. Maybe that's because she has a guest. I just hope she's able to open up to him about her problems, whatever they are. I hope she tells him how low she's been. I hope his book and his philosophy, whatever it is, helps her.

I serve them coffee followed by fresh fruit and cheese. I'm still not introduced. Maggie is happy to let the good doctor see me as the cook. I'm happy that they like my little luncheon spread. Maggie begins telling Porter her ideas for a series of reality shows. He's part of her plan—the inside view of couples in therapy. I realize that his visit is about business and has nothing to do with Maggie seeking help for herself. That disappoints me. I'm doubly disappointed that while talking to Porter she turns into the Maggie of *Maggie's World*, the TV host who makes everyone comfortable. She allows him to talk about himself which, in Porter's case, takes no effort. He goes on and on about how he'd be perfect for her reality show. He sells himself without realizing that Maggie's already sold on him. It's exhausting to listen to the man.

"For dinner," Maggie tells me later that afternoon, "do something creative. Do something with lobster. We'll be a total of five."

Well, it looks like I'm the full-time cook. I guess that's better than being the full-time nothing. Serving is a noble task. Doesn't the Lord serve us? Didn't he wash his disciples' feet? If this is God's way of bringing me closer to one of His children, so be it. If this is God's way of humbling me, I can't argue. We can all use some humbling. So I humbly traipse back down to the market and buy lobsters. From my mama's sister, who lived most of her life in Louisiana, I learned how to fix lobsters Cajun-style. I boil them and work up a strong red cocktail sauce. I remember to serve it with a dish of melted butter for dipping. I make peach cobbler for dessert. The housekeeper is off today so I do the serving as well as the cooking. Besides Dr. Porter, the other guests are TV executives who have homes in Maraqua. Every time I move in and out of the dining room, Dr. Porter is dominating the conversation.

I'm stacking the dirty dishes in the dishwasher when Maggie comes in the kitchen and says, "I'd like you to come in and sing 'Sanctified Blues,' Albertina. I told the guests you were once a singer."

Did you also bother to tell them that I'm a preacher with a college degree? I want to ask. There are a dozen things I want to ask, but I don't. I take off my apron, go to the living room, and do an a cappella version of "Sanctified Blues." It is not an especially stirring rendition but the guests are amused.

"It's wonderful that you can employ this woman," says Dr. Porter. "I'm sure you're giving her a new lease on life."

The presumption is that, until Maggie hired me as her servant, I was washed up. Everything in me wants to correct this misperception. Which is just what I'm going to do. But as I begin to speak, Maggie cuts me off by saying, "You can clear the dessert dishes now, Albertina."

Father God, I pray that night in bed, *I know your Word says that You never give us more than we can handle. I know we're continually learning the meaning of obedience. I know I have a restless spirit and sometimes a disobedient spirit. Mama told me that when I was young. That's when I first ran off and decided to sing the blues. Mama was right. I made some good choices but I made some bad choices. It took me a while to let You order my steps. You are an orderly God, I know You are, I know You know my heart. You know my ways better than I do. You know where I need to go and what I need to say and what I don't need to say.*

And maybe tonight was one of those times when I didn't need to say anything. You felt everything I wanted to say. You heard the words inside my head. You heard me cursing Maggie. You heard me accusing her of belittling and humiliating me. You heard me condemning her for misusing me. Lord, I pray that these feeling pass through me quickly. I pray to be free of the anger I feel for this woman. I want to hurt her as she is hurting me. I want to understand that I don't need to be hurt, if only I don't take it personally. I realize it's about her, not about me. It's about the mysterious sickness in her soul. I realize I'm here to address that sickness, but I also realize I don't know how. All I know is that right now I can't stand the woman I've come to help. Helping her is the last thing on my mind tonight. Getting out of here is the first thing. Like tomorrow morning. I want to pack up and leave. I want to hear Your voice say, Go home, Albertina; you've done enough; this assignment is impossible; this assignment is over. The House of Trust needs you more than this woman does. You are free to leave. I commend you for a job well done. *But here I am, Father God, telling You what to tell me. That can't be right, but that's what I want. I want to get out while the getting's good. I want to get out before I say things I'll regret. In Jesus' name I pray, Amen.*

I awake with the dawn. The day breaks fresh and new. I make myself a cup of coffee and take the Bible to the veranda where, for two hours, I read by the glorious light of the morning sun. I read in Romans where Paul says, "You are not in the flesh but in the Spirit, if indeed the Spirit of God dwells in you. But if anyone does not have the Spirit of Christ, he does not belong to Him."

As the sun ascends over the radiantly blue Caribbean, I pray that the Spirit of Christ be revived within me. I read on that "if the Spirit of Him who raised Jesus from the dead dwells in you, He who raised Christ Jesus from the dead will also give life to your mortal bodies through His Spirit who dwells in you." *Dwelling Spirit,* I pray, *dwell deep within me; refresh me; renew me; make me strong.*

I open my eyes and see Maggie standing in front of me.

"This is the housekeeper's day off," she says. "The kitchen floors need to be mopped and the windows washed."

Where is the in-dwelling spirit of Christ now? Do I give this woman a piece of my mind? Or a piece of my heart? How do I find peace when all I want to do is tell her where she can put her mop? I look at her hard and long. She looks back at me. Is this a test? Is this a standoff? Is this punishment or service? I think of Mama, the world's most cheerful housecleaner. She did it for a living without complaint or remorse. She did it *singing*! She actually sang as she scrubbed the toilets of wealthy white people. I knew as a child that her song was born not of her resignation but of certain knowledge that the joy of the living God is available to us at all times. It is our choice whether to access that joy or not.

But that doesn't change the fact that I do not want to mop Maggie's floors. I do not want to wash Maggie's windows. I would find more joy in telling her to do her own nasty mopping than in doing the mopping myself.

She turns and leaves the kitchen, leaves me to decide.

This is crazy. In the history of the world, has anyone ever been paid thirty thousand dollars a month to be a maid? What is Maggie thinking? What is she trying to prove to me? Her superiority was established long ago. She has more money than anyone. But why am I being subjected to her contempt and rewarded with her largesse all at the same time? It's absolutely nuts. I'm feeling nuts. I really don't know what to do—put on the housecoat and mop or pack my bags and get out while the getting's good.

I need a word from the Lord. I step outside on the veranda. The sound of the sea is absolute silence. The sun glistens on the water. Great winged birds gracefully soar overhead. I don't know the names of the flowers on the side of the cliff, but they're yellow and green with a touch of purple. Their fragrance is intoxicating. Down below the beach is deserted. I'm still thinking of Mama. Didn't she mop so I wouldn't have to? Wasn't she the one who told me I could achieve whatever I wanted? Well, I don't want to stay. I don't want to mop.

The Athenian

I stay. I mop. I wash. I sing the songs Mama sang—"We've Come This Far by Faith," "How I Got Over," "I'm Gonna Treat Everybody Right Till I Die." Thinking of Mama, I sing as I prepare Maggie a dinner of chicken and rice. For the rest of the day, she and I don't exchange a word. That night I sleep peacefully. The next morning I hear her crying in her bedroom. I gently knock on her door hoping I can comfort her, but her only response is, "Leave me alone." That afternoon we go sailing on a friend's yacht.

She describes her friend as a fun-loving billionaire. "He always puts me in a good mood," Maggie says. He's a tall Greek gentleman in his early sixties named George Mikos. He has bushy eyebrows and thick dark glasses and wears a colorful ascot. He's jovial and talkative and eager to please Maggie.

"This is Albertina," she tells Mr. Mikos. "She's been helping me out."

I don't know why I've been invited along. I don't know if my role is servant or companion. I don't really care because this is my first time on a yacht and I'm excited. The thing is huge. On the side of the ship I see the name written in flowing gold letters: THE ATHENIAN. There's a captain who wears a white and gold hat, and a cook below. At least I won't be cooking. The yacht is painted pale blue and is much bigger than my house in Watts. There are three bedrooms and a living room with zebra-skin couches. Piped-in opera music is playing. I don't know much about opera but it sure sounds good.

As the boat floats on the superstill waters of the Caribbean, Maggie, Mr. Mikos, and I sit on the upper deck where we're served afternoon tea and cakes. The blue of the sea bleeds into the blue of the sky. We're enveloped in blue, a sunbright blue that is breathtakingly beautiful. Like God, the blue is everything; like God, the blue is everywhere; like God, the blue inspires the imagination and has my soul singing His praises.

Our afternoon on the ATHENIAN seems to be chasing away Maggie's blues. For the first time in days she is talkative. In the extreme. She strings together all her sentences and speaks without pause or reflection. "Albertina and I are writing a book," she tells Mr. Mikos. "A spiritual book, or maybe a personal book about the evils of the Black church. Isn't that right, Albertina?" She doesn't give me even half a second to reply before continuing her rapid-fire rap.

"Albertina and I share a common trauma. We were traumatized by the paternal fathers who still run the church for their own profit and worldly pleasure. Yes, Albertina will be the first to tell you that the church is corrupt, it does far more harm than good, and it's about time to expose its vicious hypocrisy. We are sisters in a crusade against Christ, you might say, or at least the Christ our forefathers have foisted upon us. Albertina is leading that crusade. She's going on television, my own television show, to point a finger and make formal accusations. Albertina's a brave woman, yes she is, because she knows that this could and probably will ruin her career. But my Albertina is not ruled by conformity, she's ruled by truth, and, truth be told, this lady will tell the truth. She's afraid of no one. Go tell it on the mountain, Albertina! Go, sister, go! Tell the world that, when it comes to Black churches and Black life in America, God has gone to sleep."

"I'm impressed, Miss Merci," says Mr. Mikos. "You're taking on a tall task."

"No task is too tall for Albertina," Maggie rattles on, "because God is on her side. You see, she was a singer and then a preacher, and now my personal confidante, and soon to be an author, and after that probably a United States senator. I've provided the sounding board for several United States senators on my show . . ."

"Governors and presidents as well," adds Mr. Mikos.

"And a few bishops and popes. Not to mention the world's wealthiest businessman—"

"That would be me, my dear," says Mikos, "but I've never been on your show. Never wanted a public profile—"

"Sorry, George," says Maggie, "shipbuilding money was eclipsed long ago by the Bill Gateses of the world. Until you enter the digital age, you'll be relegated to the back of the boat where common everyday billionaires reminisce about a time when wood and steel still mattered."

"You'd be surprised, Maggie, by the extent of my high-tech holdings. I sail not only the Caribbean seas, but the cyber seas as well."

"Which reminds me I need to call my lawyer Bob Blakey," Maggie breaks in to say, "and see if our deal for Megatronics has come through. I'm buying the largest cell-phone provider in the country right now, a thirty-billion-dollar deal. I would have asked you to join the consortium, my sweet George, but I thought you were too busy building your little luxury liners in Athens. Albertina, go call Bob. Check on the status of that deal. Then see if his cook needs help in the kitchen. You see, George, in addition to being a theologian, Pastor Merci is a whiz with the pots and pans. Her macaroni and cheese is famous in churches all across America. I may start marketing the dish as a frozen product with her picture plastered all over the package. I want to replace Aunt Jemima with Aunt Albertina."

Mr. Mikos laughs. I do not. I excuse myself, find a phone in one of the bedrooms, and call Bob.

"How's it going?" he asks.

"I'm calling in the role of Maggie's secretary," I say. "She wants to know if the Megatronics deal is done."

"Aunt Albertina, you have to realize that she's not dealing with reality. She's on a make-believe buying binge. If I bought half the things she has asked me to buy in the past week her assets would disappear overnight."

"So you ignore her?"

"I have to, for her own sake."

"Baby," I say, "sounds like good advice. I need to do the same."

"She giving you a rough time?"

"She's on a high now, Bob. We're on a yacht owned by Mr. George Mikos and they're both talking like they own half the universe."

"Mikos is a high-class con man. He's probably trying to

pull her into some bogus venture. It sounds like you're the one sane person on a ship of fools."

"Long as I stay with the Lord, I'm staying sane, sugar. It's only because the Lord is with me."

"What about her pharmacological psychiatrist? He was supposed to fly in and monitor her medicines."

"She told him not to come. She's not taking her medicines."

"Can you gently suggest that she do so?"

"I have, and I will, Bob, but I may not be gentle enough. Right now she doesn't want to hear a word out of me."

"Yet you're the only one she's allowing to stay with her."

"For now."

"I admire your stamina, Aunt Albertina."

"It's not me, sweetheart. It's God."

That evening the three of us have dinner on the ATHENIAN. It's a Grecian feast of fresh fish. I'm not wild about octopus—it's like eating rubber bands—but the sea bass is delicate and light. I get the recipe from Nick the cook. Maggie is still off and running on her plans to buy up cable companies and shopping channels. She can't stop talking about her designs to expand her universe. When she comes up for a breath, Mr. Mikos jumps in and tries to impress her with *his* plans to scoop up satellite TV in Europe.

As they speak, I think of Solomon in the book of Ecclesiastes. Solomon was the richest man in the world. He had everything—silver, gold, wives, concubines. Yet he was depressed. Why? Because he didn't love the living God. In the third chapter of that book, it says, "There is an appointed time for everything." Maggie has everything. But I know she doesn't know the living God. I also feel like it's time for her to come to terms with Him. And time for me to testify on His behalf.

But how do I break into their conversation when, instead of inviting me to comment, she asks me to clear the table?

Do I respond by saying Jesus is Lord and it's time to praise His holy name?

Do I tell her that without God in her life she's only going to have more agony and more discontent? Do I tell her that without God she'll never find a way to fill up the hole in her soul?

On this moonlit night on the Caribbean, on this fabulous yacht, do I refuse to clear the table and instead speak my heart about the bountiful gifts that are ours if only we embrace Jesus and accept His boundless grace?

Isn't it my job to declare His sovereignty? Isn't it my job to spread His Word?

I don't say a word. I clear the table. I sit alone in the living room. I open my Bible and reread Ecclesiastes 3. "There is an appointed time for everything. And there is a time for every event under the sun." My eyes go down the page and stop when it says, "A time to be silent and a time to speak."

I walk upstairs and look out to sea. The world is silent. The only sound is the whisper of the trade winds blowing across the waters. My heart is filled with God's love. My heart wants to speak. As a pastor, I always want to speak; I always want to share the good news of Jesus Christ.

But I don't want to speak in vain. I don't want the trade winds to blow my words across the water and off into the night. I look at the sky. It looks like a vast painting. But this galaxy of glittering stars is more beautiful than any painter could ever paint. The majesty of God's awesome creation is more mysterious than any philosopher could ever discern. The Master is surely in control—the Master Artist, the Master Philosopher, the Master Healer.

How do you heal the heart of someone who decries healing?

How do you speak to a stone?

I look up and remind myself:

God created the heavens.

God removed the stone.

The Eternal City

"What in the world are you doing in Rome?" Justine asks.

"Maggie says her favorite restaurant is here," I say.

"I don't want to hear about it. Don't say a word about pasta. I can't even think about pasta. They don't have any good pizza over there in Italy, do they?"

"I don't believe they do, sugar."

"Good. If you happen to have the best pizza you've ever eaten in your life, do me a favor, keep it to yourself. Do not tell me. But do tell me what's happening with Miss Thing."

"She's in her suite, I'm in mine."

"Five-star hotel?"

"I haven't counted the stars, baby, but the view from my room looks over the whole city. I can see the Vatican off in the distance."

"Will she see the pope?"

"I'm not sure he's on her schedule."

"Who *is* on her schedule?"

"I'm not sure," I say.

"It's like she gets bored and decides to bust a move. Is she running away from something she can't face?"

"I'm not trying to analyze it, Justine. I'm just hanging in and hanging out. Seeing places I haven't seen in some time. Fact is, I haven't been in Rome since I did that tour with Joe Cocker and Leon Russell back in the sixties."

"That must have been wild, child."

"In the sixties everything was wild, honey. But tell me about how things turned out in North Carolina? Was the weight-loss program successful?"

"Moderately. But the love program . . . well, that's been extremely successful."

"Walker? Is that his name?"

"Walker Jones. And you don't have to worry about the sinful side of things, Albertina, because this is one man who is definitely not playing me. He made good on his promise. He did leave his wife. I know because of the way she looked at me when I left the fatty farm. He's coming here this weekend. And he wants to talk to you."

"How does he know about me?"

"Anyone who knows about me knows about you. I'm always talking about my pastor."

"Funny, I've never seen you in my church."

" 'Church is in our hearts,' you're always saying. And I believe what you say. Anyway, Walker needs to talk to you about Maggie."

"I wish you hadn't mentioned Maggie to him."

"He can help her," says Justine. "Bad nutrition creates depression. He's an expert on these things. The man can set her free. He just has to meet with her. Can you arrange it?"

"Hardly, honey."

"What do you mean? You're with her [...] know her every move. When you get back [...] me where the two of you are staying and [...] meet you."

"It's not that easy."

"Why not?"

"This is a very private woman. She's not meeting with any-one."

"But you have influence."

"My influence is somewhere between extremely limited and nonexistent."

"I told Walker you could help him. He wants to go on her show."

"Justine, I love you like a sister. You are my sister. But I need to tell you straight up and you need to tell him straight up: I'm not running this woman's life. He's going to have to back off."

"Maggie would love Walker. She has guests like him on her show all the time."

"There is no show right now, Justine. There's just a very lonely woman struggling to find her soul."

On the plane from Miami to Rome, Maggie made out a list of people and places she wanted to see in Italy. The list was six pages long. The list included everyone from Sophia Loren to Giorgio Armani and everywhere from La Scala opera house in Milan to a $5,000-a-day spa on a Sicilian mountainside.

"Changing scenery will do me a world of good," she said. "It's impossible to be depressed in Italy."

If that's true, Maggie is realizing the impossible because this is the fifth day she hasn't come out of her room at the Ho-

, which sits atop the famous Spanish Steps. When
get a "do not disturb" signal. When I leave the hotel to
ore the city, I slip a note under Maggie's door. "In case you
want company," I write, "I'll be back by dinnertime. God
bless."

I leave the hotel at about 10 a.m. and stop to breathe in
the sight of the city. It's early February. In contrast to the
Caribbean, the air is chilled and the sky overcast. Despite the
lack of sun, the city still inspires. Red-tile roofs, soaring
church spires, magnificent domes, the sound of chimes from
distant bell towers, the hustle and bustle of street life below.
I thank God for allowing me to be here on this very day at this
very moment.

I know something about the Word of God. I know something about the history of the Bible. But I confess that I am
not a scholar of the history of Catholicism. Growing up, I had
a few Catholic friends, and in this Catholic city, as I wander
in and out of fabulous churches and mighty cathedrals, I
hunger to feel God's presence. Sometimes I feel I do, sometimes I don't. I am always interested in seeing how our Lord
is depicted. He is painted in robes of scarlet and gold or He is
painted in robes of simple cloth. His hair is dark or His hair is
light; His face is narrow or His face is wide; His eyes are blue,
brown, or green. His passion on the cross, sculpted in bronze
or imagined in mosaic, expresses anguish, or acceptance, or
serenity, or woe. Each artist sees a different Jesus. Each artist
creates a different Jesus. Before each Jesus, I pray to the Jesus of my people, the Jesus of all people, the Jesus whose
earthly visage and bodily form didn't really matter. Maybe He
was as handsome as the models used by Michelangelo. Or
maybe His looks were unremarkable. His enduring beauty was
not of this world. His enduring beauty was not born of flesh

but of spirit. His incarnation was a miracle, not because, as Justine might say, He was fine, but because He was God formed as man, God brought to earth to lead us not into temptation but to deliver us from evil, to wash us clean and let us live in the light of His undying love.

So if many of the churches that I visit in Rome—and it seems like I visit at least fifty—are too ornate, too cavernous or too cold, too damp or too dreary, I turn my thoughts away from the décor to the divinity that inspired these sanctuaries. I turn my thoughts to God. I devote my trip to Him. I devote my day to Him. In each church, I offer a prayer. I pray for my children, Andre and Laura, both so creative in their own way, both eager to contribute to the world. I pray for my nephew, Patrick, and my parishioners whom he now leads. I pray for him to be patient and compassionate. I pray for them to be understanding. I pray that Justine will find clarity in her relationships with men. I pray that Maggie Clay's unsettled mind will find rest. *Dear Father,* I pray, *let her know Your acceptance, let her feel Your love, let her find peace.*

In early afternoon I find myself in the Vatican, overwhelmed by it all, walking down endless hallways through a museum of religious artifacts and extravagant paintings until I reach the Sistine Chapel where the story of creation floats above me like a prayer. There, too, I pray that Maggie will recognize the source of all creativity. I pray for the right words to say, or the wrong words to avoid, or the restraint that makes possible a calm and wise silence.

Map in hand, I walk back toward the hotel, stopping on a bridge that crosses the Tiber River. I'm exhausted but exhilarated. I'm all prayed up. My feet ache but my soul sings. God is on this bridge where sculpted angels holding objects from His Crucifixion—a nail, a spear, a cross—mark my way. An ancient castle looms behind me. The grey sky darkens. Cars are honking, motor scooter engines screaming, pigeons flying everywhere. I feel peace in my heart. They call this city eternal. I call my Lord eternal.

I think of the little ol' country church in the backwoods of east Texas where my mother took me so I could see where she had worshipped as a child. We arrived on a Sunday afternoon and folks were still having church up in there. The rickety wood floors had seen better days. The upright piano was out of tune. The walls were bare, but the church was alive with His spirit. Nothing had changed. "God doesn't change," Mama liked to say. "But He sure can change us." God is in the country church. God is in the Vatican. God is in every fiber of my being as I find the strength to drag my tired feet through the cobblestone streets of ancient Rome. I get lost but people are friendly and help me find my way. In an hour or so, I'm back at the hotel. My corns are on fire. I need a hot bath, but I see the red message light blinking on my phone.

"I've had it," says Maggie on her message. She's enraged. "I've had it with you. This isn't a tourist junket. I didn't bring you to Europe so you could go shopping. Today was the day I'd planned on working. Today was the day I *needed* to work. Where in the world are you? This is the sixth time I've called. I've run out of patience with you. You've had a ridiculously easy job and somehow you've managed to fail at it miserably. For all your moral superiority, you've taken advantage of me. I refuse to be used any longer. I'm sending you home. I've booked you on the first flight out tomorrow morning."

Golden Oldies

There's Aretha's "Respect," James Brown's "I'm Black and Proud," Marvin Gaye's "Heard It Through the Grapevine," Etta James's "Tell Mama," Johnnie Taylor's "Disco Lady," and, if you can believe it, Albertina Merci's "Sanctified Blues." Well, look at that.

I'm looking at the entertainment magazine music guide for the Rome–Los Angeles flight on American Airlines. I'm sitting way back in the coach cabin squeezed in between a married couple in their forties. They both have pleasant all-American demeanors. She looks a little like Sally Field; he resembles Peter Jennings. I've told them that I'm perfectly willing to change seats so they can be together, but, in fact, they seem to want to be apart. They're not speaking to each other. They're both in dark moods.

My mood is mixed. Of course I'm happy to see that my song is listed among the classics. And I have to be happy to be heading home. It's been a month. At the same time, the eviction was swift. Yesterday I was musing about the eternal beauty of Rome and the wondrous grace of God; today I've been expelled like a schoolgirl for misbehavior. In a strange way, though, I'm feeling more sad than wronged. I know Maggie's patterns. She acts out emotionally. She throws fits, and I've learned not to take those fits personally. On the other hand, my entire personal and professional life has been turned upside down by her erratic behavior. The fact that she cannot control her behavior is sad. Sad because she is in terrible pain. Sad because she still doesn't know how to reach out for help. Sad because she seems to be getting worse.

Last night when I examined my options, I considered staying. I reasoned that Maggie would probably change her mind; she would ask me to return; once home, I would just be called back to Rome or Paris or Tokyo or wherever she decides to go. At the same time, though, what has my stay with her achieved? We have yet to pray together. I have as yet not been able to offer her a truly comforting word. She has not allowed it. She has been either withdrawn or hostile. I've felt less and less useful, more and more frustrated. Humbling myself by cooking and cleaning in Maraqua was all well and good. It surely did me good. If that was a test, I'm glad I passed. But if it was my hope that by serving her I would be an example to her of how we are all called to serve God, I don't think I made my case. In any event, she made her point when I called her last night to ask whether she was certain she wanted me gone. The moment she heard my voice, she hung up.

The pilot's voice tells us we have another ten hours ahead of us. The ride is rough and I can see the lady seated next to me is agitated. I don't want to assume anything or be presumptuous, but I'm feeling her fear. My Bible is open to the

Psalms—I never tire of reading those exquisite poems of praise—and the lady looks at me like something is really wrong. I offer her a smile of reassurance.

"When I see people reading the Bible on planes," she says, "I figure they believe their time is up."

I give a little chuckle and say, "Oh no, you can't go by me 'cause I read the Bible in the bathtub."

That gets her to smile a little too, but as we hit an air pocket I see the fear is still there.

"This air turbulence is nothing more than sailing on a choppy sea," I assure her. "It's uncomfortable but there's no real danger."

"You fly often?" she asks.

"I have been recently."

"For business?"

I can see light conversation is making her feel better, so I'm happy to oblige. "I guess you can call it business, dear."

"May I ask what business you're in?"

"God's business. I'm a pastor."

"How wonderful! My husband Tom and I go to the Holy Trinity Lutheran in Pasadena. Or at least we used to go. I don't think we'll be going anymore." She looked over at Tom who was fast asleep.

"Sorry to hear that," I say.

"My name is Muriel."

"I'm Albertina."

"Where is your church, Albertina?"

"South Central L.A."

"We never go to that part of the city. We never go anywhere."

"Didn't you just visit Italy, Muriel?"

"It was our anniversary. It was supposed to be a second

honeymoon. My mother volunteered to take care of the kids. It was a dream trip, but the trip turned into a nightmare."

I don't know what to say so I say nothing. The air turbulence has diminished.

"Are you married, Albertina?"

"No, but I have been."

"More than once?" asks Muriel.

"Yes, sugar, more than once."

"Well, this is it for me. Tom and I were high school sweethearts. I've devoted my life to him and our three daughters. When he wanted his advanced degree in civil engineering, I worked at a dry cleaners to help pay the tuition. When he wanted to move from Ohio to California to find a better job, I left my family back in Columbus and stood by his side, just the way my mother stood by Daddy's side. That's how I was raised. Do you see anything wrong with that, Albertina?"

"No, I don't."

"And this dream trip, this vacation I had planned for a year . . . it was to be the most perfect two weeks of our married lives. Why would he ruin it? Why would he choose this occasion to lower the boom?"

"I don't know. I don't know what the boom was."

"I haven't mentioned this to a soul. And I've needed to. Lord knows I've needed to. Do you mind?"

"My calendar is clear for the next several hours, baby. I'm feeling that God seated us next to each other for a reason."

The reason becomes clear. Muriel is hurting deep inside. She's been dying for someone to talk to. As Tom softly snores, his wife tells me the story of how on their last week in Italy he broke down and told her what he had been wanting to tell her for some time. Tom had been involved with another woman. He finally broke off the relationship, but only because the woman found a man who would marry her. Tom and this woman had been carrying on for over a year. He didn't love her, he said—not the way he loves Muriel—but he found her sexually irresistible.

"Why would a man tell his wife something like that?" Muriel asks. "Why would he want to hurt me like this?"

"He has to be feeling guilty," I say. "He has to be consumed by guilt."

Muriel starts crying. I take her hand and say, "Crying is good. It's good to get it out, honey."

"How can I ever trust him again?" she asks. "I know you're a minister, Albertina, but please, don't even mention the idea of forgiveness. For what he did—for his months of lying and cheating—forgiveness is not possible. I can't stand to look at him."

There's no consoling Muriel, so I don't even try. I just listen. It's apparent that she loves this man. And it's also apparent he has good qualities. She tells me about the many interests they have in common, including golf and English antiques. He's neither violent nor short-tempered, and, for everything she has said, he's a good dad. The children adore him. Muriel, bless her heart, adores him. Thus the pain is that much more excruciating.

After nearly two hours of talk, Muriel has exhausted herself. "Thank you for listening," she says. "I hope I haven't been a burden."

"Quite the contrary," I say. "You are a blessing, sweetheart."

She pats my hand, closes her eyes, and drifts off to sleep. I start to do the same when I see Tom starting to stretch.

"Wow," he says. "I was really tired. I see Muriel is tired too."

I smile and don't say anything.

"Was I dreaming," he asks me, "or did I hear you two talking?"

"We did have a conversation."

He looks at me knowingly. I think he's guessing that Muriel might have spoken about him. His guess is confirmed when we introduce ourselves and he learns I'm a pastor.

"You don't take confession, do you?" he asks.

I smile and say, "I confess that I never have. At least not formally."

"We're always confessing," he says, "but usually it's in little bits and pieces. Maybe it's just being in a Catholic country like Italy that makes me want to confess everything."

"I understand what you're saying."

"You do?"

"Well, I think I do," I say. "Yesterday I must have visited a dozen churches. And I know they had an impact on me."

"We're Lutherans."

"Your wife told me."

"Sounds like she told you a great deal."

"It's funny," I tell Tom, "but when you're thirty thousand feet up in the air, suspended above Mother Earth and your normal routine, you find yourself telling strangers intimacies that you might not even tell your closest friends."

"You give me the impression of a person who does a lot of listening without doing a lot of judging."

"Thank you."

"I don't know what it is, but some people have the gift of making it easy for you talk to them."

Tom begins tentatively but winds up talking a lot. I say very little. I suppose he knows that Muriel has told her side of the story and now he's eager to tell his. Sitting between the couple I can't help but be amazed not only by the irony of being seated between them but also by how they have unconsciously alternated their sleep so the other is able to speak to me in privacy. During Tom's hour-long monologue, Muriel sleeps soundly. Once in a while I'll nod; once in a while I'll say, "I understand," or "I see what you're saying," but that's it. His need to open up is overwhelming. He speaks of the pressure of his job, the pressure of carrying the family's financial load. He has struggled to find balance between being a good employee, father, husband, and son. His own parents are ailing and require financial and emotional care.

"I want to be there for everybody," he says, "and wind up being there for no one." He says he realizes how vulnerable he is. He sees that his affair with a younger woman who works in his office was wrong. "Adultery," he says, "is always wrong. I can't believe I did what I did. I swore every time would be the last, but I was weak, the flesh was strong, and I fell, over and over again. I also realize that telling Muriel could be seen as cruel, but I couldn't hold it in any longer. I couldn't live with myself. Either she'll forgive me or she won't. But at least the truth is out."

There are many things I want to say to him, but I see that Muriel is stirring. She looks over at me, and then at her husband, and deduces that we have been speaking. She does not seem unhappy about that. At the same time, she is not interested in saying a word to him. Her pain is still evident. So is his.

Now it is my turn to sleep. Before I drift off, I open my Bible to John 15:12–13. This verse never fails to renew my spirit and remind me of what I consider the heart and soul of my Master's ministry. "This is my commandment," He says, "that you love one another, just as I have loved you. Greater love has no one than this, that one lay down his life for his friends." I feel like I've made two new friends.

I cannot remember my dreams, but the next thing I know

the pilot is talking about landing in Los Angeles. As we gather our things, Muriel says, "May I have your number, Pastor."

"Of course, sweetheart," I say.

While Muriel is in the restroom, Tom says, "Thank you for listening to me. I'm just wondering if it would be possible to speak with you again."

"Any time," I say, and hand him my number as well.

On the ground, as I stand by the luggage carousel waiting for my suitcases, I see Muriel and Tom are still not talking. They're not even looking at each other. A few minutes later, my nephew Patrick arrives to drive me home.

"Bad news, Aunt Albertina," he says. "Your church is in chaos."

Politics and Faith

I come home to a mountain of mail and messages. I sort through and I prioritize. But on the top of my mind is the crisis at church. Charles Green, my pianist, and his wife, Mary Green, a wonderful artist, have split up. I knew they'd been having trouble off and on for months, but what I didn't know was that Mary had left him for a woman in Long Beach. Things like that happen. That's life. But Charles took it hard and, in the midst of playing piano last Sunday during church, he stood up and began shouting that he could not be part of a church that housed lesbians. Rhonda Bolden and Lisa Adams were sitting in the first pew. Charles stormed out and apparently took two-thirds of the congregation with him. Now I'm staring at a list of fourteen parishioners who have called me. When I call them, most of them sound outraged and sympathetic toward Charles. I'm sympathetic as well. I've known Charles since the early seventies. Charles is an emotional musician and an emotional man. He's very sensitive and high-strung and, for what I could see, deeply in love with Mary. I can see how her rejection would wound him deeply. On the other hand, a public flip-out in church is not appropriate behavior. Yet this occurrence revealed something neither I nor Patrick had seen.

"I had no idea," said Patrick, "that so many people were so angry about Rhonda and Lisa. I feel like I carried that problem from my first church to your church."

"It's not a problem," I replied, "it's a situation. With all situations come opportunities. God is in every situation we face, as long as we allow Him in."

"What are you going to do?"

"Discuss it with those who are most concerned."

"But you don't even have a deacon board. You don't believe in church hierarchy."

"Jesus never designated a church hierarchy, baby. Jesus never said preachers and teachers should have titles. This meeting will be open to anyone who wants to come."

"It'll be very political."

"Only if we let it."

"How can you not let it? Politics and faith are always clashing."

"Or peacefully coexisting."

"I hope you'll have this meeting soon."

"Soon as I check in with my children and get over this jet lag."

My son, Andre, is excited because Nina has landed a good movie part. The film is shooting in Texas. He also found an agent for his screenplay. All is well.

Not so with my daughter Laura. She's mourning the loss of her favorite student, a girl named Jody, who was shot to death sitting next to her gangbanger boyfriend in his car. No one knows why she, and not he, was killed. Some speculate that the killing was done to horrify and torture him. Laura says that Jody had told her, the very day before she died, that she was going to meet with her boyfriend one last time. She was fed up with his gangster ways and had decided to break up with him.

"Mama," says Laura, "Jody was smart as a whip and connected to God. She wrote beautiful heartfelt poetry and loved with an open heart. She loved this guy in spite of his faults and was convinced she could change him. When he wouldn't change, she found the courage to tell him good-bye. That's when she was taken. Why, Mama, why in the name of mercy did it happen? What can I tell her grandmother? What can I tell her mother? What can I tell her little sisters? What can I tell my students?"

"You don't have to tell them anything, sweetheart. You just have to be a loving spirit in their midst. That's enough."

Together, Laura and I pray for Jody's family; we pray for her boyfriend's family as well; we also pray that God will touch the hearts of those who took Jody's life and let them see the horrible waste of their murderous ways.

Before I can get back to my bills, Justine calls.

"I heard you were back."

"You heard right, baby. How are you, Justine?"

"Dying to hear about everything. Is Maggie out in Malibu?"

"I'm not exactly sure where Maggie is. I suspect she's still in Rome."

"Then what are you doing here? I thought you two were inseparable."

"You thought wrong, honey."

"Well, when you talk to her, tell her she has to meet Walker Jones. When are you going to talk to her?"

"Don't know."

"Can you call her?"

"I can, sugar, but I won't."

"Why not, Albertina? This man can help her."

"Maggie needs her privacy right now."

"I told Walker I'd help him."

"Tell him you're doing your best, Justine, because, God bless you, baby, you are."

The phone startles me out of a deep afternoon slumber. I open my eyes and forget where I am. Maraqua? Rome? South Central?

"Maggie said you were home," says Bob Blakey. "She said you left her, Aunt Albertina."

I shake off the sleep and say, "I left her, Bob, because she insisted I do so."

"She's changing the story. She claims she's been abandoned."

"I'm sorry to hear that, honey."

"She also claims it's the best thing that ever happened to her. Now, she says, she realizes that she can't depend on anyone and doesn't need to. She's saying she can only count on herself. She's on her way back to Dallas where she wants to start up production on the show."

"I wish her well, Bob, I really do. I'll be praying for her. But I fear for her. I don't think she's ready to go back on the air. She still needs a great deal of help."

"She sounded a little better, Albertina."

"That can be deceptive, baby. I've been with her long enough to know that she has some moments of clarity. But then she gets hit hard by a spell of awful depression or she gets swept up in a kind of crazy energy."

"I'm sorry she put you through all this."

"It's been an education. And I can't complain about the pay. I can save some and put the rest into the church. I harbor no ill will toward the woman, Bob. I know underneath her pain there has to be a world of goodness. I just don't know how to get to it."

"Well, if it's any consolation to you, you've gotten to me. I was baptized last week in a church I've been attending in South Dallas."

"Baby! That's beautiful! That's the best consolation anyone can ever have! I didn't even know you've been thinking about it."

"I've been thinking about you, Aunt Albertina, and the spirit that leads you. I decided that's the spirit I want leading me."

"Praise God," I say.

The Coach

A week after I'm back from Rome, I'm finally going to have the big meeting at church. It has taken me a while to feel ready. It isn't anything I'm looking forward to. In fact, it's something I've had to pray hard about. I've prayed for a teachable spirit and a humble attitude. I've prayed that rancor will be avoided and understanding will prevail. Understanding, of course, means understanding everybody, not just those you agree with. Understanding also means mainly listening, which is what I've been doing over the past few days—meeting and listening to various church members individually.

I understand why Patrick couldn't handle the conflict. His last church had fired him over this very issue. Then just at the point when House of Trust was growing in membership and I was off with Maggie, the issue exploded again. It's no wonder that Patrick has become even more confused.

I think of St. Augustine. Confusion led him to spiritual

growth. Out of honest confusion came clarity. Without it, with only mindless certainty molding our arguments, we become dogmatic and obstinate. I tell this to Patrick when he comes for dinner. He's still unsure about how to deal with the issue. He's doubly confused because last week at his college reunion he saw a woman to whom he feels mightily drawn. As it turns out, she has a black Christian father and a white Jewish mother. She practices the religion of her mother and is, in fact, a rabbi. Her name is Naomi.

"We connected on such a deep level," says Patrick who, although extremely handsome, has never been a lady's man.

"Well, that's wonderful Patrick. I hope you see her again."

"She wants us to get together. She told me so."

"Praise God," I say.

"But I refused."

"Why?"

"She doesn't know the Lord. She hasn't accepted the Lord. She's a rabbi."

"Jesus was a rabbi," I remind Patrick.

"She doesn't believe in Jesus."

"She told you that, sugar?"

"How *could* she believe in Jesus? She's Jewish. How can I get romantic with a woman who rejects my Lord and Savior?"

"Hold on now, Patrick. You're putting a lot of words in her mouth, and you're getting ahead of yourself. You're already moving to romance. How about starting with friendship? Maybe you've simply met a new friend. Don't tell me you won't allow yourself Jewish friends."

"Of course not."

"Well then, it doesn't have to be more than that. You're both interested in the Bible, you're both passionate about God. And you have different orientations. Sounds like the basis for a fascinating friendship."

"If she'll accept Jesus."

"You're not proposing to her, baby. You're just getting to know her. You might just want to listen to her story."

"Her father's an accountant and a deacon in a big AME church in Detroit. Her mother's a lawyer who, according to Naomi, never practiced her Judaism. But ever since Naomi began studying for the rabbinate, her father won't even talk to her."

"That's unfortunate."

"But when she talks about her dad," says Patrick, "she sounds like she really loves him. She says he's a great guy."

"She sounds like a compassionate person."

"She has too many good qualities," Patrick admits. "She worries me."

I can't help but laugh. I need a good laugh because the big meeting at House of Trust is set for tomorrow night.

Bright and early next morning the phone rings. I'm certain it's a church member wanting to win me over to his side. Until now, I've just let everyone say what they've had to say. I figure that's the best way; people need to express their feelings; people need to feel like they're being heard. But I'm growing a little weary because people also tend to be long-winded inventing their feelings. People get excited by the sound of their own voice; the more they hear their opinions, the more they agree with themselves. But if they show no restraint of tongue, the Lord has advised me that I must. In this preliminary period, the less I say the better.

On the other end of the phone, though, is not a church member. It's Muriel, the woman I met on the plane from Rome.

"Do you remember me?" she asks.

"Of course I remember you. How are you, sweetheart?"

"Devastated. Tom and I are having a terrible time. I told him I couldn't stand the sight of him anymore. Our children are all confused, and . . . well, I'm just wondering if I could talk to you about it."

"Sure. You could come to my home or come to my church," I offer, but when I give her the exact addresses she's hesitant.

"I don't want to hurt your feelings, Pastor, but, well, I don't really know that part of the city, and, with all the drive-by shootings and everything, I'm afraid to go there by myself."

I'm a little taken aback. This is, after all, where I live. I don't want to take offense, and I know Muriel means none, but I feel awkward. I pause, close my eyes and offer up a prayer. *Dear God*, I silently say, *help me respond wisely*.

"You know, Muriel," I hear myself saying, "maybe you'd feel better if Tom accompanied you. Maybe you and he could both come and talk to me."

Miraculously, she agrees.

It's a Tuesday and the rain is unrelenting. It won't rain in L.A. for months, the winter can be mild as spring, but then suddenly the storms arrive, one after another, and it feels like we're back in Bible times with Noah working on his ark. I'm wondering if the heavy rains will keep everyone away, but when I arrive at the House of Trust I see that the place is already packed. The rains haven't kept anyone away.

Rhonda and Lisa are seated in the first pew where they always sit. I've gotten to know them as smart and strong women; they're not about to be intimidated by anyone. I like them both enormously. When they've called me during these recent days to see what side I'm on, we've had constructive conversations.

"If you're going to ask us to leave your church," Lisa offered, "we'll save you the embarrassment by not showing up."

"First of all," I said, "it's not my church, it's God's church, and in God's church no one who seeks Him is excluded. Wherever I worship, you are always welcome. And anyone else you wish to bring."

"The issue of same-sex marriage will come up," Lisa said. "Will you speak for it?"

"I'm not a politician, baby, and I'm not a legislator. I'm someone who wishes to glorify God with sincerity and humility—that's all I am."

I'm not sure that's the answer Lisa wanted. I'm not sure any of my answers will satisfy my congregation. Fact is, I'm not even sure I have answers. At the same time, as I walk down the aisle to take my place at the pulpit, I'm feeling peaceful.

"Let us invoke the presence of the living God," I say. "Let us pray that He remains in our hearts with every word we speak. Let us pray that He gives us the patience to listen to others, to purge our hearts of whatever prejudices may be festering in our souls, to display kindness and love to those who may not share our point of view. In the precious name of He who died at the hands of bitter intolerance and hateful prejudice so we might be gifted with the glory of eternal salvation, let us say Amen."

I look out and see that Charles Green is seated on one side of the aisle and Mary Green on the other. Several older women I've known and befriended over the years look especially agitated. They have told me in private conversations that they will not attend a church that tolerates rampant homosexuality of any kind. Several men who are also steeped in old-school church tradition have told me the same thing.

Great tension fills the air. Yet my heart remains calm. I don't know why, but I feel as though God will get us through.

"The best way to proceed," I say, "is to allow anyone who wants to speak to do so. I have a little stopwatch that will beep after five minutes. Take another minute or so and then please yield the floor to the next speaker. Who would like to start?"

There are five or ten seconds of awkwardness before Martin Simmons, who is seated next to his wife Paulette, comes to the pulpit. He is a hulk of a man—well over six feet with wide shoulders, a barrel chest, and shiny bald head. I have no idea what he's going to say.

"My name is Martin Simmons and I've only been to this church once but my wife Paulette has been attending regularly and praising your pastor here for being a woman of God. I was raised up in the Baptist church and consider myself knowledgeable in the Word of God. I accepted Christ as my Savior when I was seven and never backed down from that commitment, not once. Some of you may know that I've been coaching football at Dorsey High for twenty years. I have a reputation for winning. I also have a reputation for not putting up with nonsense. I have a reputation for dealing in discipline. Before coaching I played football at Morehouse College. I'm good at football. I was good as a player and I'm good as a coach and wanted my boy, Chuck, to be even better than I was. I wanted him to be everything I wasn't. You see, I was good but never great. So if I couldn't be great, he had to be. Not for himself, you understand, but for me. Anyway, Chuck wasn't interested in football and later I saw he wasn't interested in girls. He was interested in books, he made great grades, but I wanted him to be great at football and great with the girls.

Many a time I lost my temper with the boy. Before God Almighty, I admit that I struck him—and struck him hard—when he didn't do anything to deserve it. I told myself I was only doing what my daddy had done to me. And, well, I turned out good and so would my son. But the more I hit him, the more defiant he became. For years we didn't speak. He went to college and graduated at the head of his class. We still didn't speak. He got a scholarship to UCLA law school, he lived right across town from us, but still we didn't speak.

"Then he told us he had AIDS and my reaction—I swear to God this is what I said—was, 'Son, the Lord is punishing you. Now you'll finally see I was right.' My wife was horrified by what I said. Now, my wife is a loyal woman who has stood by me for forty years. Paulette comes from a generation of women taught not to argue with their husbands. But this was too much, even for my Paulette. She called Pastor Merci here. She didn't know what else to do.

"Pastor Merci called me and I read this good woman the riot act. I quoted Scripture about the evils of sexual sins. I told her I was raised on the Bible and the Bible was telling me I was right, my son was wrong, and I didn't want to hear a word otherwise. Your pastor here let me talk. You see, your pastor is a good listener. I have to give her that. She let me go on and on and, believe me, I did go on. But when I got through she said, 'Coach Simmons, the Word of God does not have to be argued.' Well, right there that statement made a big impression on me. But her next statement made an even bigger impression. It was short and to the point. All Pastor Merci said was, 'Love trumps everything.'

"That made me stop and think. See, I'm a card player and I understand trumping. So I got to thinking. I got to thinking how I thought I was playing my ace. My ace was my understanding of Scripture. But Pastor said that love trumps everything, even the ace. What if my ace wasn't the ace of truth but the ace of arrogance? I've been called arrogant before. Two different principals at the high school where I coach have called me arrogant. I wanted to belt them both, but they were my superiors. I wrote off their criticism as jealousy. I figured they wished they could be the coach on the field rather than be the principal in the office. But their words haunted me. Pastor's words haunted me in the same way. Was I acting out of love or out of arrogance? Was I playing according to the rules, not the rules set up by man, but the ones set up by Christ, who said love trumps everything?

"It took me a couple of days of prayer and reflection before I called my son, but I did. I followed the pastor's example. I was short and to the point. I said, 'Son, I want to see you.' He wanted to know why. He suspected I wanted to see him to tell him how I disapproved of everything about him. He was right to be skeptical. So I was short and to the point again. 'I want to see you,' I said, 'just to show you some love.' Man, did that take him by surprise! I mean, a full minute must have passed before he could say a word. And what he said was 'Okay.'

"So we met in a little coffee shop near his law school and I just listened to him talk about his life. I'd never done that before. And I can't say that everything he told me made me happy. I still wished he had turned out differently. I still wished that rather than being a star law student he had won the Heisman Trophy. I still wished he went with girls. I wasn't comfortable when he told me he's living with a guy. But I was comfortable in telling him something real simple that had been on my heart for years but I'd never said. I was comfortable when I finally said it. 'Son,' I said, 'I love you.' He said the same to me and we actually hugged. Maybe for the first time ever.

"I'm telling you all this to make one point. I asked my son,

Chuck, whether he would ever like to attend church with his mother and me. I told him we'd found a church and a minister we liked. He told me that he had spoken to Pastor Merci and he liked her too, and, yes, he would like to attend church with us. So when I leave here tonight and call him up I can tell him one of two things. I can say, 'Son, Pastor Merci's church has a new rule that says people like you aren't welcome there,' or I can say, 'Son, meet us at church on Sunday and as a family we'll all pray together.' My sisters and brothers in Christ, I leave that decision up to you."

After Coach Simmons took his seat, you could have heard a pin drop. A long eerie silence ensued. You could hear everyone thinking. You could feel how deeply everyone was affected. I waited for another parishioner to come to the pulpit, but none came, not after two minutes, not after five minutes. It was clear no one else intended to speak.

"Well," I said, "if no one else wants to speak, I won't either. I don't have anything to add to what our brother said. All I can do is pray. All I can say is, 'Father God, we exult You, we praise You, we magnify You, we lift You up for entering our hearts and allowing the peace of Your light to prevail. We thank You that no hurtful words were spoken here tonight, that no brother turned against brother or sister against sister, that we are witnesses to the miracle of reconciliation that is realized every time we turn to You, dear Father, for steady guidance and enduring strength. In Jesus' name, Amen.'"

Walker's Miracle Program of Mental and Physical Health

Bob Blakey and I are having dinner at the Biltmore Hotel in downtown Los Angeles. I love the place because it's elegant and old world and takes me back to another era before iPods and cell phones. In the hush-hush opulence of the hotel dining room, men and women are talking on their cell phones too loudly for my taste, but I let it go. I'm just happy to be with Bob who's in town to meet with one of the networks about starting up *Maggie's World* again.

"She's ready," he says. "Or at least she thinks she is."

"I'm happy for her."

"I don't know if she's back on antidepressants, I don't know if she's seeing a therapist, I don't know what's happening and I'm not about to ask her."

"That's wise," I say.

"But I do know that she's swung into action and is planning an ambitious public relations campaign to explain her absence and announce her return."

"Going back to work can be energizing," I say. "Work is a powerful antidepressant."

"So you aren't bitter?"

"I'm grateful, baby. God puts everyone in our life for a reason."

"He put you in my life so I could put Him in mine."

Our dinners arrive. In between bites I ask Bob about his personal life.

"Work, work, work," he says. "I'm still not ready to socialize. I still think of Cindy every day and every night. It's strange, Aunt Albertina, but the longer she's gone, the more my love for her grows."

"That's not strange, honey," I say. "That's the nature of love. True love deepens. And, at least from my point of view, there is no death. The spirit can't die, just as God can't die. Cindy's spirit is alive in you. That's a beautiful thing."

"My mother says I should date."

"I understand how your mother feels. She wants you to be happy."

"And she wants grandchildren."

"Me too," I confess.

"Do you campaign for grandchildren with your children?"

"I don't campaign for much of anything except the Gospel of Jesus."

"Well, you're a successful campaigner in that arena."

"Semi-successful at best, sugar. Always looking to improve."

"By the way," says Bob, "one of your parishioners contacted me. She said she was calling with your endorsement."

"Who is that?"

"Her name is Justine."

"Oh, Lord."

"So you do know her. . . ."

"She's my neighbor and close friend. Was she calling about her workout/nutritionist friend?"

"Someone like that."

"I asked her not to bother Maggie's people."

"It was no bother. Besides, any friend of yours is entitled to a favor from me. I gave her the number of the woman who books Maggie's guests. The chances of his actually getting on are extremely slim."

"I tried to tell Justine that. But Justine, bless her heart, has a mind of her own."

Over my protestations, Justine slips in the videocassette.

"You have to see this man, Albertina," she insists. "You have to see him right now."

It's Wednesday night and I'm just back from Bible class at House of Trust. Justine was not in attendance. Had she been there, she would have heard me elucidate—or at least try to elucidate—the story of Job. I had been thinking about how God challenges us, how Satan tempts us, and how only faith maintains us. Job was tested over and over again. Satan wanted to convince him that acts of goodness do not result in happiness. Satan wanted him to doubt God. But being a man of God, Job knew that his own understanding of God did not depend upon his human intellect; it depended upon his human heart. Job's heart told him that God is good. To sin, to fall into Satan's trap of trying to understand the uncertain relationship between good acts and a good life, is to fall into the trap of theological debate. Satan can win any debate because, by nature, Satan is diabolically clever. God is beyond cleverness; God simply *is*. Job rejects Satan and the sin of trying to decipher what only God comprehends. Throughout the long and painful ordeal that ripped his life apart, Job sought and found God. He heard from God. The deeper Job's anguish, the deeper his reliance on God, the stronger his faith, the more perfect his patience.

Tonight my patience with Justine is highly imperfect. As much as I love her, I would rather be alone and reread the beautiful book of Job that, beyond its enduring wisdom, has the feeling of an exquisite dramatic play. But I suppose Justine is the star of her own play, or maybe her own soap opera, and I always seem to be drawn into its unpredictable twists and turns. This latest turn, though—her obsession with Walker Jones—has me upset. He's a married man who, I fear, is using my friend. I don't like that. I also don't like that Justine called Bob Blakey without telling me.

"If I had told you, you would have told me not to, wouldn't you?" she asked.

"I would have said it's inappropriate," I answered.

"There you go," she said. "So I did you a favor by not asking you for a favor. And according to you, Mr. Blakey didn't mind my asking the favor."

"Bob's a gentleman," I said.

"So is Walker. A gentleman and a genius. I've lost thirty pounds, Albertina. You have to admit I look good."

"You do look good, baby, and I'm proud of you."

"All credit to Walker."

"You lost the weight, not him."

"He motivated me. He molded me, he scolded me, and, Albertina, if you only knew what else he did to me you'd understand why I'm feeling like a new woman, thank you, Jesus. Now sit back and take a good look at this man of mine."

On the tape, smooth Kenny G–sounding jazz plays as the words "Walker's Miracle Program of Mental and Physical Health" crawl across the screen. Justine's right. Walker Jones is a fine-looking brother with a muscular physique. His tank top is tight and so are his shorts. He has a neatly groomed moustache and gleaming white teeth. He has his rap down. He's a salesman. He's slick. He says his program is based on the three Es—exercise, eating right, and enduring energy. Enduring energy is derived from the right vitamin mix and the right emotional attitude. He uses words well, but he's too glib for me. He's like a preacher who uses words to get money out of you. Now he uses a computer to make a power point presentation; now he demonstrates several of his exercises that display the contours of his body; now he argues that his plan will even defeat serious depression; now he makes his final pitch: you can buy his six-part DVD program from his Web site for only $89.99. None of this sounds new to me; I hear it as a pile of clichés.

But when Justine asks me what I think, I fudge by saying, "Well, sugar, I just hope he can help people."

"It isn't that he *can*, Albertina, he *is*. Thousands of people. Maggie can make that millions of people. That's why she has to put him on the air. Will you help him?"

Justine is relentless. In spite of my chastising her for calling Bob, in spite of my constant refusal to intervene in this business, she keeps after me.

"I can't do anything," I say simply.

"Can't or won't?"

"Both."

"Is that because you don't approve of his relationship with me on moral grounds?"

"It has nothing to do with that, baby, but everything to do with my limitations."

"What do you mean by that?"

"I have no influence with Maggie."

"I don't believe you, Albertina."

"Justine, you are free to believe or disbelieve whatever you choose. But on the subject of Walker Jones, I've said my last word."

"It's all because you don't want me fooling around with a married man, isn't it?"

I keep my pledge. I don't say another word.

"Married men have a sacred bond," says Muriel. "They have a bond not to lie and cheat on the people who mean the most to them. When they break that bond, they deserve nothing but scorn."

Muriel, Tom, and I are sitting in my living room. They have commented on the neat and pretty appearance of my home. Their praise is so extravagant I feel like they're overcompensating for Muriel's fear of my neighborhood. No matter, I thank them for their kind words and get to the matter at hand. I feel that Muriel is bursting with pain, so I suggest she let it out. She's sitting on one end of my long couch, Tom on the other end. I'm in my grandfather's big blue easy chair facing the two of them. As Muriel speaks caustically, I see Tom squirm. He cannot look at her and she cannot look at him. When he tries to break in, to make an excuse or correct a perception, I stop him by saying, "Tom, let Muriel speak. Then it'll be your turn. It's better if we don't interrupt each other." He nods in agreement. After a while, though, she stops the story of the betrayal and begins assaulting his character. It's easy to understand why. He has wounded her and now she wants to wound him. I gently stop her and suggest we give Tom a chance to speak.

"I don't know what he possibly has to say," she says. "Is he now going to lie to me and say he was lying before? Is he going to change his story and say this nightmare never happened?"

"No, I'm not going to say that," says Tom. "It happened."

"Well, I don't want to hear about it."

"I listened to you," Tom reminds her.

"As damn well you should have. I wasn't the one who scarred this relationship. I wasn't the one who spit on our marriage vows. That was you."

"Maybe we should just let Tom talk for a little while, Muriel," I suggest. "I know it's painful for you. But getting through the pain is the aim here. We can't get through it if we don't face it."

"I'm facing it," Muriel bursts out with renewed anger. "But what about him? He didn't have pain. He had pleasure. And I wonder—how many times did he have that pleasure? That's what I want to know. And when he was having that pleasure, where was I? Picking up his clothes at the dry cleaners? Taking the kids to the dentist? Making sure the meals I prepared were to his liking? Was that painful for him? What kind of pain did he feel when he was checking in with his floozy at the Hyatt Hotel? That's what I want to hear about. I want to hear how that hurt him. Tell me, Tom, tell me about the pain you and this bimbo suffered at the Hot Sheet Motel, or wherever you took her."

"I don't know how to answer that," says Tom.

"Of course you don't," Muriel shoots back, "because there wasn't any pain. None of this was painful for you. You're not in pain now. You're just looking for a way to cover your behind and worm your way back into the good graces of your family. Well, that's not going to happen. Your family detests you. Your family will always detest you for destroying the most beautiful thing in the world—trust. Isn't that the name of your church, Pastor, the House of Trust? I thought we had a house of trust

but, boy, was I wrong! It was a house of lies and you're looking at the head of that household, Pastor, you're looking at
America's number one liar and cheat!"

And with that, Muriel breaks into tears. Tom goes over to
try to comfort her, but she waves him away. She will not be
consoled. When he starts to say something, she gets up and
runs out of the room.

Now Tom and I are alone.

"Now what?" he asks.

"We pray," I say. "Father God, we pray the prayer of Job
who said you can do all things, that no purpose of yours can
be hindered. Job said he had to deal with things he did not understand. It's true of us, too. Every day we deal with things we
don't understand. We don't understand Your grace, we don't
understand Your forgiveness, we don't understand why You
love every one of us with undying passion. But even if we don't
understand these things, we believe in them. We believe in
You. We believe that miracles happen, and we need a miracle
down here today, yes we do, Father, a miracle of forgiveness
and grace. In Jesus' beautiful name, Amen."

Muriel doesn't return for another twenty minutes. When
she does, she says, "Don't believe a word he tells you, Pastor.
This man is not to be trusted."

"Do you trust him to take you home?" I ask.

"I have no choice," she answers.

"That's how I feel about living a life based on love," I say.
"I have no choice, sweetheart. Anything else is dangerous and
dark."

Woman of the Week

Springtime in L.A. is no big deal. Most of the time it feels like spring here anyway. But this year the rains came heavy and winter had a nasty edge. Now the April afternoons are warm and the evenings fragrant with the night-blooming jasmine I planted by the front door.

It's been a year since Maggie had her disturbing episode on TV, a year since I learned about Cindy's cancer. I'm still not sure I've had time to absorb the changes this chain of events unleashed in my life. I am glad when I think about Bob's latest report—that Maggie seems better—but I can't help but be skeptical. I can't imagine her on an even keel. And the truth is that she hasn't left my mind. When I see her name in magazines or hear her name on television, I always stop to read and listen. I'm grateful to have a normal life again, but I'm just as interested in Maggie as ever. Maybe more so.

When ABC News announces that Maggie Clay is the

Woman of the Week, I am careful not to miss the feature on her. I sit in front of the TV, a hot cup of green tea by my side, and carefully watch the story.

Glamorous journalist Diane Sawyer looks into the camera and says, "It's been a little over a year since rumors began swirling about Maggie Clay. It began with an upsetting episode on *Maggie's World*, in which the famed talk show host appeared emotionally distraught, causing considerable concern. When the show went off the air for what was described as an 'indefinite hiatus,' concern grew. Tabloid speculation ran the gamut from complete nervous breakdown to terminal disease. Fortunately, those speculations have proven false. This week Maggie Clay appears on the covers of no less than four national magazines, looking as elegant and svelte as ever, telling a comeback story of hope and renewal. When I sat with her in her lovely home in Dallas only a few days ago, I saw a woman who at age fifty displayed the energy of a teenager. She was focused and determined to reestablish her position in the hotly contested talk show ratings. And when it came to revealing details of her personal life and private struggle, she responded with unusual candor and confidence."

The camera cuts to a tape of Diane Sawyer and Maggie Clay sitting in Maggie's modern art museum–like living room. Maggie looks composed and happy. She's wearing a stunning pants suit in a subtle shade of mauve. A diamond bracelet sparkles on her left wrist. A lovely oval jade pendant graces her neck. Her hair is cropped fashionably short. Her face seems less drawn, her long torso more alert.

"What happened last year?" Diane Sawyer asks her directly.

"Mental and physical exhaustion, Diane," Maggie replies. "My hours were incredibly long and the pressure was unbearable. I was simply trying to do too much too soon. In the midst of this, I learned that one of my producers, a young woman who was my protégée, had been diagnosed with terminal cancer."

Maggie has the time line all wrong. She had her unfortunate episode on television *before* she knew about Cindy. She didn't learn about the cancer until she came to the party at Cindy's apartment where she and I met for the first time. This misstatement of facts upsets me. It's as though she's using Cindy to gain sympathy for herself.

"What got you through it all?" asks Sawyer.

"Fortunately I have a wonderful support system," says Maggie. "I have dozens of close and caring friends. One friend in particular . . ."

Here Maggie pauses. I can't but wonder if she'll mention me.

"A very special friend," she continues, "whose support, under difficult circumstances, was nothing short of a godsend. I'm talking about Dr. Oliver Porter, the author of *Mind Over Matter: Making Every Day Count*. Oliver took special interest in me during my challenging times. He came to see me when I was staying in the Caribbean. In quite specific ways, he showed me how to apply the wisdom of putting mind over matter. His positive influence and positive energy got me through, Diane. I must say, he's an amazing man. In fact, he and I are writing a book together about my difficult days and how I overcame these challenges. The publisher is so excited about the story they're rushing it out to stores next month."

"My word," says Sawyer, "you must have written it in a hurry."

"I do everything in a hurry, Diane. That's part of my problem but also part of my solution. I apply positive solutions quickly. Too many of us moan and groan about the same problems for years without taking action."

"But getting back to your problem, Maggie. One source told us that you experienced a deep and even clinical depression. Another source said your recovery involved religion. Are our sources wrong?"

"I'm not a psychologist, Diane, and I don't know the exact technical terms. I was not suicidal, if that's what you mean. I was certainly down. And no, traditional religion, while I respect it, did not play a part in my recovery."

"We had heard, in fact," Sawyer says, "that you had sent for a preacher to live with you."

"I am blessed to have so many friends in so many fields who were concerned for my welfare. Those friends include religious leaders. I thank them all for their help. But no, I did not have a spiritual epiphany. As our book explains, my recovery was based on practical principles."

"Were you taking antidepressants?"

"I am now. Like millions of people worldwide, I have learned that they have their place in combating mood disorder."

"Were you diagnosed as bipolar?"

"Again, Diane, I'm not sure these terms are useful or even applicable. My self-diagnosis now is that, as Dr. Porter says, the potential of the mind to heal itself is a reason for all of us to live with hope."

There is more discussion about Maggie's upcoming shows and the celebrities who will be her guests. The more Maggie talks, the deeper I look into her eyes. Her words make sense. Her hand gestures are not erratic. She's not talking manically as she had been for months. She doesn't seem irritable or volatile. And yet I see something disturbing. There's a void behind her eyes. Maybe I'm looking too deeply; maybe I'm looking for something that isn't there. But I can't help but believe that something is still wrong.

If I'm right, Father, I pray, make it right for Maggie. Settle her unsettled mind. Give her peace. Grant her serenity. Let her live without fronting or fooling anyone. Let her be calm and truly rested. Let her know and rely on You. In Jesus' name, Amen.

Passover

Rabbi Naomi Cohen lives in a garden apartment in Park LaBrea, a sprawling complex off Fairfax Avenue in the middle of Los Angeles. I know the area well because my good friend from high school, Florence Ginzburg, lives just up the street by the Whole Foods store. Florence is a lawyer who late in life gave up her legal practice to become a psychologist. She and her husband, Bernard, an upholsterer, traveled to Israel with me a few years back. It was my third trip, and we had a fabulous time. Driving over to their side of the city, I remind myself to call Florence and see how she's doing.

I'm in the car with my nephew Patrick. Rabbi Cohen has invited him to her Passover Seder and he asked whether he could bring his aunt along. "Of course," the rabbi told him. "I'd love to meet her."

"Am I acting as your bodyguard?" I ask Patrick.

"I want your opinion of Naomi," he says. "I know there's something about this woman that can't be right. Maybe you can pinpoint it."

"I'm not looking for faults, baby. I'm not that type."

"You see through people, Aunt Albertina. I just want you to read her."

Naomi's apartment is pleasant and modest and filled with books. She's a beautiful woman with medium brown skin and dark curly hair shaped a little like an Afro. Her eyes are kind and her smile sincere. She's small and demure and speaks with a soft eloquence. Her speech is neither mannered nor flowery. She speaks plainly and from the heart. I wouldn't call her shy—she's a confident woman—but neither is she boisterous. She greets me with great warmth and shows me around her place. The walls are covered with photographs of her family, her parents and her two brothers. As she points to pictures of her various relatives, I enjoy the aroma of baked chicken. I'm looking forward to a delicious meal.

Naomi has invited three other people: Zeola and Larry deYoung, an African-American couple in their early thirties; and Clifford Bloom, a white man whose name and voice I know because I've heard him deejaying on the local jazz station. He resembles a light-skinned uncle of mine, my mother's brother, who was six feet eight and the first in our family to attend college.

As it turns out, Zeola and Larry are Jewish and members of the rabbi's reformed congregation. They became friends with Naomi when all three, along with Patrick, attended UCLA as undergraduates. Clifford Bloom, on the other hand, is a Jew who became a Christian ten years ago. He's seventy-five but looks much younger.

"I love cultural and religious diversity," says Naomi. "I love being with people whose search for God takes them to unexpected places."

I agree.

I'm not sure Patrick agrees, but I can feel him restraining himself from saying so. I can feel how smitten he is with Naomi.

We have a beautiful Seder service during which Naomi succinctly explains the deep meaning of the holiday, the eight-day observance that celebrates freedom and the exodus of the Jewish slaves from Egypt during the reign of Pharaoh Ramses II. We are each given a Haggadah, the manual for conducting the at-home service. There are songs, Psalms, prayers, explanations, little dialogues, choice words from wise rabbis, and the famous four questions. The overall question that stays in my mind is, "Why is this night different from all other nights?"

This night is different, of course, because I am sitting in the home of a young unmarried female rabbi who seems interested in my young unmarried pastor nephew. It is different because an extremely sweet couple—Larry deYoung is a banker, Zeola is a dance instructor—are explaining their love of Jewish rituals. It is also different because Clifford Bloom, whom I have listened to on the radio for many years, is telling me about his conversion to Christianity.

"I wouldn't call it a conversion," he says. "I'd call it a continuum. I love being Jewish and will always be Jewish. I would never renounce Judaism. I merely see Christianity as the next logical—and holy—step in the development of Judaism's basic theology. In some ways, I see Christ as the ultimate and perfect Jew."

"Amen," adds Patrick with great enthusiasm.

I wonder if Mr. Bloom's position will lead to dissent. It doesn't.

"My parents were secular," says Larry deYoung, "and my best friend growing up in Boston came from a household of observant Jews. I loved being over there during the holidays. I loved the sense of history and the warmth of family togetherness. My folks divorced when I was six."

I wonder about Zeola's background. "My mother is Catholic but my father is Jewish," she says. "My father strongly influenced my view of theology. He was very articulate about his Judaism. Mom didn't like to talk about her religion. From an early age, I associated Judaism with scholarly books and serious reading. I liked that connection. I was a philosophy major in college, and, because of my background, was well prepared. I thank my father for that."

"What about you, Patrick?" asks Clifford Bloom. "I hear you're a preacher. How did that come about?"

"My aunt right here is probably responsible," Patrick replies.

"Oh please . . ." I say.

"Really," he insists. "She doesn't preach the teachings of Christ. She lives them."

"Imperfectly," I add.

"Are you a fundamentalist?" asks Larry deYoung.

"I fundamentally believe in Jesus Christ," I say, "but I also fundamentally run away from labels. In his day, they didn't call Jesus a fundamentalist or even a Christian. They called him Rabbi."

"My father is a fundamentalist Christian," says Naomi. "So I know a little something about that point of view."

"And you're a reformed Jew, I take it," Clifford adds. "You're a liberal Jew with a different outlook on traditional ritual."

"I am," Naomi confirms.

"Doesn't it hurt to have that gap between you and your dad?" Patrick asks.

"It hurts a great deal," Naomi answers.

"All these differences are interesting," Clifford remarks. "I for one would be interested in attending your church, Pastor Merci."

"I'd love to have you. I'd love to invite everyone here to my church," I respond. "I'd be honored to have you pray with me."

"I think he likes you," Patrick tells me in the car on the way home.

"Who, baby?"

"The deejay. Clifford Bloom. He knew your records."

"Music is his line of work."

"But the way he was talking to you, Aunt Tina, the way he was looking at you . . ."

"Please, child, if there was romance in the air, it was coming from your side of the table. And Naomi's."

"Did you like her?"

"Lovely person. And a wonderful cook."

"It's amazing that she's such a rebel."

"She didn't call herself a rebel."

"Well, she denied her father's church."

"That doesn't mean she rebelled, honey. It just means she followed her path."

"She called herself a liberal. That bothered me. In seminary, religious liberals are seen as the Enemy."

"What she means by 'liberal' and what they mean could be two different things. That's why labels are so dangerous, sugar. They separate people who might well be of the same heart."

"You didn't get into religious differences with her," he says. "You didn't challenge her."

"Now think about it, Patrick. If someone of a different faith invites me to her home, includes me in her sacred holiday service, cooks and serves me food, am I supposed to *challenge* her? I'm sorry, baby, I just wasn't raised that way, and neither were you."

"When you were talking about Jesus, I saw how uncomfortable she was," Patrick says.

"I saw no such thing. When she and I were talking in the kitchen, she said several things that led me to believe she had studied early Christianity extremely closely."

"Studying and believing," says Patrick, "are two different things."

"I believe she is a woman who loves the Lord."

"Which Lord?" asks Patrick.

"There's only one, honey," I answer.

"From Virginia Hogobin, Executive Producer, Maggie's World"

open the FedEx overnight envelope. My curiosity is keen.

Dear Pastor Merci,

You might recall that I met you in Dallas at Cindy's loft during that wonderful party you hosted. I also saw you at her funeral. Cindy and I were great friends and all of us at the show miss her terribly. I'm writing you today on a happier note. Miss Clay would like to invite you to appear on her program. In two weeks, she'll be doing a show based on her recovery. She is inviting all those people who have been instrumental in helping her. You are included in that group of six people she considers absolutely essential to her well-being.

Of course we will provide you with a first-class round-trip ticket and accommodations at the Fairmont Hotel.

I cannot imagine doing the show without you, Pastor Merci, and we are hopeful you will accept this invitation. If you have any questions at all, please feel free to call me.

Virginia Hogobin

I call her.

"Virginia Hogobin?" I ask.

"Yes."

"Albertina Merci."

"Good morning, Pastor. Good to hear your voice."

"Thank you, sweetheart. I'm just a little confused by your letter."

"How so?"

"Well, to be honest, Virginia, I'm not at all sure that I helped Maggie. And I'm not at all sure she thinks I did."

"But she does, I can assure you."

"Furthermore, dear, I'm not sure if I have anything to say about helping her. I don't want to contradict her other guests. I don't want to confuse the issues. I'm not sure about the whole thing."

"Maggie and I have discussed this at length, Pastor, and she's perfectly willing to have you say whatever you feel. There are no restrictions. I think she intends to simply ask you what is it in your philosophy that helps people get past depression."

"My philosophy revolves around Jesus Christ."

"I know that, Pastor, and so does Maggie. Anyone who knows you knows what you stand for. And I believe Maggie is eager to have your point of view stated, clearly and powerfully, to all her viewers."

I pause to sigh.

"I understand your reservations, Pastor," she continues. "I know Maggie's moods have been erratic. And I know you've seen a great deal of volatility on her part. But I can assure you she is sincere about giving you this public forum. If that weren't the case, I would not be extending this invitation."

"Well, thank you, dear."

"So we can count on you?"

"Give me the day to think it over. May I call you first thing tomorrow?"

"Of course."

Justine is hysterically happy.

"Walker is going to be in Dallas at the exact same time you're appearing on Maggie's show! He's conducting a seminar there all week. It's all meant to be, Albertina! This is too good to be true! It's God's will! It *has* to be!"

"Not so fast, Justine. First of all, I haven't decided if I'm going—"

"Oh, you're going alright. You're going and you're going to put in a good word for Walker with Maggie's people. He's going to meet the woman who books her guests that same week. You probably know her."

"I don't know her."

"Well, you can meet her. And you can get Maggie to meet Walker. You can hook up the whole thing. It's beautiful how God works, isn't it, Albertina? Didn't you say God gives us the desires of our heart?"

"All I'll say is that my understanding of Maggie Clay diminishes with each day. I'm not at all sure what this turn of events is all about."

"After all is said and done, Albertina, it's clear that this woman sure enough likes you. If she didn't, she wouldn't keep sending for you. Maybe when you're with her she gets in a bad mood now and then, but she winds up giving you money and buying you chruches. Ain't that proof enough?"

"And what can I say on her show about how I helped her when, in fact, I don't know how I helped her. Or even *if* I helped her?"

"Of course you helped her. She's back and better than ever. You saw that first show. She looks terrific. She sounds terrific."

"There's something about the whole thing I don't trust," I say.

"Aren't you supposed to trust the Lord?"

"I do trust the Lord, honey."

"And isn't it clear that the Lord has placed Maggie in your life?"

"Clear as a bell."

"Then go on and ring that bell, girl! Get to Dallas, go on her show and tell the whole world how you love Jesus! Isn't that what you want to do?"

"I always want to talk about my love for Jesus, yes."

"Then praise God, Albertina, because you will finally have your chance to testify on national television!"

"Did you hear about my invitation?" I ask Bob Blakey.

He's in his office in Dallas. I'm home in L.A., still trying to figure out what to do.

"Yes," he says, "I saw Virginia's letter to you."

"What do you think, Bob?"

"I mentioned it to Maggie. To tell you the truth, Aunt Albertina, after all that happened, I did find her invitation strange."

"What did Maggie say?"

"She said, 'Albertina is Cindy's aunt. Albertina is a marvelous person. She was of great comfort to me. Why wouldn't I include Albertina in this show?' "

"And she said nothing more?"

"Nothing more."

"And you believe her, baby?"

"I have no reason not to."

"So you think I should come."

"I think you should do whatever is comfortable for you."

"That's praying. I'm always comfortable praying. Can we pray together, Bob?"

"Please, Aunt Albertina. No one else is going to call me today and invite me to pray. I love it."

"We love *You*, Father God, and we worship You with open hearts. You know our hearts. You are in our hearts. You *are* our hearts. We pray that deep inside our hearts we find the resolution that comes with Your divine clarity. We pray that You sustain us in our daily decisions, and our indecisions, in our certainty and in our confusion. We pray that You sustain us with every word we utter. We pray that You envelop us in your astounding and extravagant love. We pray that we extend that extravagance to others. And that through us, they feel You. In the precious name of Jesus, Amen."

Muriel is holding a Bible. She and Tom are sitting on opposite sides of my couch, even further away from each other than last time. She opens the Bible and says, "Hebrews 13:4. 'Marriage is to be held in honor among all, and the marriage bed is to be undefiled; for fornicators and adulterers God will judge.' "

"An auspicious beginning to our second session," says Tom.

"You do believe the Bible, don't you, Pastor Merci?" Muriel asks.

"I do, sweetheart," I assure her.

"Well, then," she adds, "the text couldn't be plainer."

Tom stays silent.

"May I ask you a question, Muriel?" I say.

"Yes."

"What if this meeting had begun differently. What if Tom had brought a Bible and read the passage from Colossians 1:13–14 that says, 'For He rescued us from the domain of darkness, and transferred us to the kingdom of His beloved Son, in whom we have redemption, the forgiveness of sin.' How would you have responded?"

"I would have referred him to Hebrews 13:4."

"So we'd have a Bible battle, is that it?" I ask.

"What is your point, Pastor?" Muriel wants to know.

"I get uncomfortable when the Bible is used for personal attacks," I say.

"Is that what you see me doing?" Muriel asks.

"Any woman in your position would be angry," I answer. "Any woman in your position is entitled to be angry. I'd be the last person in the world to ask you to deny or suppress that anger. I'm just not sure that our anger needs to be linked to God's wrath and God's judgment. I prefer to see that wrath and judgment as strictly God's domain, not ours. When a boxer claims he's going to win because God is on his side, I wonder about the legitimacy of that claim."

"I have a legitimate right to be furious," says Muriel.

"Of course you do, sweetheart," I affirm. "And my heart is with you. But my heart is also with Tom."

"That's the part I can't understand," Muriel states emphatically. "How can you have sympathy for him knowing what he did?"

"I don't have sympathy for him," I say. "I have love for him."

"That's even more inconceivable."

"It's hard to conceive that God loves us after we've done the things we've done," I explain. "It's very hard to conceive that He forgives us, after we've denounced Him, rejected Him, and violated His commandments. But inconceivable love and radical forgiveness are part of the very nature of the God we worship."

"I don't want to think about that," says Muriel.

"You don't have to think about it," I say. "But you might want to try to *feel* it. It feels wonderful."

"To you," she retorts. "Not to me."

"What do you think about forgiveness?" I ask Tom. "Do you think you can forgive yourself, Tom, for the pain you have caused?"

He hesitates before answering. When he does answer, he utters a barely audible "No." And with that he breaks down and cries.

Muriel instinctually gets up and begins to go to him, but she stops herself. She sits back down, turns her head from him and begins to weep.

I close my eyes and say, "Father God, we just thank You for allowing these powerful feelings of pain and regret to flow through us. We thank You for this day, for this moment, for the healing power of tears, for the healing power of Jesus Christ. In His holy name, Amen."

D/FW

I'm not crazy about D/FW Airport. It's too big, too busy, too sprawling and unmanageable. It doesn't even feel like Dallas to me. It feels more like Chicago or New York. Everyone in a hurry, everyone frantic, everyone shoving and pushing and practically running you over.

I miss that lazy old Love Field that was close to the house I grew up in. I miss walking over to Bachman Lake where, as a little girl, I'd watch the prop planes take off and land. Sometimes my daddy would take his fishing pole and try his luck in the lake while I waited for the 3:30 Pan American flight from Chicago to make its dramatic descent just over our heads. I wondered whether I'd ever get to fly in an airplane, whether life would allow me to travel to faraway places.

Life has allowed that, and much more. I thank God for all my blessings. As an entertainer I've been to every continent and more countries than I can count. Every place interested and excited me. Every place made me grateful that God was showing me still another one of His wonders—a different landscape, a different language, a different culture. I was thrilled to go to Tokyo, Japan, and thrilled to go to Toledo, Ohio. As the kids say today, it's all good. The road has its drawbacks, but the road was my teacher for much of my life. In these past twelve months, however, why that road keeps leading me back to Dallas remains a mystery.

It's Wednesday morning and the airport is teeming with people rushing to and fro. My trip is just three days long, so I'm traveling light. I checked one small piece of luggage. Miss Hogobin said a driver would be waiting for me in baggage claim. Sure enough, a fine-looking brother is holding a sign with my name on it.

"I'm Pastor Merci," I say.

"I'm Walker Jones," he says with a smile that extends from ear to ear.

"Well, I'll be," I say. "I knew you solved health problems, Mr. Jones, but I didn't realize you solve transportation problems as well."

"Any problem, Pastor Merci, any problem at all."

I am not comfortable with this situation, but there's not much I can do except ask, "Are you working as a driver for Maggie's show?"

Walker laughs a hearty, confident laugh. "No, Pastor, not at all. To be perfectly candid—and I'd like you to know that I am a perfectly candid and honest person—I arranged this. Justine said you'd be coming in today, and with a few calls I got in touch with the limo service, contacted the driver, and told him that, as your relative, I'd like to pick you up but would pay him for his trouble. So I did."

"And that's honest, Mr. Jones?" I ask.

"It's an honest expression of my desire to meet you, Pastor

Merci, and express my admiration for your ministry. You're doing wonderful work, and it's an honor to assist you today. It's an absolute honor to be in your service."

"Well, thank you, Mr. Jones . . ."

"Please call me Walker."

"I didn't realize anyone around here knew anything about my ministry," I say.

"Justine carried the word to me. She has to be one of your most devoted disciples."

"I hardly think of Justine as a disciple," I observe, "but she is a wonderful and devoted friend."

"That's exactly how I feel about her."

The luggage arrives and Walker, dressed in a dramatic white linen suit, scoops it up. A fancy Lincoln Town Car is waiting at the curb. When I start to climb in the front seat, he stops.

"Please," he says, "you'll be more comfortable in the back."

"Mr. Jones, this is not 'Driving Pastor Merci,'" I insist. "The front is fine."

He opens the door for me and soon we're off. I know what the man has in mind and I'm curious to see how long it'll take him to get to his agenda. It doesn't take long.

"You know, Pastor," he says, "I'm envious of your relationship with Maggie Clay. She's such a fascinating woman. It must be a great blessing to have her in your life. And a blessing for her as well."

I don't know how to reply, so I don't.

"Justine tells me that you met her through your niece," he says.

"That's true," I confirm tersely.

"And that your niece worked for her," he adds.

"She did," I confirm.

"And that you've been in close contact with Miss Clay for over a year."

"I'm not sure I'd categorize it as close contact."

"Well, according to Justine . . ."

"Mr. Jones—" I begin.

"Walker—" he corrects me.

"Okay. Walker . . ." I continue, "Justine has a wonderful imagination. Like all of us, sometimes her imagination corresponds to reality and sometimes it doesn't."

"Justine told me you and she watched my tape together," he says, switching gears.

"Yes."

"And I hope you found it enlightening."

"I did," I say.

"If you don't mind, I'd like to tell you a little bit more about my program and the work I'm doing in this Dallas seminar. Nothing would please me more than to have you come by for a session. And if you'd like to bring Miss Clay with you, I'd make sure the situation was private—no press, no outsiders. I think she'd be interested in what I'm doing."

"Don't know her well enough to say."

"Well, if an opportunity opens up you might—"

"Mr. Jones . . . I mean Mr. Walker . . . I mean Walker, please don't take this the wrong way. I'm sure your program is fine, but I'm really in no position to lean on Maggie for any favors. I hope you understand."

"Of course. I understand completely. But if you're hesitant to speak to Miss Clay, you might know a Miss Alice Taylor, the woman who books guests for Miss Clay. I'm sure you've spoken to her."

"Actually I haven't," I say. "I spoke with a Virginia Hogobin."

"She's even better. She's Miss Taylor's boss. She's the show's executive producer. I'm wondering, Pastor, if you'd be kind enough to let Miss Hogobin know that you and I are working together and—"

"Working together? Is that what we're doing?"

"Well, chatting. And I like to think forming a friendship. You see, my grandfather was a pastor. I have a deep respect for pastors and a great love of the Lord. I've been a church boy all my life and I've tried to live by God's commandments."

Then how about this business of cheating on your wife with Justine? I want to ask him but don't.

"That's wonderful, Walker," I tell him, "but I'm not sure I'll have much time to speak with Miss Hogobin."

"Maybe when it's time for you to go to the show tomorrow, I can again have the honor of driving you."

How can I refuse? I don't. I just don't say anything.

When we arrive at the fancy Fairmont Hotel, Walker tells me that he has taken the trouble to check my accommodations and was able to get the manager to upgrade me to a deluxe suite.

"When he found out who you were," Walker explains, "he was more than happy to move you to more comfortable quarters."

"Thank you," I say, "but I'm comfortable most anywhere."

Walker carries my bag to my suite, which is so opulent and expansive I feel a little uneasy. He tells me that he's staying in the same hotel. "Please let me know if I can help you in any way, Pastor," he says.

"Thank you, Walker. I just need a little rest right now."

On the gilded coffee table in the living room is a huge bouquet of flowers and a note from Maggie and Virginia Hogobin. "Welcome. You grace us with your presence." There's also a large platter of fruits and cheeses and tantalizing desserts. I decide to take a bath.

I'm taking a post-bath nap in the king-sized bed when the phone rings.

"Mom, it's Andre."

"How are you, son?"

"Blessed, really blessed, Mom. Got an offer for my screenplay."

"Wonderful, Andre."

"Not huge money, but decent. And serious producers. They're serious about making the movie."

"I'm proud of you."

"But that's not the only reason I'm calling. I remembered you said something about going to Dallas. It took me a minute to put two and two together, but I just called cousin Patrick in L.A. who said you were in Dallas right now. Well, it turns out Nina's in Dallas as well—her movie, which was shot in Dallas, is premiering there tonight—and it also turns out she's staying in the same hotel as you. So if you want to go to the premiere tonight, she's looking for a date."

"Oh, son, I'm so tired. The plane trip wore me out and—"

"She's got a limo picking her up in two hours. Throw on a dress and have yourself a good time, Ma. You don't have to stay for the after-party."

"Well . . ."

"Well, nothing. Just go. You'll have a blast. Nina will be calling your room in a few minutes. Look, Mom, this is all meant to be or it wouldn't be so easy. All you have to do is put on a dress and get in a limo. Is that so hard?"

"It's just that—"

"I'm calling Nina right now. Have a great time tonight."

Five minutes later the phone rings.

"Pastor Merci, it's Nina."

"Hi, honey."

"I can't believe you're here! I can't believe we're staying in the same hotel! What room are you in?"

"Eight twenty-five."

"I'm in eight-o-one. We're even on the same floor! You have to come with me tonight! You just have to! I was going to go alone, but this is just too perfect!"

"Alright, dear. I'm going to have to wear the same outfit I'm wearing on television tomorrow . . ."

"Andre said you're going on *Maggie's World*. That is *so* exciting! Maggie is supposed to be at the premiere tonight. I hope you'll introduce me."

"Why . . . of course I will," I say, but in the privacy of my mind, I add, *Help me, Jesus.*

"The Couch"

I get to the lobby a little before Nina. When Nina arrives, she causes quite a commotion. Heads turn—mainly men's heads. She's dressed provocatively in an extremely short black shirt and black blouse that leaves nothing to the imagination. She has a superb figure and I certainly understand why actresses feel compelled to show off their anatomical assets, but suddenly I feel very concerned for my son.

"It's wonderful to see you, Pastor," she says. "I can't believe we're here at the same time! You are such a doll to accompany me to the premiere. I'd be a nervous wreck without you. This is really my first semi-starring role."

A publicist from the movie studio is waiting for us in the limo. Nina introduces us. The publicist couldn't care less who I am or why I'm there. "She's like an aunt," Nina explains to deaf ears. All the publicist cares about is preparing Nina for the red-carpet entrance.

"I'll point out which photographers are from the big magazines, and which reporters are from the national media," she says. "I'll lead you through this thing. Miss . . . what was your name again?" she asks me.

"Merci," I say. "Albertina Merci."

"I'll have someone take you through the back door to the VIP room," the publicist explains to me. "Just wait there until further notice."

"I've never been this excited in my life," says Nina. "I'm not sure I can take all the attention."

I almost say, *I think you'll handle the attention just fine*, but I don't.

When the limo pulls up to the curb, I see that we're in front of the Majestic Theater on Elm Street in downtown Dallas. As a little girl, this was the theater where I went to see Duke Ellington and Jimmie Lunceford's big bands. African Americans were allowed to sit only in the balcony. That hurt my heart since the bands were all Black, but once I heard their music, the pain went away. Their rhythms and melodies set me dreaming. Only a block or two away sits Neiman-Marcus, scene of more dreams, pains, and nightmares. I take my head out of my past, though, and think of Nina. Tonight is her dream. She's entitled to be giddy and beside herself with anticipation.

"The two big stars—Sean Penn and Penelope Cruz—are off shooting another movie," the publicist explains, "and couldn't make it here. So we're focusing a great deal of attention on Nina, who has third billing but a major and explosive role that should put her on the map."

The photographers are waiting as the door opens and the publicist leads Nina down the red carpet. I'm escorted around the back of the theater into a rear entrance. Ironically, that's the entrance I used as a little girl to climb up to the balcony. This time, though, the balcony is roped off for VIPs. It is a private party that includes an even more exclusive party in an ornate reception room. I'm brought inside, where a jazz trio is playing softly. Women in gowns and men in tuxes mingle among platters of fancy food. I feel underdressed. In the corner I see Maggie Clay. She towers over the admirers surrounding her. She's wearing a long silver dress sprinkled with black sequins. She spots me out of the corner of her eye and waves for me to approach her.

"Pastor!" she exclaims. "I had no idea you went to movie premieres. How liberal of you!" Maggie seems clear but her mannerisms just aren't right. I feel her fighting something in her spirit.

"My son's girlfriend is in the movie," I say. "I've accompanied her."

"How wonderful."

"Thank you, Maggie," I add, "for inviting me on your show."

"I'm thrilled you could make it, Pastor. Tomorrow should be quite a show."

"I'm just glad you're feeling and looking well."

"Never felt or looked better, wouldn't you say?"

The people surrounding Maggie all say, "Yes!" in unison.

I hear a voice from behind my back say, "Excuse me, Pastor Merci, but what a wonderful coincidence that we're both here."

I turn around and see Walker Jones dressed in a midnight blue tux. He extends his hand to Maggie and says, "I'm Walker Jones, a close friend of Pastor Merci's. It's a pleasure to meet you."

"Pastor keeps all the fine men away from me," says Maggie. "She knows my weakness."

"Physical and mental strength are my specialty," says Walker. "I'm sure Pastor has mentioned my program to you. One of her parishioners is among my biggest endorsers."

"Tell me about it, Mr. Jones," Maggie urges.

I leave them to go fetch some celery and peanuts. I don't want to hear Walker's pitch. I'm also a little peeved that he introduced himself as my close friend. But if that's how he plays his game, I'm not about to get involved.

Fifteen minutes later we're escorted into the theater. I'm seated next to Nina who's still tingling from the press attention.

"It was fabulous," she whispers to me, "just fabulous. Is Maggie here?"

"Yes."

"That is *so* perfect," says Nina. "I'm sure she'll be at the after-party. You just *must* introduce me."

Before I can say anything, a man leans over and says, "Pastor, you just *must* introduce me."

It's Walker. He's sitting behind us. I introduce him to Nina. They exchange pleasantries and, if my interpretation is right—and I'm sure it is—meaningful stares.

The film begins. It's called *The Couch*. Sean Penn is a psychiatrist. So is his wife Penelope Cruz. Nina is his patient. In what is evidently a psychological erotic thriller, Sean falls for Nina. Twenty minutes into the film, Sean and Nina are making passionate love—and I do mean passionate—on his couch. I don't know the literal definition of pornography, but this has to come very close. Nina is completely naked and the simulated lovemaking is graphic. I am terribly uncomfortable. I wonder how Nina feels about this. Forty minutes into the film, Sean and Nina start in on another lovemaking marathon. This time the explicitness is even more graphic.

"Please excuse me, sweetheart," I say to Nina, "but the

plane trip really knocked me out. I think I better go to sleep early tonight."

"But the after-party," Nina reminds me. "You were going to introduce me to Maggie."

"Maggie will know who you are, baby," I say. "Everybody will know who you are."

Outside in the lobby I find the limo driver and ask if he'll drive me back to the hotel, only a few minutes away. He does so.

In the limo, my head is swimming. I'm thinking about Nina, thinking about my son, thinking about propriety and prudishness and the way boundaries of discretion no longer seem to exist. Am I angry? Am I disappointed? Am I confused? I'm tired—I know that much. And though there is a voice in my head that says, *Call up Andre and give him a piece of your mind for urging you to go to a movie that he knew would make you uncomfortable*, I resist that voice. I know I need sleep. I need rest. Tomorrow is the show and I need some sweet sleep.

But my sleep is neither restful nor sweet. I'm awoken by a dream about Dexter Banks, my first husband who betrayed me while we were living in an apartment on McKinney Avenue, less than a mile from this fancy hotel. I block out the details of the dream. But meanwhile, my head is aching and my throat is dry. I need cold water but am out of ice. I put on my robe and head to the ice machine. The clock says 3 a.m. The hallway is long. I scoop up the ice, put it in the bucket, and am carrying it back to my room. As I reach my door, I hear voices behind me, way down the hallway near the ice machine. The woman certainly looks like Nina; the man certainly looks like Walker; and it certainly looks like they're entering the same room. But I'm tired, and perhaps I'm imagining things. Back in bed, I try to sleep but sleep doesn't come easily.

At brunch the next morning I put the thought out of my head, but it doesn't stay out of my head for long because I look up to see Walker and Nina entering the dining room together. They come right over to my table.

"Look who I just met on the elevator," says Walker quickly. I can hear the wheels of his mind spinning like crazy.

"Mr. Jones says he's friends with your best friend," says Nina.

"Yes," I say.

"Sorry you missed the rest of the movie," Nina adds. "It got a standing ovation. And the after-party was beautiful. Maggie came and she couldn't have been nicer. Wasn't she great, Walker?"

"Couldn't have been greater," he says.

First she called him "Mr. Jones." Now he's "Walker." I just want to finish my eggs. I do so in a hurry. I'm just not comfortable. Besides, I don't mind getting to the show early.

"I've arranged to drive you," says Walker.

"That won't be necessary," I say firmly. "I've called a cab."

There is an icy silence that I break by excusing myself.

Earlier that morning Patrick had called to say many House of Trust members were congregating at his place to watch the show. He said they would be praying for me. Justine also called to say that of course she, too, would be watching. She wanted to know if I'd seen Walker. I had, I said. "Isn't he wonderful?" she wanted to know. I changed the subject and got off the phone in a hurry.

When I give the cab driver the address, I realize that Maggie's studio complex on Lemon Avenue is only a few blocks from my childhood home. She has renovated three huge warehouses to accommodate her recording facilities. I can't be in this neighborhood without feeling tremendous emotions from my past coursing through my veins. I try not to think of Andre and Nina, of Justine and Walker, but I fail. It's hard to get that stuff off my mind.

In my highly emotional state, I must tell the country of my love for Jesus and His ability to heal hearts. Well, I'll do what I have to do. And what I have to do is pray. In the silence of Maggie's green room, I shut my eyes and silently say, *Father, this is the day You made. I am the servant You made. I want to serve You today. I want to speak from my heart, not my head, and express my love for You and Your awesome ability to settle the mind and calm the spirit. Let acrimony and suspicion be supplanted by Your light of understanding and love. Let old animosities be quieted. Let only positive healing energy inform my words. Let my words glorify You. In Jesus' precious name, Amen.*

When I open my eyes I see Bishop Henry Gold, wearing his diamond watch, and Dr. Oliver Pratt enter the room. Bishop Gold does not recognize me. He does not remember that we've met before and that I spoke at Cindy's funeral. The man pays me no mind. Dr. Pratt, on the other hand, comes over and greets me.

"We met on Maraqua," he says. "I still remember that fabulous meal you cooked us. Bishop Gold, this is Maggie's cook. I forget your name, dear."

"Albertina."

"Well, Albertina," says Dr. Pratt, looking over the platters of food in the green room, "it looks like you've outdone yourself again. This is quite a spread you've prepared."

I'm about to correct him when Virginia Hogobin walks in the room. I recognize her from the party at Cindy's loft. She's tall with reddish blond hair.

"Bishop Gold and Dr. Pratt," she says, "my assistant will accompany you to the stage."

The assistant leads the men out, leaving me alone with Virginia.

"Pastor Merci," says Virginia, "I'm afraid I don't have good news."

"Oh . . ."

"At the very last minute, Maggie seems to have changed her mind. She thinks three guests speaking of her recovery would be too many. She has decided that one from the secular world and one from the religious realm would be enough."

"I see."

"I feel just awful about this, Pastor. Just dreadful. Taking up your time. Having you go to this trouble. I . . . I just don't know what to say."

"Baby, you don't have to say anything," I say. "This wasn't your decision. It was Maggie's."

"Thank you for understanding."

"I've always understood."

"You mean, you foresaw this possibility?"

"Sure did, honey. Thought about it any number of times."

"And yet you came."

"I came because I was asked to serve," I say. "Where I come from, you don't turn down a chance to serve."

"Right now you're serving as an excellent example of patience and fortitude," says Virginia.

"I'm glad of that, baby."

"And you're not angry? You're not disappointed?"

"I'm both, but I'm also grateful to God for letting you and

me have this conversation. Feels like you, Virginia, have a heart for the Lord."

"If the Lord gives us the kind of character I see in you, then, yes, I do have a heart for the Lord."

"Have you ever accepted Jesus, Virginia? Have you ever gotten on your knees and asked him to enter your heart as your Lord and Savior?"

"I can't believe you're asking me that right now, Pastor. Not here in the green room, not with the show about to go on the air . . ."

"Please, Virginia, understand that I'm happy to wish you well and send you on your way. But I'm also happy to sit and pray over you for a second or two."

"I . . . I think I want you to do just that. I think I want you to pray over me, Pastor."

I do. I place my hands on Virginia's head. I pray. I quote Romans 10:8–9, "The word is near you, in your mouth and in your heart, that is the word that we are preaching, that if you confess with your mouth Jesus as Lord, and believe in your heart that God raised Him from the dead, you will be saved. . . ." Virginia confesses; Virginia believes; Virginia is saved.

"That was beautiful," she says. "That felt so beautiful."

"I love you, my daughter," I say. Tears are in my eyes. Tears are in her eyes.

"I have to go," she says. "I have to see about the show."

"I love you, sweetheart."

"I love you too, Pastor."

"Glory to God," I say, falling to my knees.

"Payback"

James Brown had a song called "Payback." It came out in the seventies at a time when James was interested in having me join his troupe as backup singer. I love and respect James. He is the Godfather of Soul and no one will ever replace him. The man is a superbad singer, brilliant writer, and ridiculously talented dancer. His grooves are forever. As a band leader, he's a disciplinarian who demands the best of his musicians, singers, and dancers. I like his attitude about going for perfection. I remember what Paul said in 2 Corinthians 13:11: "Aim for perfection, listen to my appeal, be of one mind, live in peace. And the God of peace will be with you."

Going on the road with James did not hold the promise of peace for me. My instincts told me so. When I heard the haunting start of "Payback"—"Got to get to payback—revenge!"—I knew my life had to move in a different direction than the coast-to-coast James Brown tour.

When I return home to LAX from Dallas, I know the same thing. The minute my nephew Patrick meets me at the baggage claim, he says, even before saying "hello," "I know we preach forgiveness and I know we're supposed to be forgiving souls, Aunt Albertina, but this is too much."

"There's nothing to do except pray for her, Patrick."

"I have friends in the press," he says. "One of them wants to interview you about the whole experience."

"I won't agree to any interview," I say. "I can't be part of that story. I have no idea how he'll twist the facts and recast the tone. I have no desire to hurt anyone."

"She hurt you."

"Being hurt is part of life, baby. Yes, I'm hurt. I'll grant you. Hurt and tired. It was a trying trip."

"I think you're compromising your integrity, Aunt Albertina."

"Did Christ compromise His when He wouldn't retaliate against those who humiliated and tortured Him? Did he ask the Father to rebuke them or did He ask the Father to forgive them?"

Patrick doesn't respond. My baggage arrives. We are silent. Patrick drives me home and I go to sleep.

Sometimes I remember my dreams; sometimes I don't. This dream I remember in detail: James Brown, Little Richard, Al Green, and Elton John are standing in front of a huge church. Each has his own pulpit. But they aren't speaking, they're singing. In four-part harmony they're singing a song that says, "The Kingdom of God is alive, the Kingdom of God is inside." I have never heard this song before. I am in the first pew, sitting with my children. Darryl is alive and a very young boy. Andre and Laura are adults. I'm so happy that all three of my children are alive and well. Then the music gets to grooving so hard and the message is so strong that I fall out. I pass out. From the floor I see Justine, dressed in a nurse's uniform, offering me smelling salts. I'm revitalized, and when I get back up I find I'm in the Paris Opera House, where Bishop Henry Gold is dressed in tights and singing the part of a clown. He's Pagliacci. The audience is made up of schoolchildren. They won't pay attention to the Bishop, who becomes agitated and starts screaming. Maggie appears onstage. She is introduced as the Queen of France. She is dressed as Marie-Antoinette. She raises her hand and order is reestablished. She points to me and orders me out of the opera house. Soldiers appear on either side of me and escort me outside. The great boulevard of Paris turns into the runway at Love Field where a giant jumbo jet is about to land in the exact spot where I'm standing. I run. I hear a voice that says, "You don't have to run. You can stand just where you are. You are safe just where you are." And with that, I wake up.

An hour later, Justine comes over. I realize it's time for our daily ritual of watching *Maggie's World*.

"If you can't manage it today," Justine says, "I understand."

"I'm afraid I can't, sweetheart," I say.

"That must have hurt so bad."

"It wasn't fun," I admit.

"I'm so sorry, Albertina, I really am."

"I know you are."

"It turned out so bad for you, but in the midst of it all, it turned out so good for Walker. He and I can't thank you enough for introducing him to Maggie. He said you were wonderful about it. Maggie told him that she'd talk to the person who books her guests. He's meeting with that person today. So maybe that was the purpose of your trip, Albertina. You know how you always say that we never know God's purpose, but we can only pray for it. But maybe that was God's purpose. Maybe my prayers have been answered."

"Justine, I have to say something."

"What?"

"I don't trust that man," I declare.

This takes her aback.

"Why?" she wants to know.

"I can't say exactly . . ."

"Did he do something? Did he say something?"

I don't want to go into details. I don't want to make presumptions. I was not in the room with Walker and Nina if in fact they were the couple I saw going into the room. I was tired. Maybe I was seeing things. Who knows?

"It wasn't anything he said or did, it was his manner," I explain. "I'm not judging him, baby, but just observing. And from what I saw he puts himself before anyone or anything."

"He has to. He wants to have a great career. He's driven. Is anything wrong with that?"

"No, sugar. But something isn't right."

"If you can't be more specific, Albertina, I wish you wouldn't say anything at all. Frankly, I don't think you understand him."

"I'm sure I don't."

"Then don't judge him."

"I said I'm not judging him."

"I think you are. I think you're judging us for being together while his divorce still isn't final. That's what I think."

"Oh, baby," I tell Justine, "I just want you to be happy."

"I'd be happy, Albertina, if you'd stay out of my personal business."

With that, Justine leaves.

Next day Muriel and Tom come over for another three-way discussion. Before we start, Tom hands me a check for $400.

"This is to cover your time so far," he says.

"I can't accept this," I say. "I'm not a licensed counselor."

"Then I'll donate it to your church."

"That's fine," I assure him. "Thank you. Now how are you both doing?"

"Not great," he says.

"Tell me," I urge.

"You speak first, Muriel," he urges.

"I told the children," she blurts out.

"Oh," I say. "What prompted that, honey?"

"I guess they call it payback. I wanted to pay him back for how he hurt me. I wanted our kids to see that their father isn't the man they think he is. I wanted the truth out there."

"You wanted revenge?" I ask.

"Yes."

"And did you get it?" I ask.

"The kids are devastated," says Tom.

"Is that true?" I ask Muriel.

"They found the news disturbing, yes."

"And what was accomplished?" I ask.

"The truth is out," she answers. "No more secrets, no more lies."

"Did you and Tom talk about telling the children before you actually told them?" I ask Muriel.

"That wasn't his decision to make," she says. "It was mine. I'm the injured party here. Not him."

"Muriel, I'm going to say something to you that might sound shocking, but it's something I'm feeling strongly in my spirit. I think you should leave Tom or ask him to leave."

"Pastor!" Tom breaks in, "I thought the purpose of this was reconciliation."

"Sometimes reconciliation takes a different turn," I say.

"I don't see how that will help anything," Muriel states.

"Then you don't want to leave?" I ask her. "You don't want him to leave?"

"I'm not ready to make that move," she says.

"The more he stays," I say, "the more you're punishing him."

"And doesn't he deserve it?" she asks.

"Your home is toxic with acrimony and vendetta. It's not a healthy home now. Something should be done," I say.

"What?" Tom wants to know.

"If Muriel won't leave or isn't ready to ask you to leave, I'm going to ask that at least once a day the two of you pray together," I suggest. "I won't prescribe your prayers. Just pray from your heart. Speak to God. But pray in each other's presence. Pray out loud. That's all I ask. That's my only assignment. If you're willing to do that, I'm happy to keep talking to both of you. If you're not, I'm afraid there's nothing more for me to do."

After a few seconds, they say yes, they are willing.

Later that night I learn the sad news: Paulette and Martin Simmons's son, Chuck, has died. The cause was an AIDS-related stroke. I'm devastated. The funeral is later this week. They want me to officiate. I ask God to give me the words to say because right now no words seem right.

There Is No Death

I'm surprised at how emotional I am. I can't remember ever being this emotional at a funeral, even with my mom and dad, even with Cindy. I guess everything has built up. I still haven't said a thing to Andre about Nina. Justine has stopped talking to me—that hurts—but I don't want to accuse her boyfriend of something I can't prove. I detest gossip and slander. I know that being rejected one more time by Maggie has had an impact on me. I've brought out something mean in that woman and I'm struggling not to take it personally. I don't think it's personal, but I must symbolize something she resents, something she wants to destroy. I know it is God's will that I not react—and with God's help I have not reacted—because reaction would only trigger more from Maggie. She wants to get into it with me. She wants me to rant and rave at her so she can rant and rave at me. I know I need to pray for her from afar.

At Chuck's funeral, most of my church family has come to pray with Paulette and Martin. House of Trust is overflowing with mourners, many of whom are young people, Chuck's friends and colleagues. It is a sad, sad day. In Los Angeles we call the early summer months June gloom. The sky is overcast in the morning, but by early afternoon the sun breaks through. It's two o'clock in the afternoon but the sun still has not broken through.

Rather than speak at length—the right words still have not come to me—I ask anyone who wishes to speak to do so. Many come forth. All have something moving to say. Chuck was much loved for his kindness, gentle spirit, and bravery in the face of disease. The diversity of his friends is amazing—a Korean woman who is a fellow law student, a Hispanic man who met Chuck in high school, several of his teachers, his uncles, his aunts. A man who lived with Chuck speaks of Chuck's "exquisite sensitivity." Chuck's parents are too grief-stricken to speak. I see Martin trying to contain himself, but he cannot. Coach Simmons weeps openly.

I read several Psalms. We sing hymns. A man who knew Chuck well sings an a cappella version of Luther Vandross's "Power of Love." Now many are weeping openly.

We drive to Forest Lawn where Chuck's body will be buried. As I stand beside the casket, his family and close friends by my side, all holding hands, the words finally come to me. The sun finally comes out. I feel the Son. Thank you, Jesus.

"There is no death," I say. "There is only life. Jesus promised this. Jesus exemplified this. Jesus brought this transition into being. There are no more beautiful words in Scripture than John 8:12 when the Lord says plainly, 'I am the light of the world; he who follows Me will not walk in darkness but will have the light of life.' Chuck has the light of life. That light is inextinguishable. His light and God's light are now one light. Chuck is forever illuminated by a force of love so immense our minds cannot grasp its beauty, its power, its eternal joy. God wasn't born and God didn't die and God never goes away. God simply is. Jesus brings us to God because Jesus is born of God. Jesus is God. Jesus is our link, our loving link to God's forever grace. Because God cannot know death, and because Jesus defeated death, we too live in His glorious victory. There is no death. There is only God's infinite spirit. Chuck lives in that spirit. Chuck's human consciousness, limited as all of our consciousnesses are limited, has given way to the unalterable beauty of Christ consciousness. So we praise the power that brought Chuck forth. We praise the power that reconciled this loving family. We praise our Lord Jesus Christ for reconciling all of us to the Father, to God Almighty, whom we worship in gladness and with gratitude for life—bountiful creative life—that goes on forever and forever and forever. In the holy name of Jesus, Amen."

That night, in the quiet of my bedroom, I read over the book of John. I stop at the forty-seventh verse of the sixth chapter: "Truly, truly, I say to you, he who believes has eternal life. I am the bread of life. Your fathers ate the manna in the wilderness, and they died. This is the bread which comes down out of heaven, so that one may eat of it and not die. I am the living bread that came down out of heaven; if anyone eats of this bread, he will live forever; and the bread also which I will give for the life of the world is My flesh."

I carefully copy down the words on a beautiful card and address the card to Paulette and Martin. I sleep peacefully.

"I'm sorry I spoke harshly to you," says Justine. "You're my best friend. You're the best friend anyone could have. You'd just gone through a hard time and there I was, giving you a harder time. Please forgive me."

"You're forgiven, sweetheart."

"I'm on way to Dallas," Justine adds.

"When?"

"Tomorrow."

We're sitting at a French bistro in the Grove, a pleasant outdoor mall near Rabbi Naomi Cohen's house. Justine has invited me to lunch. At two o'clock I'm meeting my friend Florence Ginzburg, who lives right across the street.

"So why are you going to Dallas tomorrow?" I ask Justine.

"Walker is making his debut appearance on Maggie's show."

"Oh."

"I'm surprising him. He doesn't know I'm coming."

"Do you think that's wise?"

"I think he'll be thrilled when he sees me standing up in the audience, cheering him on. Your friend Bob Blakey made sure I got into the audience."

There are so many things I want to say, but they are not especially loving. I thank God for restraining my tongue. For the rest of the lunch, Justine discusses why Walker's methods of weight reduction can change anyone's life and his affirmations can defeat anyone's depression. She eats a green salad. I have pasta.

Florence and Bernard Ginzburg live in a pleasant 1930s three-bedroom apartment off Third Street. They've lived there for nearly forty years. Bernard has retired from his upholstery business but Florence keeps seeing patients. That's because her work as a therapist began when she was in her sixties. I admire her for switching professions late in life. She simply tired of being a lawyer, went back to school for more degrees, and found happiness helping people in a different way.

"I knew you'd do great as a therapist, sweetheart," I tell her, "because you're such a good listener."

"That's only because it's less tiring to listen than to talk," she says jokingly.

Florence is a small woman. She's slightly bent and suffers from osteoporosis. She has brown eyes that sparkle when she speaks, curly white hair that she has never dyed, and a wonderful collection of Israeli shawls. Because the air-conditioning in her apartment is going full-blast, she's wearing a sheer turquoise shawl across her shoulders. Bernard is out playing golf.

She serves me delicious chocolate cookies. We settle into easy chairs facing each other. Sunlight streaks through the living room window.

"I can't tell you how much I love having a forever friend like you," I say. "It's amazing how many years we've known each other, Florence."

"I feel the same, Albertina. Once I accepted that it was you and not me who was class valedictorian, I was fine. It only took me ten years to get over my jealousy!"

"I never felt any jealousy," I say.

"I was good at hiding it."

I smile and get right to the point. "Florence, I'm here to talk to you in strict confidence about a challenging relationship I have with Maggie Clay."

And talk I do. I start with Cindy and go all the way through to the latest fiasco in Dallas. I try not to leave out any important facts. It takes me nearly half an hour and when I'm through I'm exhausted.

"Wow," says Florence. "That's quite a story, Albertina."

"I tell you all this, honey," I explain, "not only to unburden myself—and I thank you for that—but to ask you whether my understanding of this situation, seen from my scriptural point of view, makes sense to you as a psychologist."

"Well, Albertina, it's obvious that this woman's psyche has been deeply injured."

"I guess what you call 'psyche,' I call 'spirit.'"

"The terms probably mean the same thing. It feels to me like Miss Clay has not dealt with the many elements that have so deeply hurt her."

"She keeps so much bottled up," I say.

"Fame and adulation are not always conducive to mental health. Neither is excessive wealth."

"Amen," I add. "Jesus said it's easier for a camel to pass through the eye of a needle than for a rich man to enter heaven."

"When celebrities feel pain, they have so many ways of anesthetizing it. They win an award, they buy a house, they buy someone else a house. They escape their confusion with extravagant gestures."

"Maggie is good at escaping," I say.

"But eventually she can't escape her own mind," adds Florence. "She thought she needed you to reclaim her mind or what you call her spirit. But she resented needing you. Maybe she saw herself as being weak in needing you. Then she found her game face again. Using whatever props were at her disposal—you'd know better than me what those props were—she built herself back up. At the same time, her anger over her own weakness—and the fear of growing even weaker—is connected in her mind to you."

"Exactly," I concur. "So to satisfy her sense of being in control, she turns her fear into something devilish. She won't give up the control to God. She has to be in control herself. . . ."

"So she reminds you of her power and gives you one more kick in the behind, just for good measure. I'm surprised you didn't react, Albertina."

"What for?"

"Well, you're right. Most people aren't that secure in themselves."

"In dealing with Maggie, I've felt like I've been guided by a good spirit."

"That's your faith, Albertina. That's the spirit that keeps you healthy and whole."

"I call it the spirit of God."

"Look, I'm a trained psychologist, but I could not have handled this situation with any more love and gentleness than you have granted this woman."

"I serve a loving and gentle God, Florence."

"I know you do, Albertina. I can feel it."

The National Enquirer

I **hear it** in Justine's voice. I hear it in the way she says my name.

"Albertina," she says, "I'm still in Dallas."

"Hope everything's okay."

"Everything's not okay. He saw me but he didn't see me. I was sitting in the first row. I stood up and cheered when he was introduced. But he never looked my way. During commercial break, I waved at him. He looked right at me but never waved back. Like I wasn't even there. After the show, I had a pass to go backstage. Your friend Bob Blakey got me that pass. Walker was in a room talking to a bunch of people. Finally I was able to say something to him. He kinda pecked me on the cheek and whispered that this wasn't a good time. He'd be real busy for the next several days. Nothing about, *Oh my God, you flew here from California!* Nothing about, *What a surprise to see my baby!* Just cold. Ice cold. He left the studio without saying another word to me. So I've been calling his room. Leaving messages. But he hasn't called me back. So I'm going to wait down in the lobby until he shows up. He has to show up."

"Don't do that, Justine. Don't do that, honey."

"Why not?"

"You don't want to hurt yourself like that."

"I want to hurt him."

"That'll only hurt you," I say.

"I'm talking about physical hurt. I want to lay this sucker out."

"He's a former football player."

"That'll make it even more humiliating for him when it hits the papers."

"Come home, Justine. Just call a cab and come home."

"And go down in defeat?"

"You don't have to look at it that way, baby. It's growth. Sometimes we need pain to grow."

"I feel like the dumbest woman in the world."

"You're not. The Lord loves you just as much today as He did yesterday, Justine. Lean on the love of the Lord, baby. Lean on the love of the Lord."

Sometimes the best thing you can do is go to the supermarket. I mean it. Sometimes the weight of the world and all its heavy problems are lessened by shopping for produce. It feels good to express gratitude to all those farmers and farmworkers who cultivated and grew and picked all those fruits and vegetables that are displayed so beautifully. Our bountiful life is nothing to take for granted. Fact is, some folk might be able to pray better in the produce section than in church. You could say, *Father God, thank You for our bountiful life. Thank You for making a world of abundance, a world of fresh fruits and vegetables that look beautiful and taste divine. Thank You for our sense of taste and our sense of sight. Thank You for sustaining me another day so I can walk up and down the aisles of this supermarket and enjoy the brightly colored packages. And thank You for providing me with the means to pay for my food. Lord Jesus, my heart is filled with gratitude. I even thank You for the consciousness of gratitude because without it I wouldn't know what to do.*

My cart is filled up with food. My heart is filled up with joy. I don't even mind waiting in the long line. Happy to wait in the long line. Happy to be alive. But not happy to see, off in the distance, sitting in a display case right next to the checkout stand, the *National Enquirer*. I'm not happy to see a big picture of Maggie and Walker Jones photographed as they got out of a limo. Not happy to see the screaming headline, "MAGGIE'S GOT HER GROOVE BACK—HE'S A HUNK, AND HE'S MARRIED!"

I do not buy the magazine. I do not intend to give that publication a cent of my money. I am tempted to read it while waiting in line, but I do not. I do not care what it says. I do care what it says. But I do not care to read idle gossip since I do not trust the magazine. I also do not trust Walker Jones. I never have. I think about Andre and Nina. I haven't heard from them in a couple of weeks. I want to call my son, but he calls me first. In fact, the phone rings an hour later while I'm putting away the groceries.

"Hi, Mom."

"Hi, honey."

"Calling with good news."

"I always like good news."

"Nina will be on *Maggie's World* next week to promote the film. Isn't that great?"

I hesitate, but I say, "Yes."

"Funny how things work. She has this new personal trainer, this famous nutritionist she met in Dallas that weekend. Well, he's close to Maggie and he arranged her appearance."

I don't say anything.

"Mom, are you there?"

"I'm here, son."

"Are you alright?"

"I'm fine."

"I know the movie made you uncomfortable. I thought about that after I urged you to see it. But I guess I was so excited about you and Nina being in the same city and the same hotel at the same time, I forgot that the movie's pretty explicit. I hope you weren't offended."

"Well . . ."

"Were you offended?"

"You know, Andre, this is a different world we're living in. Women are taking off their clothes and simulating sex in mainstream movies. It's just something I find . . . well . . ."

"Offensive?"

"Yes, I do find it offensive."

"And do you find Nina offensive?"

"I don't know her that well."

"You don't like her."

"I don't know her well enough not to like her."

"You're beating around the bush, Mom."

"When mothers warn sons about women, I'm always afraid the advice will backfire."

"So you're warning me about her. Is that what you're saying?"

"I'm saying I'm uneasy, baby."

"I don't think you really know this woman."

"I already admitted that. I don't. But I have met Walker Jones. He's a married man who was Justine's boyfriend. He threw her over as soon as he was able to get on Maggie's show."

"Well, he's not involved with Nina."

"I thought you said he got her on the show."

"Well, I wouldn't call that 'involved,' would you?"

"Look, Andre, I've never told you how to live your life or who to live it with. And I'm not starting now."

"But you're planting doubts in my head, Mom. You have to admit that's what you're doing."

"Mothers naturally protect their children. Not to give you my straight-up opinion of this man would go against everything in me, son."

"I don't think we should talk about this anymore, Mom."

"Agreed. I don't want to belabor my point."

I don't want to think about the picture in the *National Enquirer*. Don't want to think what it will do to Justine. Maybe she won't see it. But of course she will. Working at Target, where they sell the magazine, how can she miss it? It's going to hurt her bad, infuriate her, get her ranting and raging about Walker and Maggie.

Maybe by making myself a bowl of soup and a nice salad I can put my mind elsewhere. A light supper will let me focus on my sermon for Sunday. I'm teaching from Acts and loving the story of the early church. I want my church to be like the early church where all focus was on the Lord. I love the early church because of all the excitement surrounding the good news of Christ. I love Luke, who wrote Acts, and Paul because

Paul was on fire for the Lord. The more I read, the more I feel myself back there with His students and disciples. I'm proud to be His student and His disciple. And just when I'm feeling happiest about the joy that Jesus brought into the world, my phone rings. I don't want to answer it, but I do.

"Pastor Merci, this is Clifford Bloom."

"Mr. Bloom, how are you, sir?"

"Fine. Am I disturbing you?"

"Not at all. Just working on a sermon."

"That's why I'm calling. I'd love to hear you preach."

"Wonderful."

"Would you be good enough to give me the address of your church and the time you'll be preaching?"

I give him both.

"And I thought that afterward, if you're free, I'd like to invite you to brunch."

This takes me by surprise.

He reads my hesitation and says, "Or if you're busy, perhaps another time."

"Well," I say, "I usually don't eat right after church. I need a little while to settle down from the excitement of the service."

"I can understand that, Pastor. Maybe we can meet for lunch during the week. We can talk about that another time. But there's something else I want to mention. As you might know, I do a show on seventies soul music and sometimes I have guests. I was hoping you could come on the show and let me interview you. I'd consider it a privilege."

"That's kind of you, Mr. Bloom. Yes, sometime in the future we could certainly do that."

"Wonderful. Then I'll see you Sunday."

"You will indeed."

Strange call. Strange man. But maybe not so strange. Maybe I'm the strange one. Maybe I'm reading too much into it. I'm remembering how Patrick said he was interested in me. My first thought is that he's older than I am—he's seventy-five. But who am I, at seventy, to say that someone's too old? He's an interesting guy, being a deejay and all, and I've enjoyed his program when I've listened to it from time to time, but the last thing I need or want right now is a beau. Then I remember my advice to Patrick when he was worrying about Rabbi Naomi Cohen. Don't go jumping ahead. A new friendship is always a nice thing.

A New Friendship

"I feel ridiculous," I tell my nephew Patrick. "I feel like I'm acting like your chaperone again."

"You're my aunt," Patrick says, "and you're my pastor, and I like being with you. I told Naomi that you and I already had plans to be together and so she suggested I take you along. That's all."

"But we didn't have plans," I remind Patrick.

"We do now."

Indeed we do. It's Saturday night and we're walking down the Promenade in Santa Monica, a long street of shops that prohibits cars and encourages street entertainers—jugglers and mimes, steel drummers and sidewalk sketch artists. It's only a few blocks from the ocean so the air is fresh and clean. Seems like the whole city turns up here on a Saturday night. Parents pushing their babies in strollers, teenagers running in and out of jean stores, older folks like me taking it easy and just enjoying being outdoors.

We're headed to the big Barnes and Noble bookstore. That's where Rabbi Naomi Cohen invited Patrick to hear a man named Professor Tim Tyler speak on his new book, *The Spirit Within*. The rabbi described Tyler as a theologian from the Harvard Divinity School whose philosophy embraces elements of all the world's great religions.

Naomi is waiting for us by the front door. She looks adorable in a loose-fitting light gray summer pants suit. She appears to be a perpetually happy woman with a disposition that manages to be both sunny and serious. She couldn't be more respectful of me and seems delighted I've come along. Clearly Patrick is smitten with her, but he's just as clearly uncomfortable with the attraction.

Toward the rear of the store, there is a cluster of folding chairs set up in front of a small podium. The three of us take a seat. A few minutes later the store manager introduces the professor who, in turn, introduces his ideas.

I like the professor. He is plain-spoken, well-mannered and sincere. His ideas revolve around the fact that the unifying principle of universal morality is based on love. He shows how this works in a variety of cultures and religious systems. He speaks of metaphors and mythological storytelling. He doesn't argue or preach. He teaches. I enjoy his lesson.

Afterward, Naomi, Patrick, and I walk down the Promenade and stop for frozen yogurt.

"You two sit and talk," I say. "I feel like stretching my legs."

I see a little panic on Patrick's face at the thought of being left alone with the rabbi. But I figure he can handle it. I get up and let the young people enjoy some private time.

I like window shopping. I like living in a culture where there's so much variety. When I was a little girl, the idea of walking over to a bookstore and hearing a learned man speak of different world religions wasn't part of my world picture. Now it is. And I love it. I love wandering into the record store and seeing whether they have any compilations of my old recordings—they do—and whether there are any new gospel CDs I might like. There are several. I buy Helen Baylor's latest. I kill a bit more time in the record store by putting on a headset and listening to a new edition of Mahalia Jackson singing with Duke Ellington. Mahalia said she'd never sing with a jazz band but Duke wrote a religious suite and convinced her to change her mind. She sings a song called "Come Sunday" that never fails to give me goose bumps. I stand there with my eyes closed and imagine the miraculous atmosphere of this recording session back in the fifties. She also sings a version of "The Lord's Prayer" that she and Duke's orchestra made up on the spot. Another miracle.

Feeling renewed, I stroll back up to the yogurt shop where Naomi and Patrick are deep in discussion.

"We're talking about pluralism," says Naomi. "I thought Professor Tyler made the case for pluralism tonight, didn't you?"

"I'm not sure he was making a case, darling, as much as pointing out the common threads that bind us all," I say.

"God is not pluralistic," Patrick offers. "God is one."

"But we Christians believe that his oneness has three central components. Isn't that what the trinity is all about?" I ask.

"Those three components are indivisible," says Patrick. "Three equals one."

"There are three of us here tonight," says the rabbi, "yet we are one in believing that the essential character of God is love."

"Amen," I say.

Later, when Patrick is driving me home, he says, "Weren't

you bothered by the professor's attitude that a different god is perfectly okay for a different culture."

"I don't think that was his attitude. I think he was saying it's the same God."

"But is God inside of us, as he contends, or is God in heaven with Christ by his right side?" asks Patrick.

"You remember Mark 4:30 where it asks, 'How shall we picture the kingdom of God, or by what parable shall we present it? It is like a mustard seed, which, when sown upon the soil, though it is smaller than all the seeds that are upon the soil, yet when it is sown, it grows up and becomes larger than all the garden plants and forms large branches; so that the birds of the air can rest under its shade.' The Scripture is saying that the kingdom of God is within us. When Christ died, we died with Him. When He rose, He rose within us. He is our mustard seed."

"The professor wasn't talking about Christ."

"Everything he said applied to Christ. Nothing he said contradicted Christ. I was thinking of Christ every minute he was speaking," I say.

"But he wasn't. And neither was Naomi."

"Well, honey she certainly seems open-minded when it comes to ideas about God," I say. "She certainly doesn't have an axe to grind."

"But is she saved? Is she willing to be saved?"

"She was certainly willing to spend a delightful evening with us. The weather was wonderful and the lecture was stimulating. What more could you want, baby?"

"I'm not sure I should see her again."

"I'm sure you will, Patrick. I'm sure you will."

Letter From Dallas

Dear Pastor Merci,

I've been meaning to write you before this, but, as you know, my job is incredibly time-consuming and lately it's been crazier than ever.

One thing that has not been crazy, though, is my commitment to Christ that you so magnificently facilitated when you were here in Dallas. I told you then, and I tell you again, how flabbergasted I was at the quickness and intensity of our encounter. If a person had told me that, in a three-minute meeting with a minister, I would accept Jesus as Lord and Savior, I would have told them they were stark-raving mad. I've tried to understand what happened, and, quite frankly, I'm convinced that at that amazing moment I saw Christ in you, Pastor Merci. Seeing Him, feeling Him, experiencing Him operate in another person made me hunger to have Him operate in me.

As a child, I went to a Methodist church with my mother. I was an obedient child, never a rebel, and so I was happy to have Mother dress me up and take me with her. I did feel a certain calmness and sense of well-being in church, but it was not strong enough to sustain me as an adult. I married and divorced a man who was an adamant atheist. His atheism was not the reason I divorced him, but his atheism did bother me. There was a coldness somewhere inside his soul that made me wonder whether I, too, lacked the warmth that comes with a spiritual connection.

From time to time I would pick up the Bible. Occasionally I would read a Christian book or even think about going to church. But the pressures of this job overwhelmed almost all other parts of my life. When Cindy became ill, I spent some time with her. I watched how you ministered to her and found that extremely moving. The fact that she never seemed panicked or desperate impressed me deeply. But even then, I never considered returning to church or seeking some contact with God.

When it happened, it really was a miracle. The day that Maggie decided to cut you out of the show was unbelievably hectic. She was in an absolute rage, and there was nothing I could do but listen. That was trying. But the most trying part was thinking of how to tell you. I hated having to convey the bad news to you. It felt awful. So the miracle came in your receiving that news with grace. You didn't take it out on me. I was sure you would. Maybe because that's Maggie's method—to blame the messenger, to rag on whomever's around. You did the opposite. You touched my heart by being so sensitive to me. I think you also read my heart. And when you asked me about Christ and receiving Christ, I found the question so disarming, so utterly sincere, I responded not with my head but with my heart. I simply said, "Yes."

That simple "yes" has changed my life, Pastor. I'm in a Bible class with other professional women; I've joined a small church whose preacher, a woman, has great passion for the Lord. I'm going to a Philosopher's Forum where Christian theology over the centuries is explained and discussed. In short, I can't hear or read enough about the Lord. I want to tell the world about this love. Which brings me to Maggie . . .

As you know, I'm with her practically every day all day. It's a challenge. She's in this hyperactive state again, working feverishly, pushing ahead like never before. She's also involved romantically with a man who spends much of his time flirting with the young women on her staff. It's all quite crazy. I know she needs the Lord more than ever. I would love to share what I have found, but am hesitant to do so. Not only do I not want to endanger my job, I also don't want to proselytize when it won't do any good. I'm sure you faced this dilemma with Maggie as well and I wonder how you resolved it.

Your advice is much needed and valued.

God bless you, Pastor Merci, and thank you again.

Your sister in Christ, Virgina Hogobin.

Dear Virginia,

I know you're busy, dear, so I'll be brief.

Words can't convey my happiness for you. God is truly good and the fact that He has entered your heart is not just good news, but the best news we can ever receive.

You are a blessing to me and, I'm sure, a blessing to all you encounter.

I'm sure that goes for Maggie as well. She's a brilliant and explosive woman and I feel the smartest thing you can do is listen to her and be there for her. We're here to serve each other, and I know you do a beautiful job serving her. Being a blessing, though, doesn't mean trying to convert someone on your timetable. We need to be on God's timetable. We remain quiet to listen for the Holy Ghost stirring within us. God will instruct you when to move to action. Speaking to her about Christ—and having your message sink in—depends upon being sensitive to her, even super-sensitive to her.

Don't rush it, sweetheart. God never rushes anything. He is a gentleman, never pushy or rude. His is the way of patience. He creates opportunities and openings. Such an opening will surely come your way.

Meanwhile, may you find even deeper peace and comfort in your walk with Christ. I cherish our new friendship.

In His Grace,

Pastor Albertina Merci

Patience becomes the subject of Sunday's sermon. I feel inspired by Virginia's letter and Virginia's miraculous conversion. I cite Mark 10:46 where Bartimaeus, a blind man, sits by the side of the road and feels the Lord approaching. He cries out, "Jesus, son of David, have mercy on me!" We don't know how long he's been sitting there. Hours, days, months, years. But we do know that his senses, heightened by faith and prayer, are perfectly attuned to God's timing. He asks to be healed and so he is. He can see. Similarly, if we are tuned to God's timing—that if we are patient, if we are vigilant in faith and prayer—we too will receive our heart's desire. The cobwebs will be removed from our minds; the residue will be removed from our eyes; clarity will be ours—moral clarity, emotional clarity, spiritual clarity. It will be clear that God is real and His spirit of love a dynamic and healing force capable of overcoming anything.

After my sermon, Clifford Bloom, who has been sitting on the first pew, greets me with words of praise.

"Magnificent, Pastor," he says. "Stirring words that I won't soon forget."

"Well, thank you, Mr. Bloom."

"Clifford, please," he corrects me, "and I'm really looking forward to our interview later this week."

The jazz station studio is on La Cienega Boulevard. I arrive at five in the afternoon and feel immediately comfortable. On the walls are photos of everyone from saxist David "Fathead" Newman to trumpeter Johnny Coles. I know practically every last one of the musicians and singers whose images line the hallways—Nancy Wilson and Dakota Staton, Hank Crawford and Stanley Turrentine. Clifford greets me and escorts me to his recording studio. He introduces me to his audience by playing "Sanctified Blues."

"In the golden era of soul," he says when the record is over, "no sister sang more soulfully than Albertina Merci. We're honored to have her with us today."

"Thank you for inviting me here, Clifford."

"Last Sunday I was privileged to attend your church, the House of Trust, on Adams Boulevard. I say privileged because your sermon was as soulful as any song you ever sang. For those in the audience who may not know, Albertina Merci became Pastor Merci some time ago. And I must say, Pastor, that you've made the transition from secular to sacred with exceptional poise. What I'd like to ask you today is, how do you reconcile these two vital aspects of your life?"

"Well, Clifford, let me take a quote from you," I say. "Not long ago we met for the first time and you were talking about being a new Christian. You said—and this is something I'll never forget—that it wasn't a matter of a conversion; it was a continuum. I love the word 'continuum.' The Old Testament continues into the New. One book leads to the other. The same was true with me. My life in show business led to my life in the Lord. My love for the Lord was modeled for me by my mother. I always loved Him. But by singing from my soul, by practicing this beautiful art form known as 'soul singing,' I learned that expressing true feelings is the most wonderful thing an artist can do. And the deeper I got into my soul, the more I realized that Christ *is* my soul."

"And what about the famous irreconcilable difference between secular and sacred music, the conflict that seems to be such a recurring theme in African-American culture?"

"I don't accept the difference, Clifford. I believe God is underneath it all. Jazz is as much God's music as gospel. The Bible just says, 'Make a joyful noise.' The key word is 'joyful.' Jazz is about joy. Even blues, which is looked on as being sad, is about joy because in singing the blues you lose your blues. The act of singing transforms your heart, turns you happy, sheds light on the darkness. You can be listening to the saddest B.B. King blues, but your spirit gets happy because he's releasing hurt in himself and, at the same time, releasing hurt in you. That's God working through B.B. That's God using music to heal. I'm telling you, Clifford, it's all God."

"And it's all good," Clifford adds. "So good to have you

here, Pastor. Now for another one of your vintage recordings on wax . . ."

Afterward, Clifford suggests we go to Roscoe's Chicken and Waffles on Pico for a snack. I suggest we go to Canter's Deli on Fairfax. I have a sweet tooth for New York cheesecake.

Canter's is filled with older Jewish people. I don't feel in the least out of place. Clifford feels a need to tell me that, unlike many men his age who are dependent on walkers and wheelchairs, he's in top-notch shape. He goes to the gym five times a week. He hikes in Topanga Canyon. He plays eighteen holes of golf and never uses a cart. He works out with weights. "Never been sick a day in my life," he says.

"Wonderful," I reply.

"The quality of my life is so high," he says. "And meeting you has only made it higher."

"Thank you, Clifford."

An awkward silence hangs over us. I really don't know what to say. I feel the genuineness of his sentiment, but I'm not at all inclined to respond in kind. I know that he wants me to, but I simply can't.

"It's been nearly twenty years since Grace died," he tells me. "We were married thirty years. Wonderful woman. Elementary school teacher. Born in the South. Her parents were sharecroppers."

"She was African American?"

"Yes. As you can well imagine, when we married things were not easy for mixed couples. It was rough, but we prevailed. Love always prevailed. The odd part is that she was a Christian who prayed for me to accept Christ. But it never happened when she was alive. Why do you think it happened only afterward?"

"I'm just thankful it happened," I say. "God sets up these situations so He can be glorified. The setup has intricacies beyond our understanding."

"Did He set up this meeting between you and me?" he asks.

"He sets up everything," I answer.

Clifford smiles broadly. He takes my hand. I'm afraid I've led him on. I can't withdraw my hand without being rude. I'm not comfortable with the way he's looking at me. I see he's a very lonely man.

After a few seconds, I withdraw my hand.

I hope he reads me right. My eyes are saying, *You're a good man, Clifford Bloom, but right now romance is not on my menu.*

Let My People Go

When the phone rings in the dead of night it's always alarming. Being shocked out of sleep startles the body and the brain, not to mention the resting spirit. And when the voice on the other end of the line is screaming profanities, it's hard to know what to do.

"You call yourself a pastor! Why, you're nothing but a fraud!" It took me less than a second to realize it was Maggie Clay. "You set up this thing to get me back! You and your conniving manipulative devil mind concocted this scheme, thinking I wouldn't see through it. But let me tell you something, woman, I smelled you out. You're crafty and you're cynical. I understand the damage you wanted to inflict on me. You're an angry and frustrated old lady. You're sanctimonious and pathetic and for you to put this man in my life is one of the lowest acts of mean-spirited manipulation I've ever seen. This Walker Jones. This cheater, this liar, this low-life serial womanizer. You brought him to Dallas. You made sure he was at that party. You introduced me to him. You set up the scenario, sister, with one aim and one aim only—to strike back. To put an arrow through my heart. To pay me back for everything I did to you. Well, I got news for you, you little Bible-thumping schemer, I am *not* going down. This fool of a man is going down. You are going down. This is going on the news. This is going out to the media. Believe me, this is going on the internet. Extra! Extra! Read all about it! *Jackleg pastor hooks up with male hooker to scam Maggie Clay!* Well, Maggie Clay ain't about to be scammed. Maggie Clay is going public. And the public loves Maggie Clay. The public trusts Maggie Clay, not some muscle-head idiot, not some phony pastor hell-bent on biting the hand that feeds her. You realize how much money I've given you? You realize—"

"Maggie, I'm sorry," I say, "but I'm going to have to put down the receiver—"

"You do and I'll—"

I put down the receiver.

I shrug off Maggie's tirade and fall back to sleep. I fall into an amazing dream. I'm in a high school pageant playing the part of Moses. Maggie is playing the part of Pharaoh. I'm asking her to let my people go. A choir led by Paul Robeson is singing behind me, "Let my people go." Maggie says yes, she will let my people go. Everyone in the auditorium, dressed as slaves, gets up to leave. "No!" Maggie screams. "I've changed my mind. You can't leave. You're staying here. Your leader has betrayed you. I have not. I love you. And you should love me. I am your true leader."

The slaves don't know who to believe.

"Moses isn't even a man," Maggie says. "She's a woman pretending to be a man. She's a fraud."

"God lives through us all," I say. "God wants us free. God is no fraud."

She calls for her guards to put me away, but I see I have wings and I can fly. I fly over the audience. I fly over Love Field, my childhood home. I fly over the downtown Neiman-Marcus store. I fly over the House of Trust where all my parishioners are waving at me. I fly over Maggie's house in Malibu and her house in Dallas. I fly down to Houston to the medical center where Cindy is alive and smiling and greets me with a hug. And my mother and father are there, and relatives I have never seen. And on the grounds of the medical center we have a picnic. Joyful music is playing. We dance to the music. I wake up refreshed and amazed at how I remember every last detail of my dream.

I drive my PT Cruiser to Pasadena to the home of Muriel and Tom. I am grateful for the dinner invitation. Before I left the house, Virginia Hogobin called to say that Maggie told her how she had excoriated me. Virginia wanted me to know that Maggie had caught Walker with another woman and had flown into a mad rage. I told Virginia I understood and was not taking Maggie's attack personally. I told her that I understood it had nothing to do with me, and that all we can do is pray.

"I want to quit this job, Pastor," Virginia said. "I want to leave right now."

"Do what you think you need to do, baby, but if you can hang in with her for a while it would be good. Right now, more than ever, she needs someone around her who loves the Lord."

———

Muriel and Tom live in a split-level home built in the sixties on a quiet street not far from the Rose Bowl. Tom greets me at the door.

"We're so glad you could come," he says.

"I'm glad to be invited."

"Muriel's in the kitchen preparing a feast," he says.

Muriel's wearing a yellow apron with smiling sunflowers. She herself is not smiling. She grasps my hand and says, "It's been difficult, Pastor. Extremely difficult."

"I understand, sweetheart," I say.

"Dinner should be ready in fifteen minutes."

"Please let me help you," I offer.

"Oh no, it's all under control. The children want to meet you."

Their three girls—Dora, Joan, and Belinda—are adorable. They range in age from five to twelve. They all have stories to tell me about their schools and teachers and their orange cat named Miss Boots.

I insist on helping Muriel serve dinner.

When we are all seated, I'm asked to lead them in prayer.

"We thank You, Father," I say, "for this food. We thank You for this family that You have blessed, for Dora and Joan and Belinda and their wonderful parents Muriel and Tom. We thank You for bringing us all together—and keeping us all together—so we can glorify Your name and relax in the bosom of Your love. In Jesus' name, Amen."

After dinner, little Dora, the youngest, asks me if I would read her some books. I'm delighted to do so. She loves stories of Babar, the elephant king. As I read, she rests her head on my shoulder.

When the children have gone to sleep, Muriel, Tom, and I sit in the den and share a pot of hot tea.

"I can't help but wonder," I say, "whether you've been praying together."

"Yes," says Tom.

"My prayers are very short," says Muriel.

"Nothing wrong with that, sugar," I tell her.

"My prayers are nothing more than asking God to give me the motivation to keep praying," she adds.

"That's a beautiful prayer," I say. "A perfect prayer. How about you, Tom? What are your prayers like?"

"I pray for patience and forgiveness."

"That prayer has already been granted," I tell him. "God has already forgiven you."

Muriel starts to say something, but stops herself. We remain silent for several seconds.

"If you don't mind," Tom says, "I'm just going to turn on the television to check the weather channel. I'm flying to Chicago tomorrow and I'm concerned about thunderstorms."

The storms have passed. Clear skies over the Midwest for the next several days. As Tom inadvertently flips through a few channels, I see Maggie's face on Fox News.

"Would you mind stopping there?" I ask.

"Late-breaking bulletin," the announcer says. "Maggie Clay was rushed to a Dallas hospital late this afternoon. She's reported to be in critical condition. The circumstances are still unknown."

Darkness

"I don't think I should go," Patrick tells me as we drive down Century Boulevard on our way to LAX. I'm taking the early flight to Dallas.

"If I weren't leaving," I say, "I'd go with you to Naomi's temple for the High Holiday. Yom Kippur is the holiest day of the Jewish calendar. The day of atonement. It's a beautiful holiday, and I'd love to see Naomi lead the service."

"If you were here," says Patrick, "maybe I would go. But going alone, I'm not sure. It's going to seem so obvious that I'm only going to see Naomi."

"How about going to worship God, baby?"

"In a sanctuary where Jesus is rejected?" Patrick asks.

"I'd be surprised if Rabbi Cohen speaks about the rejection of Jesus in her service. I believe she'll be speaking about atonement."

"Do I greet her after the service or just leave?"

"You do whatever feels right," I say. "To me, it would feel right to greet a friend."

"I don't know, Aunt Albertina, you have a strange notion of friendship. You call Maggie Clay a friend. But all she does is call you vicious names and treat you like dirt."

"She's ill, baby."

"She can afford doctors."

"Doctors haven't helped her."

"But I'm not sure you have either, Aunt Albertina."

"You're right, honey."

"But you're still going."

"I'm going because the two people closest to her, Virginia Hogobin and Bob Blakey, have asked me to go."

"Was it really a suicide attempt like the paper says?"

"I really don't know, Patrick. All I know is that the woman is hurting."

Presbyterian Hospital in Dallas has an exclusive floor for celebrities and big shots. Press is not allowed. Visitors are closely screened. Virginia Hogobin and Bob Blakey are sitting in the waiting area adjacent to Maggie's suite.

"We've been praying," says Bob.

"Praying that you'd come," adds Virginia.

"How is she?" I ask.

"She swallowed a bottle of pills," says Virginia, "but they were able to pump her stomach in time. The doctor says she's out of danger now, but her mood is dark. I've never seen it this dark."

"I'm hoping that the three of us, just staying by her side and praying for her, might make a difference," says Bob.

"Do I hear voices out there?" Maggie's voice calls from the other room. "Who's there?"

We walk into her room, a united front. She looks awful, puffy bags under her eyes, her eyes half-closed, her mouth drooping and sad.

"Oh no," she says, looking at the three of us, "the Christ crew. This is part of your little conspiracy, isn't it, Albertina? You Jesus-ize my two closest associates, then you bring a two-timing dog into my life so he'll destroy whatever peace of mind I might have, and now you gather the troops in the hopes of some melodramatic death-bed conversion. Is that it? Well, girlfriend, I got news for you. I ain't dying and I ain't converting. So you and your little Bible thumpers can leave me alone and get your asses out of here."

"We'll be outside if you need us," I say.

"Are you deaf, stupid, or both? I said I don't want to see any of you—*not now, not ever!*"

With that, she picks up a vase of roses sitting next to her bed and smashes it on the floor.

Bob, Virginia and I are back in the waiting area.

"I feel like praising God," I say.

Virginia and Bob look at me quizzically. Their facial expressions say, *Given the circumstances, why in the world would you want to start praising God now?*

"If I don't praise Him," I say, "the rocks will cry out. So I praise Him for our friendship, for the airplane that brought me here and the pilots who flew it, for the doctors and nurses who work in this hospital, for the workers who built this hospital, for our determination to stick by our friend. For the Holy Spirit that informs our hearts to offer unceasing love, unceasing understanding. Love free of rancor, love free of revenge, love pure and powerful as the love that allowed our Lord to suffer the cross, to bring us salvation, to make us right with God, to link us to eternal life, to prompt us to exchange our life for His, to live in us every day in every way, increasing in strength, increasing in faith, increasing in compassion, increasing in the love we offer to all those who surround us, increasing in the confidence and security that come with Christ consciousness. Permanent peace, peace in the midst of turbulence, peace in the midst of chaos, peace in the midst of stormy seas, precious peace that comes only with the sweet heart knowledge of Jesus doing for us what we cannot do for ourselves. Thank You, Lord. Thank You, Lord. Thank You, Lord."

From Maggie's room we hear her screaming, *"Get them out of the hospital! I want them out of here! Get those sanctimonious fools out of here!"*

Love Field

Love Field is back in business. Southwest and a bunch of other commuter airlines fly in and out of here. The airport, while no match for the behemoth D/FW, is buzzing. I'm glad. I'm driving around my old neighborhood, thinking of days gone by, thinking about Mom and Daddy and my brothers, thinking what it was like being raised up in Dallas when it was a sleepy ol' Texas town just getting started, when there were no superhighways and just two or three tall buildings downtown, when in our neighborhood everyone knew our name and if our folks weren't home to look out for us other folks would.

I'm thinking of my daddy and how he resisted the Lord until his best friend Al was killed in a barroom down the street from Love Field. Daddy was seated on the stool right next to Al when a man came in and shot Al between the eyes. Turned out Al owed the man fifty dollars. That's when Daddy turned to God. My brothers Calvin and Fred never did turn to God, or at least not to my knowledge. They struggled through life without Him.

When do people turn to God? And how do you help them make that turn?

Turn, turn, turn.

I know Maggie grew up in a neighborhood like mine. I know she grew up dirt-poor like I grew up dirt-poor. I know she suffered deep wounds like I suffered deep wounds. No need to compare the two of us. No need to figure whose wounds are worse. God blessed Maggie Clay. God blessed me. God blesses us all with His grace. Maggie knows she's blessed. That's why she keeps turning to me, keeps trying to connect with me. But the spirits war within her. One spirit is righteousness. One spirit is rejection. *Seek* God, *spurn* God. Run *to* God, run *from* God. How do you settle the unsettled mind? How do you tell someone who's filled up with fear to replace that fear with faith?

You don't. God does. God does it by setting up the circumstances in their life in a way that forces them to come closer to Him. Sometimes we resist those circumstances. Or we read them wrong. We miss the cues, we think we're in charge, we're calling the shots, we're getting what we want because we're God. But only God is God. Only God can set us free. We can't do it for ourselves, and the more we try, the greater our frustration.

Daddy lived a life of frustration. My brothers Fred and Calvin too. So did Dexter Banks, my first husband. These were men who, in different ways, suffered from financial frustration. They wanted money, they deserved money, they had skills to make money, but the money never came. My mother never had money, but she had the Lord. My mother didn't know frustration. She knew Jesus and would sing His praises doing the most mundane tasks imaginable. When I made money singing the blues, I was seeking a satisfaction this world couldn't give me. Being as close as I've been to Maggie, hearing her moaning and crying in the midnight hour, I know that the satisfaction she seeks cannot be found in worldly things. I have not told her that—not once—because telling her would only have recharged her resentment. So I speak to God in secret. I say, *Father God, satisfy her soul. Let her find the honey in the rock. Minister to her spirit, save her and make her whole.*

The next day when I arrive at Presbyterian Hospital, Virginia and Bob are waiting for me by the first-floor reception desk.

"We've been barred from the hospital," says Bob.

"What do we do?" asks Virginia.

"Pray," I say.

And we do.

Later that afternoon Virginia and I are walking around Bachman Lake, the same lake where Daddy took me fishing and the planes descended directly over our heads as they prepared to land at Love Field.

September can be murderously hot in Dallas, but last night's thunderstorms chased off the heat and left the city refreshed and cool. Virginia said she just wanted to get away from Maggie's production office, where chaos and uncertainty ruled, and be with me. I suggested we go for a walk.

"Now the entire fiscal integrity of Maggie's empire is threatened," Virginia explains. "No one knows anything anymore. No one knows what to do. Who knows when or if she'll ever be back?"

"But your spiritual integrity is intact," I say. "That's what counts, baby."

"I wonder about that."

"Why?" I ask.

"In figuring all this out—how to put the show back on hiatus, how to deal with the network, what to tell our fifty-odd employees—Bob was been invaluable. He has devoted himself to Maggie's well-being and the well-being of her complex business affairs."

"He's wonderful, sweetheart, he really is."

"That's the problem, Albertina. He's too wonderful."

"In what way?"

"I'm . . . I'm, well, I'm attracted to him in a way that . . ."

"I understand," I say. "You feel guilty about Cindy."

"That's for sure. And I have no idea how he feels about me. To express romantic feelings in the middle of everything that's going on now seems ludicrous. It's confusing."

"And wonderful," I add. "Love is always wonderful, sugar. When it comes, we can't help but praise its source."

Light

Patrick is panicked. We're sitting in my tiny office in the back of House of Trust and he's opening his heart to me.

"I think I'm in love with her," he says. "I'm afraid I'm in love with her."

"Is this a confession?" I ask.

"I suppose it is. I want you to tell me to stop. I want you to tell me never to see her again."

"How does she feel, sugar?"

"I think she's confused. I don't think either one of us expected this. It's powerful, Aunt Albertina, more powerful than anything I've ever experienced."

"Well, time will reveal more. God will reveal more."

"And you can't?"

"I can't, baby. I can't prescribe relationship formulas for others."

"But you can say that she's a nonbeliever and I've gotten

myself involved with a nonbeliever. You can say that, can't you?"

"You're saying that, Patrick, and I know you're feeling that. So you'll have to see where that feeling takes you."

"You think I can get her to accept the Lord?"

"Only the Lord can get people to accept the Lord," I suggest.

"She never will. She's a rabbi, for God's sake."

"For God's sake, people do all sorts of things. People change in all sorts of ways."

"So you're suggesting . . ."

"Nothing, baby. I'm suggesting nothing. I'm just saying that something deep is happening here, and I'm not sure what it is. My powers of understanding are limited, like everyone else's."

"That doesn't help. That doesn't help me pick up the phone and tell her that I intend never to see her again."

"If you do that, you must do it on your own."

On her own, Justine has finally slammed the door on Walker Jones. After his fiasco with Maggie, he came back to Justine. He wanted Justine to convince me to intervene on his behalf. He wrongly presumed that I was close to Maggie; he thought he was going to persuade me to persuade Maggie that he really wasn't having an affair with a woman on Maggie's staff. He was so adamant in pursuing his pleadings that he flew from Dallas to Los Angeles and showed up at Justine's door. That's when she went off. She called him names that would shame the devil and nearly caught his nose in the door when she slammed it closed with such ferocity that the windows up and down the block rattled as though we were having an earthquake. Boyfriend ran out of there in a hurry.

I have a surprise visitor myself. It happens two weeks after I'm back from Dallas. It's eight o'clock in the evening. I've been reading my Bible. I'm into Mark, one of my favorite writers. His gospel was written first, and it's about faith. Recorded at a time when followers of the risen Christ were suffering humiliation, torture, and death, Mark reassures those followers that Christ's suffering initiated the ultimate freedom from pain. Christ's suffering led to eternal bliss, eternal life, salvation of the soul, and glorious reconciliation with the Father. To achieve that reconciliation, though, is not a matter of legalistic mumbo jumbo. You don't achieve it by mouthing the right prayers or reciting the right Scriptures. In Mark 7:6, the Lord reflects on Isaiah's opinions of those who give God only lip service: "Well did Isaiah prophesy of you hypocrites, as it is written, this people honoreth me with their lips, but their heart is far from me."

I'm lost in thought, thinking how God has no use for hypocrites, when the doorbell rings. I look through the peephole and see Maggie Clay.

I open the door. "Welcome," I say.

"Do you mean that?" she asks.

"Of course," I answer.

She motions her driver, who has parked the limo by the curb, to wait for her.

I don't know what to expect. Perhaps more chastisement, or praise followed by chastisement. I'm just glad to see that she looks much better than she did in the hospital. She's wearing khaki pants and a plain white blouse. She seems tired. Her eyes are relatively clear, although sad. She looks like she's been to hell and back.

"Might I have a cup of coffee?" she asks.

"Of course."

I make us a pot. She notices that my Bible is open to Mark 7 and starts reading to herself.

"You've been reading about hypocrites," says Maggie. "I know about hypocrites. I was raised among them. I . . . look, Albertina, I didn't really come to talk about how I was raised. I came to apologize."

"No need," I say.

"Big need. Very big need."

"I'm glad to see you, Maggie. And I want to hear about the hypocrites. Who were they?"

"Church folk."

"The kind Christ was talking about?"

"The kind my mother was convinced would make our lives better and take us into a better neighborhood. They were men."

"You mentioned something about that when we first met."

"They were handsome, they had money, they had position in the community. They had everything my mother thought she needed. Everything she thought I needed. She chased them, or they chased her, I'm not sure which."

"And your daddy?"

"He never wanted anything to do with me until I started modeling and he figured I had money. By then I wanted nothing to do with him. Later I learned he had died of a heart attack. Anyway, it was just me and mom and her many men."

"And did they harm you?"

"Not physically, not sexually, but emotionally they twisted me into knots. Mother would dress us up in matching outfits. Lavender dresses. Lavender hats. Lavender gloves. She would seat us in the front pew, in full view. The preacher couldn't miss her. The preacher would perform for her, for me. The preacher would be magnificent. Articulate. Brilliant. Bombastic. The preacher would bring down the house. I was in awe of the preacher. I was in awe of the whole ordeal. When the preacher came for dinner, I felt like the luckiest little girl in the world. When I was shipped off to my aunt's after dinner, I didn't understand. When one preacher disappeared and another showed up a month or two later, when we changed churches, when the whole business started all over again, I began to understand. It took a while, but at a pretty young age I had a solid comprehension of hypocrisy. Not one of them proved true. They were users and Mama, bless her heart, was too needy to see what she was doing. It was the same type time after time. He was usually handsome; he was usually married; he was always a dog. I saw all this before Mama did. I'd scream and yell at her, but it'd do no good. The last one was a famous one, a preacher from TV, known from one end of the country to the other. He hurt her the most because he promised her the most. When he dropped her—like every last one of them dropped her—she nearly lost it. He dropped her at the height of his popularity. At the time I was seventeen, and I swore I'd show them all. I'd become more famous than any preacher anywhere. And I would never ever step foot in a church again as long as I lived."

"I understand, baby," I offer.

"But the part I never understood, and still don't, was that, despite all the hypocrisy, something in those churches reached me. That something had nothing to do with the preachers. It was something strong and good and reassuring, something I felt inside."

"We all seek that something," I say.

"Psychologists have told me I've been looking for Daddy my whole life," Maggie says.

"All of us are. Except the Father is not of this world."

"It's hard for me to accept that. It's hard to accept diagnoses of myself as bipolar. And, Albertina, I have to say that it's just as hard to accept the existence of the devil."

"But you do see the reality of depression?"

"I'm not blind. Of course I see it. But you aren't calling depression the devil, are you?"

"I'm just saying, baby, that depression is the negative force. It's the opposite of the life force. It's the death force. Given enough power, it will kill us. Isn't that what you've been going through?"

"I've been battling. God knows I've been battling."

"Well, I say surrender, sweetheart. I say put down the sword. Give the devil his due. But know that nothing can overwhelm God's love. God's victory is established fact based on undying faith. The devil achieves victory only when he fools us into thinking his power is unbeatable. You're too smart for that, Maggie. You've worked too hard, learned too much, been too successful to let the devil bring it all down. The devil wants you to think that you're God. He wants you to buy into that arrogance and false sense of power. Then once you have it, he snatches it away leaving you with doubt and feelings of unworthiness, anger, fury, shame, even depression so severe you want to take your life. But the smartest thing the devil can do is convince you he doesn't exist. That way he can work his trickery with free rein. That way he has you where he wants you."

"Why couldn't you have told me this when we first met?"

"Because you couldn't have heard it."

"You were so patient with me, Albertina, until I didn't know what to do. I hated your patience and understanding. Maybe I still do. But my conscience has convicted me—that's all there is to it. I stand convicted."

"You stand forgiven."

"I know I have the right team of doctors now. I've researched it. And I have researchers who have researched it. I'm no fool."

"I know you're not. You're a brilliant woman, Maggie."

"But that doesn't keep me from falling apart. The right meds have not kept me from falling apart. The right meds are important, I know that. I can't function without them. I believe in intelligent medication."

"I do too. The chemistry of the brain is a complicated matter, and when it's unbalanced it must be dealt with."

"Well, I've been dealing with it, and I still am. My team of doctors has prescribed the right psychopharmacological cocktail. But something is still missing. And when I go back and think about that feeling I used to get in church, that 'something' that was so strong but so elusive, I can't find it, Albertina. I look for it, I pray for it, I even dream of it, but it's gone . . . it's gone. . . ."

Maggie begins to cry. Soon she begins to weep. The weeping is deep and long lasting. The weeping is profound, as if all the saints in heaven are weeping with her. I get up and go to Maggie, sit beside her, take her in my arms. She's weeping so intensely her body is shaking.

"Baby," I say. "That 'something' is not gone. It can't be gone. It was always here. It's here now. It will always be here."

Say a Little Prayer

A **Few weeks** have passed. Patrick has been coming to church every Sunday and helping me with my Bible class on Wednesdays. Strangely, though, he has not said a word to me about Naomi. Then last Sunday I look up and see her seated in the last pew of the House of Trust. Afterward, she congratulates me on my sermon, taken from Mark 6:31 when the Lord tells His disciples, "Come away by yourselves to a secluded place and rest awhile."

"Today, Pastor Merci," says the rabbi, "you provided rest for me. And I thank you."

"The pastor always provides that rest," adds Clifford Bloom, who has become an active member of my congregation.

Patrick, however, is nowhere in sight.

Maggie has also slipped out of public sight. Bob and Virginia tell me she's resting at a rehab facility in Big Sur. Then word comes that, after this second hiatus, her show is going back on the air.

It's Monday morning. Andre calls with the news that he has proposed to Nina and she has accepted. Will I officiate at their wedding in New York this coming winter? I silently sigh, close my eyes, pray for wisdom, and say, "Yes, baby, of course I will." I don't feel great about this engagement but reason that there's no way, not now, to effectively challenge my son. He's ecstatically happy, he's floating on a big emotional high and anything I tell him will be ignored, resented, or both.

So, with Andre still on my mind, I return to prayer. The prayer doesn't last long because Justine is banging on my door.

"You've prayed enough for one morning," she says. "You've prayed enough for one lifetime. You warm up the TV while I make the coffee. Your gal's back on the air today. And if I see she's got that fool trainer on the show with her, I'm putting my foot through the screen. I'm just warning you—I *will* get violent."

"You'll behave, sweetheart," I say, "like you always do. Or usually do. Anyway, recently promoted sales supervisors of Target do not get violent."

Justine makes the coffee extra-strong. I make some sourdough toast and cover it with apple butter.

Maggie's World begins.

Maggie looks okay. Maybe even normal. She's wearing a mint green dress that's quietly elegant. Her demeanor is calm.

"Today," she says, "after our latest much-discussed hiatus, we're going to continue our discussion of bipolarity with several experts. And as you might suspect, I have something to say about the subject. But before I say that, I want to express gratitude for the healing I've been feeling in my heart. I do not see my show as a platform for proselytizing. I do not intend to use it for that purpose. But I do have to say that I've been battling with the devil. Call that devil what you want. The names aren't important. But what is important for me to declare is my belief in Christ and my belief in God. I've been running from that belief. I've been tortured by that belief. It's a belief I've fought and resisted my whole life. But now I'm a witness that without that firm faith I have neither sanity nor salvation. With that faith, I have a peace that surpasses all understanding. So all I can say, as so many others have lovingly said before me, is, 'Thank you, Jesus.' Now let's get on with the show . . ."

"Amazing," says Justine, looking over at me. "You did it, Albertina. You actually did it."

"No, baby," I say. "I didn't do it."

"Then who did?" Justine asks.

"God."

1. What are some of Albertina's favorite scriptures? How do they provide guidance for Albertina and others during the course of the narrative?

2. How does Cindy's illness affect the other characters in the novel? How does her death affect Albertina? Bob? Maggie?

3. How does Bob differ from the other men in the novel? Can you describe through his actions how he is different? Also describe Bob and Albertina's relationship. How would it have been different had Cindy lived?

4. What kind of preacher is Bishop Gold? How does his approach differ from Albertina's? Their perspectives clash during Cindy's funeral and during the awards show. How does Albertina handle these situations?

5. What events from Albertina's past constantly pervade her thoughts and dreams throughout the novel? How were they significant to her spiritual development?

6. Albertina Merci possesses the humility and strength of spirit to admit when her actions or thoughts interfere with God's plan. How does this affect Albertina's decisions? Do other characters help steer Albertina toward God's will? If so, how?

7. Maggie Clay has fierce mood swings that cause her to lash out at the people around her. Do you think you could have put up with Maggie? How would you have handled her?

8. Albertina always offers scriptural advice, but often likes to steer clear of meddling in other people's lives, which causes her to stay quiet during some potentially explosive situations. Describe some of these instances in the novel. Do you agree with her actions?

9. Patrick, like his Aunt Albertina, is also a Christian minister. At times it becomes evident that his fervent conviction to Christianity and short temper put him at odds with people around him. How do his beliefs affect his actions in public and in private? How does Albertina help him develop patience? Does he remind you of someone you know?

10. What taboo issue causes unease in the House of Trust? What event triggers the issue to emerge as a topic of concern? How is it resolved?

11. Justine has terrible taste in men. Describe the events surrounding her last two relationships. How does Albertina guide Justine? Do you agree with Justine's actions?

12. Albertina believes firmly in the healing power of prayer.

Describe the events surrounding the married couple Tom and Muriel, and the events surrounding Coach Martin Simmons and his son Chuck. Does prayer help in these two situations? Discuss moments when prayer has helped you deal with or come out of a difficult situation.

13. The radio station disk jockey Clifford Bloom makes an interesting point during his interview with Albertina when he says that Pastor Merci made the "transition from secular to sacred with exceptional poise." How does this statement help the reader's understanding of Albertina? How does Albertina respond to the comment? Does her view of herself differ from how you view her?